Praise

"Reasonable Lies may just be the best book I will ever read. The author has surpassed all expectations with this one. Be sure to have the tissues ready when you start it because you will definitely need a box…or three. I highly recommend that everyone read this book as soon as possible. It is one you will never forget." *Sarah Jayne Harry, Author*

"I finished this beautiful story in one day of starting it; it was so good I could not put it down. This book is a must if you need a good cry. It's well written with such feeling and compassion, it had me crying happy, sad and angry tears all the way through. This book resonates so clearly that life is too short. It will leave you appreciating everything a little bit more."
Natalie, Instagram Book Reviewer

"Wow, Wow, Wow! I highly recommend everyone read this. The story is just absolutely beautiful, powerful and heart breaking. I laughed & cried lots and once I closed the book, I smiled. I just couldn't put it down & you will need tissues towards the end of the book." *Jess Dickinson, Instagrammer*

"Well, what can I say, this was a wonderful book from start to finish. The author tackles a very sensitive subject matter that so many families have to deal with, but she does it in such a thoughtful way. Be prepared for some tears. I defy anyone to not shed at least one tear when reading this. A fantastic first novel, which I recommend everyone to read."
Nicola, Amazon Customer

"Well, this book broke me. I cried like a baby and I am not ashamed to admit it. The storyline is obviously heart-breaking and difficult to read, but it's well written with the perfect amount of humour and happiness for balance. One of my favourite things about this book was the friendship between Jane, the protagonist, and her life-long best friend Sarah. Their relationship was well developed, you can really tell that they're more like sisters without it having to be said. The support Sarah provides to not only Jane but her whole family is incredible, what a brilliant friend she is – I think we could all do with a friend like her! There is a plot twist involving one of the characters that I did not see coming at all. I thought it was a really interesting way of forming interweaving connections between the characters that all come to light towards the end of the novel. Highly recommend!"

Zoe, Bookstagrammer

"Be ready to feel overwhelmed with emotion. I stumbled across Reasonable Lies. And I am so happy about that. I just finished reading it in the last hour or so and am finding myself just stopping and thinking. The realisation that I'm bloody lucky. The actual tears I cried for these exceptionally developed characters (this has happened only once before!). The story covers love, heartbreak, friendship, and relationships like nothing I've read before, along with the illness itself. This is a beautifully written piece of literature that will stay with me and I'll definitely recommend this to my friends and to any of you who haven't already read it. If this ever got made into a movie, I'd be watching it! (Though I doubt it'd be half as good as the book). I'll wait patiently for the next book from this exceptionally talented author."

Donna, Bookstagrammer

"Wow, what an emotional book this was & yes, I did shed a tear or two. We follow the journey of the main character, Jane, seeing how this amazing woman tried to stay strong for her husband & twins. She finds solace & friendship in a man called James at the cemetery where her father is buried, but all is not what it seems. Beautifully written & is a book that will stay with me long after reading it." *Stacey, Goodreads Reviewer*

"Wow!!! What a book!! Sometimes you read something, and it touches every part of you. This has really hit a part of my heart, I've smiled, and I've cried…A lot!! This is a book which needs to be read, a perfect example of not knowing what someone is going through. This is such a beautiful read, with real life issues covered sensitively and delicately. A definite 5 star read, even though it made me cry." *Vikki. Bookstagrammer*

"Wow, just wow. T.A. Rosewood's compelling and thought-provoking storytelling brought tears to my eyes. So much so, I had to put the book down (only for five minutes), then I had to find out what happens afterwards. Jane's story is something that more and more of us are having to live, deal with or find out, Reasonable Lies are around us. A gripping novel with beautiful characters set in the lovely Cambridge. A must-read with a box of tissues needed. A five-star read; I can't wait for more of Rosewood's work." *Holly, Bookstagrammer*

"Wow! An emotional, provocative and compelling punch of a read. This book actually floored me. The big, fat, ugly tears that I cried are best not spoken about. I nearly did a Joey, from Friends, by putting the book in the freezer (the only thing that stopped me is that it's on my kindle). I highly recommend this book. A big well done to the author on this debut novel, you've done yourself proud!" *Emma, Bookstagrammer*

"Tear jerking and Amazing. I absolutely loved this book. It made me laugh, made me cry and experience a whole rollercoaster of emotions. A truly beautiful story that is thought provoking and so well written that I never wanted to put it down. I would recommend this to all who want to read a good book and maybe have a good cry too." *Candice, Bookstagrammer*

"Honestly, I'm not usually one for picking up books from new authors. I read a lot and I tend to stick to my favourites - the big dogs. More recently, however, I've tried to broaden my horizons and actually found the author of this novel via my bookish Instagram account. The first thing that grabbed my attention was how this novel was inspired by the work of JoJo Moyes, who is without doubt one of my favourite authors. I figured - why not? - and downloaded a copy to my kindle. I picked up this book at around 3pm today and have finished it now, having hardly put it down all evening. Written in what felt like a simplistic, easy to read and down to earth manner; this novel really held its own. I'm certainly glad that I gave it a chance!" *Kim, Instagram*

"What can I say but wow! This book has touched every part of my soul and i know that I won't be able to start another until I've grieved for this one. Please be prepared to ugly cry from this. Reading on Christmas day probably wasn't the best of ideas but what a book" *Kelly, Instagram*

"Utterly brilliant. A heartfelt story that is so easy to read, I couldn't put the book down. You really get involved with the characters & in some way or other you relate to them & what they are dealing with. There is also a twist which I didn't see coming. Cannot recommend this enough & can't wait for the next book." *Janet, Amazon Customer*

Reasonable Lies

To Karen,

Best Wishes,

[signature]

T. A. ROSEWOOD

To Leonardo, with love.

"Love as powerful as your mother's…
leaves its own mark.
To have been loved so deeply, even though
the person who loved us is gone, will give
us some protection forever."

J.K. Rowling

Prologue

"I can't believe this, you never play the lottery," shrieked Karl excitedly again.

"I know, who would have thought it," Jane replied trying her best to give a huge smile as he kissed her forehead and held her arms with his strong, yet gentle, trembling hands.

The reasonable lies had begun.

With a deep breath, she continued her story.

"Hey, you know we've always wanted to take the kids on holiday to Florida, let's do it now Karl, let's book it today and surprise them. It's nearly the end of term, so it's an ideal time to go. We don't have to worry about taking them out of school, they'll absolutely love it." Jane reached behind her into the kitchen drawer and pulled out a brochure they had picked up a few months back after seeing a programme on television about a family moving to Florida.

They'd discussed how great it would be to have a longer

length family holiday there soon, and the kids had already been busy choosing the biggest rides and theme parks that they wanted to experience.

They'd been too busy for the past few months to think about it, and money had been a little bit tight. It had remained just a dream for a while, but now, they could have their dream holiday come true; thanks to this lie.

"Yes!" shouted Karl with joy, "Let's get online and book it now. The kids are going to be so stoked." He hurried over to his laptop bag on the kitchen table where he had left it after getting in from work earlier. Jane had called him to come straight home from work as she had urgent news to tell him.

"We should go for a few weeks, Jane, really have a fantastic holiday to remember," Karl said as he tapped away on his computer finding the best deals for Florida holidays and excursions to go on. "We could even visit Miami like you've always wanted to if you like?"

His enthusiasm was so cute, and she watched intently as he read out to her about the parks and attractions that they could go and visit. It became a blur to her as she was enjoying watching his fun-filled face, knowing he would be the last person she ever loved. The next few months would be the most special time they would have together; whatever lies she had to tell.

"It's not a fortune, but wow, we can relax a bit at work now and enjoy some family time before the kids are too old to come away with us. I'm sure Adam wouldn't mind letting me have a bit of time off work. He owes me anyway for all those extra hours I put in for the Brews Project this month," Karl continued. "Do you think you will be okay with getting the time off or using up your holiday time?" He didn't glance up once, he was so busy looking at places they could visit.

If only he knew that this was going to be the last holiday they spent together. Times like this would now be precious moments that Jane would treasure more than she had ever before, and all in secret.

"Yes, I'm sure it will be fine, Karl. Let's not tell the kids until the day we leave though, make it a complete surprise for them like we've always wanted to do; they will love that." Jane hugged him from behind the dining chair, watching his computer screen change rapidly as he typed in the many theme parks and attractions. Her bronzed arms gently wrapped around his chest. He smelled wonderful. His rich aftershave was intense, manly, and she loved it. She had bought it for him for Christmas the previous year. Before that, he hadn't really liked to wear any sort of aftershave, but this fragrance had grown on him, and he enjoyed the way it made her feel. She realised that she must remember to get him a new bottle soon as it was getting low.

Jane looked intently at her gorgeous husband as she took a seat on the chair beside him. He was running his fingers through his black hair in anticipation, overwhelmed with the excitement of what was to come. He was smiling so widely, like a Cheshire cat, as they say, like the cat that got the cream. He was so happy, and Jane knew this was the only thing that she wanted to see over the next few weeks, months, and, hopefully, years; just happiness, smiling, love, and her family close by for the time she had left with them, but without them suffering in the knowledge that only she knew right now.

The holiday would be the start of fulfilling their lifelong dreams and as much as she could make them happen, she would, no matter what. For however short a time scale, whatever she had to do, she would.

Knowing the truth was heart-breaking enough for her, and she just couldn't face telling her beloved husband of eighteen years and their beautiful teenage twins, Robbie and Cassie, at this time. It didn't make sense to her just yet, so why upset them now? She wanted joy in their house, not pain and broken hearts. This was her time to protect them for as long as possible.

Jane had not known where to turn when she got the news, and this was her only way of coping and keeping her family from months of stress and worry.

The time was now, and she had to do this for them; even if she had to lie to the most important people in her life.

Nothing else mattered from this day forward…

Chapter One

Jane Walden was a beautiful brunette (although not entirely natural anymore), aged thirty-nine and living in Cambridge, England with her slightly older husband, Karl, and their twins, Cassie and Robbie, who had just turned teenagers.

They thought of themselves as a 'normal' family of four, all living busy lives, with Karl and Jane having successful careers in law and accounting and luckily, both now based in the city of Cambridge. The children were in secondary school and were both enjoying it and the challenges that it brought for them each day. This was made a little easier by the fact that they were both extremely bright, talented children and mostly excelled in whatever they tried even if they didn't really like it, such as flute lessons.

Robbie loved his computer consoles and had dreams of working for one of the top games' companies in LA or New York one day. He had even set up an after-school session for teaching coding to other members of his year group.

Cassie absolutely adored art and dance with media studies being her favourite lesson, and although she doubted her abilities at times, she was particularly good at art, and her teachers encouraged her at every opportunity.

The Waldens had always been a happy-go-lucky family and loved their new home in the outskirts of Cambridge just a few minutes' drive from the centre of the city, but far enough away to not be right in the hustle and bustle of it all. They had managed to buy it eighteen months earlier as Karl had been given a great promotion to a senior position within the law firm where he worked.

Cambridge was a thriving hive of activity all the time, with many student buildings, apartments, and townhouses popping up, but their house was located on a tree-lined road, which they had seen previously when visiting the city during the spring. It had looked so beautiful with pink cherry blossom adorning every tree. They had fallen in love with the street immediately, taking photos of the trees and various houses, hoping that a place would come up for sale. After a few months of keeping a close eye on the housing lists, it did, and the timing was perfect, so they purchased it and moved in within six months.

They lived right at the end of the cul-de-sac, so the drive to their house was a pleasing experience which they enjoyed every day, but especially during the springtime when the trees were in full bloom with bright and colourful blossom.

A block paved driveway swept its way up to the symmetrical, modern house which had Greek-style pillars on each side of the large front door and gorgeous sash-style windows. The driveway was finished off with some small shrubs that Jane's mum had planted and shaped for them as their 'moving in' present.

Karl had bought a name plaque with 'Walden House' engraved on it with an etched red rose, which was Jane's favourite flower. She had made him fix it on the front wall as soon as she had unwrapped it. He didn't much like DIY projects, but as Jane loved it, he immediately got the job done for his beloved wife.

Everything was going smoothly in the Walden household, and their lives were moving in the right direction for the future. The kids were settled and happy at school, and both their workplaces were busy and doing well, but, when a charity fundraising event took place, early in June, it would change their lives in a way Jane could never have imagined and shake their idyllic family to the core within only six months.

Jane's workplace, Smith & Co Accounting was taking part in a breast screening cancer awareness campaign and everyone from the office was involved, with the exception of the few men who worked there.

The company employed mostly women, so when they had discussed which charity to choose, they had all been in agreement that this type of awareness day would be the most useful for everyone. She and her co-workers were determined to raise lots of money for such an amazing cause.

Jane had also arranged to have pink ribbon pin badges, to be sold in the reception area for staff and visitors to buy in the weeks before, raising even more funds. Cassie had helped make them, putting her creative talents to good use, and enjoying being able to spend time helping her mum. They'd spent a few evenings beforehand, pinning them all together and presenting them in a wicker basket with a small donation box.

Mornings were always a little hectic at home, but they usually managed to get at least ten minutes together before they all left for work and school. Sometimes, for Jane and Karl, it was just watching the kids eat while they sipped on their juices or munched on their toast or cereals.

"We have our charity day today," Jane said, setting the table for breakfast as Karl walked into the kitchen with Robbie and Cassie following. Robbie was still tugging his crinkled shirt on, dragging his blazer, and his tie was crooked as usual.

"Oh, yes. You should be able to raise a good amount of money for that. Here…" He reached into the pocket of his suit trousers. "This should get you started." He handed her a crisp twenty-pound note as he turned to help Robbie straighten his tie.

"Aww, thank you, darling," She leaned forward over the breakfast bar to kiss him on the cheek as she took the note. "That'll make a nice start to the fundraising and with Cassie's lovely ribbons, we should do really well today." She winked over at Cassie, who was devouring the strawberry smoothie that Jane had prepared. "Do you want a coffee, darling?" she asked, waving his 'Best Dad' mug at him.

"Sorry, no, I'm good, I had one after my run earlier. I've got to rush off actually, as we have a potential new receptionist coming in for a second interview. Melissa is off on maternity leave in about a month, so we thought we'd better get organised with the new cover. I'll call you later and see how you got on." Blowing her a kiss, he grabbed his laptop bag and keys, made his way into the hallway, and opened the front door calling back, "See you all later. Love you." Then he was gone for the day.

Jane put the mug back into the cupboard and finished up her own coffee, then turned to start loading the dishwasher.

"We've got some tests today, Mum, Maths and English. I'm dreading the Maths one," said Robbie as he sipped his orange juice and devoured another slice of Marmite on toast.

"Oh, I'm sure you'll be fine. You love Maths, don't you?" Jane asked reassuringly.

"I hate Maths," interrupted Cassie, who was now picking off some grapes and slicing them into her favourite bowl, spilling a few onto the floor as usual. Jane laughed as she collected the surplus fruit rolling off the side and chucked them into the bin.

"But you're great at English. We can't be good at everything, can we, Robbie, you'll do great, just try and relax and think about each question before answering. You remember what we always say?"

"Try your best," he mimicked, taking in her advice as he took a last mouthful of toast while watching a video on his phone. Both children were obsessed with their phones but for different reasons. Robbie liked to watch videos of gaming hints so he could get better at the online games on

his computer, and Cassie loved music videos as she had dreams of dancing for a famous pop star one day or even doing her own choreography. She idolized Ariana Grande and Jane had been keeping a lookout to get her some concert tickets as soon as her tour was announced.

They were soon all finished with their breakfasts and ready to set off for the short ten-minute walk to school. Jane always loved to see them set off before she worked her school-hours' shift. She liked to spend as much time with them as possible and would usually meet them by the front door as the three of them arrived home at roughly the same time each day.

She hadn't gone back to work until they had started full-time nursery. But time had seemed to fly by, and they had grown up quickly. Before Jane and Karl had known it, they'd finished primary and to be at secondary school already felt crazy. Jane often thought about where the time had gone, and what they'd all done over those years; fitting so much in and thinking back to the many fun times so far that they had to reminisce about together.

She recalled their first day at nursery so clearly. They had both toddled in without giving her or Karl a second glance, and she was the one who had spent the day being emotional, tearful, and worrying if they were both okay. They'd always have a fabulous time at every session, so she began to relax after a few weeks and got herself back to working, part time to begin with, so she still had those precious hours with them after nursery.

"See you both later," she called as they walked to the end of the garden path with their fully stocked backpacks.

"Good luck today, guys, smash those tests."

They both turned and waved briefly with their phones still stuck fast in their hands.

Jane stood for a moment, thinking about what she used to do on the way to school when mobile phones weren't around; probably listening to Rick Astley, Bros or Madonna on the Walkman cassette clasped to her belt. She chuckled quietly to herself as she remembered what it was like to be a child of the 80s. The loud outfits and techno style music back then – how times and fashions had changed.

Grabbing her set of keys and closing the front door, she made her way to the garage and jumped into her small VW Polo. She loved her little run around car. It was compact, but it was enough to get her to and from work and zoom around the city when she needed to. Karl had the bigger sized car for when they all went out as a family on longer journeys or holidays or trips. It was a large silver BMW and had been his dream car for about a year and a half. He'd been overjoyed at being able to purchase it after his promotion.

Closing the garage with the remote control, she fastened her seatbelt and turned the radio on to hear one of her favourite tunes by Robbie Williams: Angels. She couldn't help but sing along.

She sang along to the music, smiling and laughing to herself, glancing back to ensure that the garage had shut behind her.

It was a warmer than usual summer day in early June with a slight refreshing breeze. As she drove into the car park at work, she noticed that the large charity screening lorry was already in position and the medical staff were getting prepared to begin calling people in for their turn. '*They are organised*', she thought to herself as she passed the vehicle's side door after parking.

There was also a small team of breast cancer nurses in one of the larger meeting rooms just inside the main reception area. They were going to be showing everyone the correct way to check for lumps or abnormal signs in their breasts and handing out leaflets during the day to everyone. Although the men who worked there had decided they weren't going to have an examination, each one had agreed to have a time slot where they were going to talk about men checking themselves. Noticeboards were being erected with lots of information and diagrams and it all looked great.

"Do you have everything you need?" Carol asked the ladies at the lorry. She was the managing director of the firm and was busying herself, as usual, making sure everyone was okay before she settled into her always hectic work schedule for the day.

"Yes, everything is perfect. Thank you so much, Carol," one replied. "The cakes and biscuits are wonderful too, very much appreciated."

"No problem at all. Let us know when you need the coffee re-stocked or any more biscuits." She gave a wink and smiled while giving them the thumbs up. Carol turned around to see Jane passing by and gave her the usual air-kissing welcome.

"Morning my lovely" She was always so friendly with

everyone she met. There was something about her that made people smile, and she didn't have a bad word to say about anyone. Jane had never seen her angry or down in the fifteen years or so that they had worked together.

"Morning Carol," Jane replied, returning the air kisses with a big smile, "Hey, Karl gave me this to start off the fundraising today" She passed Carol the twenty-pound note from her purse.

"Oh, bless him. He's a keeper that one Jane" She winked, nudging Jane's arm jokingly. They both laughed. It was something she said to everyone who had a partner in their lives, no matter how long they'd been together, "I'll pop it into the kitty my darling. Right, got to crack on this morning, so much to sort through today. Speak later darling," she continued, hurrying off into the hub of the main offices and grabbing her mug of coffee from the reception area. On her way, she answered her seemingly, constantly ringing mobile phone as Jane took a breath for her almost. She loved how funny Carol was and admired her business head, even if she was a bit scatty at times.

After a few hours in her office, Jane's appointment time for the screening was approaching, so she made her way downstairs. It was all straightforward, and she didn't have any worries about it. She just wanted to help raise some money for this cause and have a chat with the ladies while they were there. She had felt a slight lump just beneath her left breast, so she thought this would be the ideal time to speak with one of the specialists before her initial breast screening. Doctors' appointments were never her strong point. She often felt like she was wasting their time and was never poorly enough to warrant going. The NHS had enough on their plate at the best of times.

"So, Jane, how can we help you today?" asked Paula, one of the senior breast screening nurses.

The team of nurses all had light pink shirts on with black trousers and black shoes with white name badges; a comfortable looking uniform for their job.

Paula had short, light brown hair, a clear complexion with a pretty smile and a caring look about her. Jane noticed her deep brown eyes and long eyelashes; she'd always wanted to have lashes like that, but she was stuck with buying the latest mascara on the market to make hers appear longer. She preferred that over the false eyelashes that she could stick on and get in a muddle with. Makeup wasn't her strong point.

"Well, it's probably nothing, but I thought since you were here today, I could get some advice on a little lump that I have felt for the past few months or so." Jane smiled her usual glowing grin, now feeling a little nervous. "You see, I don't really like going to the doctors…"

"Okay, that's fine Jane, would you like to show me where it is? Then we'll take a closer look for you?" asked Paula, pulling the fabric screen around them both.

Jane unbuttoned her red blouse, removed her bra, and pointed out to Paula where she had felt the lump.

It had been there for more than a few months, more like five months or so, but Jane had just put it down to some scar tissue that had been caused from a breast reduction operation that she had over three and a half years before.

Paula felt the lump for a few minutes, examined her

right breast for comparison and then looked carefully at the lump once again.

"Okay, look, we would like to check this further for you using the mammogram machine. Would that be okay? Do you have a time slot booked with us?"

"Yes, it's in ten minutes," Jane replied, glancing at her watch. "It's nothing to worry about though, is it?" she asked, suddenly becoming a little more anxious.

"It's best we get a check on it to make sure we know what we're dealing with," she replied as she wrote some notes down and took Jane's details. "The ladies will carry out your mammogram as planned in a moment, and we will be in touch in a few days with results and any information if necessary. If you would like to sit in the waiting area just outside the unit, that would be great. They'll call you in shortly, I think they are running over by a few minutes, but it won't be too long."

Jane buttoned up her blouse and made her way to the seats where she fidgeted nervously as anxiety set in but after a few minutes, she was called into the screening area inside the unit which disrupted her thoughts.

As she entered the lorry via the steep metal steps, she glanced inside. The mammogram machine was, or seemed, massive. The whole space was gleaming with cleanliness and was more clinical in appearance than she had thought it would be; a little weird after seeing the outside as just a big lorry with some graphics on the side. Jane began to feel more at ease because it looked so clinical, clean, and professional. It was all routine and, obviously, for a really good cause.

Another friendly nurse explained the whole procedure as she went along, and Jane shivered at how cold the lady's hands were as she undressed again.

"Sorry, my hands are a little chilly," she said as she placed one of Jane's breasts into the machine, which also freezing.

Gasping a little, Jane replied, "They are cold. Is there no heating in here?"

"Unfortunately, no, sorry, it's better for the machines to have a cold environment." The nurse tried rubbing her hands together to warm them before touching Jane's skin again, but it didn't do much good.

After the instructions and positioning, the screening began. It was noisy and quite uncomfortable but not as bad as she had imagined. She felt quite relaxed about everything once again, and before she knew it, the procedure was over. As she moved away from the machine, Jane wondered to herself how the ladies dealt with doing this sort of job all day, every day. Squashing breasts into a machine was not something she'd ever want to do if she was honest. She also wondered how many people had been saved by having this procedure carried out, how many cancers had been detected early enough to save them; she hoped many hundreds or thousands even. It was a great idea, even if it wasn't the most pleasant of experiences and she was glad to be part of it.

"We will be in touch if there is anything further to discuss," replied the nurse as she placed her hand on Jane's shoulder then opened the door.

Thanking her, Jane went back into the main building,

popping to the toilets to warm herself up with the hand dryers.

As she made her way to her own office, she chatted with some of her other colleagues about how the procedure had gone for them.

"It's a bit painful, isn't it?" said one.

"Oh, it was fine," said another.

"My poor excuses for boobs were hard work to get in the jaws of the machine. The poor nurse was embarrassed for me I think," another chuckled.

After some laughter as they drank coffee during their breaks, Jane returned to her desk, not thinking much else about it. It had been an experience but for the good of the cause and she felt better for it if she was honest. Now she just had to wait for the results.

Chapter Two

"How did the screening event go today sweetheart? Sorry, I didn't call in the end, it's been one of those days, you know, the long ones," laughed Karl as he returned home from work looking a little worn out.

"Oh, it was fine actually. Everyone was really nice, and it was amazing to see how much is involved. The men in the offices had a talking to as well to make sure that they check themselves. I picked up a leaflet for you, babe. Here, a bit of bedtime reading for you." She continued after a few breaths, "And the ladies from the clinic were so helpful, and friendly. Let's hope we raise plenty of money for it, everyone was giving so much in donations. Oh, and Carol said thanks for your contribution. It was a nice boost to start it off."

She kissed Karl on the cheek as he placed his keys on the white sideboard in the hallway, then they made their way to the kitchen where dinner had been sizzling away.

They were having chicken fajitas with spicy rice, and it was filling the air with a sweet and exotic sort of aroma. It was the twins' favourite meal, closely followed by pizza and spaghetti Bolognese.

The children were busy doing their homework at the breakfast bar, but both got up to give their dad a hug as he and Jane entered the room.

"Hey, how are you two doing?" he asked as he put his arms around them, kissing their heads in turn.

Cassie promptly replied, "Dad, it was so much fun in art today…" and continued to tell him all about what she had done in her art lesson. "We used all sorts of materials and different types of paint…" She went on with joy all over her face. She had loved art since she was a toddler, experimenting with hand painting and splash art. With many pieces of her artwork up around the house and an entire wall in her bedroom of creations that had been drawn or painted over the years. She especially liked using charcoal and had produced some amazing images. She'd already decided she would be taking this subject in her GCSEs later on in her schooling and set her heart on going to art college as well as being a movie star or a dancer for a pop star. Jane admired her creativity and enthusiasm for everything.

"Sounds like fun, darling, I can't wait to see all your work," said Karl as he sat down opposite her. "Wow, this looks lovely, babe," he said to Jane as he started tucking into the nachos already served up.

"Stop it you!" She playfully tapped his hand. "Wait until it's all ready, greedy guts."

He gave her a cheeky tap on her bottom as she turned back to plate up the dinner, chuckling to himself at getting told off, and winked cheekily at the children.

"How were the tests then, kids?" asked Jane as she tossed the chicken in the pan for a last turn.

"Actually, they were okay, Mum," Robbie replied.

"Well done. Cassie, how about yours?"

"Meh," Cassie humphed without any enthusiasm, so Jane decided to leave it at that and just chuckled to herself. Teenagers and tests, especially ones they do not like, were not a good mix. Cassie would talk about it when she was ready.

They were a very loving family and had no problems with showing affection to each other. Even the kids got on most days and fist-bumped each other in place of hugs as they'd grown. There was always time for a chat and a cuddle when needed. Schoolwork was extremely important, and they hoped that the kids would eventually make it into Cambridge University when they reached that milestone. It would be amazing for them both, as Jane and Karl had been there and had loved every moment.

Nothing more was said about the screening that evening as they carried on with their normal routine and enjoyed their delicious dinner together while chatting more about the children's school day. Jane and Karl settled down for the night in the lounge once the kids had gone off to their rooms to catch up on playing computer games and their all-important Snapchat and Instagram social media updates.

Jane always enjoyed cuddling up on the sofa with Karl before they went to bed and regularly indulged in sipping a glass or two of wine. They either chatted the night away, watched some Netflix series or read a book, and Karl would usually give Jane's feet a little massage at the same time.

~

The next morning arrived and at around nine o'clock, Jane got a call on her mobile just before she arrived at work.

She had decided to leave her car at home and get the bus for a change, although it seemed busier than usual for some reason this morning. As she hurried off the bus, she heard the phone ringing and rummaged to fetch it out of her handbag. Nearly dropping it, she managed to answer it before it rang off.

"Hello, is that Jane Walden?" said the voice.

"Hi. Yes, it is. How can I help you?" She waved at a work friend who had just got into the lift in the foyer of the glass-fronted office opposite the bus stop.

"Hi, Jane. It's Paula from the mobile breast screening clinic yesterday. We wondered if you could come in today to have another look at the lump you found and discuss the mammogram that we carried out for you. I've spoken to one of our senior doctors, who's also had a quick look at the results, and she would like to see you as soon as possible."

"Oh, okay. I could probably get there today on my lunch break, around one o'clock?" Jane replied a little anxiously. "Is everything okay with it?"

"We just wanted to have a chat, face to face if that's alright with you?"

"Erm, sure, yes that's fine, could you email or text me the address over?"

"Yes, of course. We have your email, don't we?" She

paused. "Yes, we have it here Jane. I'll email over the info now and look forward to seeing you at lunchtime."

"Okay, thank you, goodbye," Jane said as she hung up.

Placing her phone back into her bag, she glanced at her watch and hurried into the lift. The email came through shortly after she reached her door, so she checked Google Maps for the location. It worked out that the clinic was only up the road from the office block so not too bad for time scales, just enough time to grab some lunch on the way.

Jane's room was a reasonable size space with full-size windows that reached ceiling to floor and had off-white vertical blinds for when the sun made its rare British appearances during the year. Her desk was large and modern, finished in white gloss, and two silver photo frames adorned it. One was of their wedding day and the other, a picture of the kids on the last family holiday that they'd had in Lapland a few Christmases back.

Next to the frames was a pen pot, which Cassie had made out of clay in her first year of primary school. It wasn't the greatest looking of items, but Jane loved it, nonetheless. Robbie had also made a letter holder, which was on the other side of the desk. Jane kept her business cards in there as letters were opened too quickly to linger. He'd made it in woodwork class, and it had the word, 'Mum' burnt into it.

Her chair was grey and finished in a fine, soft padded fabric with a high back for added comfort. She'd had a few problems with her back, so comfort at work was essential as she spent most of the day sitting down. They had talked about getting stand-up desks, but budgets hadn't allowed for those yet. She just made sure that she tried to get up and walk around every so often to take some pressure off her back, and that worked fine for now.

"Good morning, Jane," Perry said as he knocked gently on her door. He was the mail guy in charge of making sure everyone got their daily post. He didn't have anything for her today but, as always, liked to say hi to everyone each morning whether he had letters for them or not.

Perry was in his late twenties with jet-black curly hair and piercing brown eyes. He always wore a cap with NY on it and he'd told Jane previously when she'd commented on it, that it was his dream to get to New York one day. His blue shorts and crisp white polo shirts were always fresh and pressed to perfection. Jane had often thought that he must really love ironing or have a lady who did it for him but never liked to ask. He was one of the few men in the building but didn't mind at all as he only worked a few hours each morning as he delivered the mail, and he got on with everybody.

"Hi, Perry. How are you today?" Jane gave him a huge smile as she looked up from her laptop bag, grabbing the notebook and new pens that she'd bought a few days earlier to stock her pen pot up. The company supplied basic pens but she preferred bringing in her own.

"Great, actually. Now that you ask, I have some awesome news to tell you today, and you're one of the first people I get to tell in here."

"Oh, sounds interesting…" Jane moved closer to the doorway, intrigued.

Perry never walked into the office unless he had post, so she met him at the door as he replied, "I'm going to be a daddy." His face beamed, and his eyes sparkled with joy and excitement.

"Oh, Perry, that's wonderful news. Congratulations. When's the baby due?" Jane said as she rubbed his arm.

"December sixteenth. Ironic really, it's due on my birthday. It was a bit of a shock at first, but we're both really happy now. My mum is beside herself, and she's already buying baby grows or whatever those things are called." He gestured a hand with a funny, puzzled expression on his face while shrugging his shoulders up. "Emily has been out shopping with her already as her mum died last year so it's nice that they can be so close."

"Bless her, how wonderful for you all, and how exciting too." Jane remembered back to the moment when she told her mum the news about becoming a grandma for the first time. Then to tell her a few weeks later that there were two coming. She had nearly fainted, and Pops, Jane's father, had to have an extra shot of Scotch that day to calm his nerves.

"Yep... so exciting. Can't wait to tell everyone here. Right well, on that note, I better be off and get these letters out to the rest of the gang. Have a great day, Jane." Perry waved his special little wave and went on up the corridor, whistling a tune and pushing his little mail trolley along.

"You have a great day too, Perry. See you tomorrow," she called to him as she watched him deliver his fabulous news to more of the ladies working in the middle section of the room just outside the main offices. She then carried on unpacking her things onto her desk and set to work on a pile of customer folders.

Jane was an accountant and bookkeeper for some major firms in the city and some smaller businesses around Cambridge and surrounding areas. She had studied this at university as it was all she'd ever wanted to do, and she was very good at it too. She'd often thought about having her own firm but as she was so happy in her job with Carol, she never took it any further. There was no need for the added stress of being self-employed, and she loved where she worked. So, why change anything?

She and Karl had been on the same university campus when they met and fell in love. A fancy-dress party for the end of term had brought them together; she was dressed as Marilyn Monroe and he, the one and only King of Rock 'n' Roll, Elvis. What a combination they were, but, surprisingly, they looked great as a pair.

As in all good love stories, their eyes had met across the crowded room, and Karl had nervously asked her for a dance soon after. She was smitten there and then. Even with his funny Elvis greased hair and frilly shirt with the widest of white trousers she had ever seen, he still looked handsome, and his eyes glistened in the disco lights as they caught each other's eyes while dancing.

These were among the first things she had loved about him, his dark blue-green eyes with lashes that ladies would die for. She was drawn in within minutes, as he was with her. And, as they say, the rest is history.

Interrupting her thoughts, Carol appeared. "Jane, darling, would you mind taking a look at this client's file for me please?" She knocked and entered the office with a large yellow file in her hand. "They're a little unsure on some receipts, and I can't seem to work it out. I know you are better at that sort of stuff than I am." She grinned and gave her a cheeky wink.

"Yeah, sure. I'll take a look after my lunch break if that's okay. I've got to pop out to see someone, but it shouldn't take me too long."

"Okay, no rush. Thanks, sweetie. Are you okay?"

"Yes, fine, I just have an appointment with an optician; my eyes have been a little blurry lately, so they said they could fit me in at lunchtime," she fibbed. She didn't want to explain about the breast clinic ringing, nor did she want to cause unnecessary worry. Not being one for telling lies, she felt uncomfortable doing so but had surprised herself that she had come up with the scenario so quickly.

"Right. That's good then. I can never get an appointment, so I just stick to the old 'buy over the counter' ones. They seem to work okay for me, to be honest, and they cost a whole lot less I tell you," she replied as she spun some dark-rimmed glasses round in her hand. "Oh, and, Jane, did you hear Perry's exciting baby news? Cute, hey. We'll have to club together for a gift when the little one arrives, maybe give him a baby shower a few weeks before? Be a bit different, hey, a blokey one."

"Yes, it's lovely news and of course, I'm up for chipping in for a present for sure. Let me know what you need from me and when; he's so sweet, isn't he?"

Jane again began to think about when the twins had arrived. They had received so many gifts from so many people in the office. She'd never seen so many flowers and balloons in one place. All her colleagues had decorated her office for the baby shower before they were born, and then there were even more decorations when she had brought the twins in for their first visit to meet everyone.

The work atmosphere was always fun and friendly, and everyone would enjoy celebrating each other's achievements, whether it be a wedding, engagement, birthday, babies, or just a good job done. They loved celebrations, even including divorce parties for a few of the team members over the years.

One time, there was even a raunchy hen night organised with bare-butt, naked butlers serving the drinks alongside the caterers who had been drafted in to supply a grand feast of a meal for twenty of the ladies. What an interesting night that had been. It was one that some of the ladies preferred to forget, she was pretty sure of that fact.

Above everything, it was a great place to work with a fabulous team. Some of her colleagues had become close friends as well as workmates, especially Carol. How much more did they have to experience together as a team in the coming months? Jane couldn't imagine working anywhere else, anytime soon.

Chapter Three

Lunchtime came around fast, so Jane grabbed her handbag and bottle of water before making her way out of the office and into the street. She hurried along to the clinic to meet with Paula for her appointment as planned.

The clinic was only a five-minute walk away, so she quickly ate the chicken salad roll that she'd picked up from the deli across the road from the office, trying not to spill the lashings of extra mayonnaise that she had asked for down her blouse.

Cambridge was a busy city with people rushing everywhere on foot most days and most times of the day. There wasn't really a time when it was quiet, but it was noisier during the day especially and the number of bikes on the roads was increasing tenfold each year. But she had become used to the hustle and bustle and much preferred it over her previous workplace in the centre of London where everything and everyone seemed frantic and extremely stressed twenty-four hours a day. Having to clamber on and off trains, the tube, buses, and black cabs to reach work, hurrying around making sure she was on time was just a hassle. But, since moving to work in Cambridge, her daily routine was now a little slower and more relaxed. She still rushed about being the busy person she was most days, but without as much worry as before and, of course, without the hour-long commute it had taken to reach her office each day.

As she scuttled along the street, sipping her water in between bites of the roll, her phone rang in her trouser pocket. She quickly stopped by a bench to juggle her roll and answer it.

"Hello." She hadn't looked to see who was calling as she was trying not to make a mess with her lunch. She balanced the bag on a nearby bench and cupped the phone between her ear and shoulder.

"Hi, honey, it's me, Sarah. Where are you?"

"Oh, hi, sweetie. I'm just in town, got an appointment in five minutes… you okay?"

"Yes, fine, honey. I just popped by the office to see if you wanted to grab a bucksie with your old mate."

Bucksie was their pet name for their favourite coffee shop, Starbucks. Jane always had a soya cappuccino, and Sarah had a full-on double shot Americano. They nearly always grabbed a large double chocolate chip cookie to share too.

"Oh, sorry, I can't do it today. Are you okay? Nothing wrong is there?"

"No, not at all. I just had an extra half hour to kill

between clients. I'll speak to you later, have fun," Sarah said and sounded a kiss down the phone.

"Okay, bye, love you…" Jane threw the virtual kiss back to her. They always ended their conversations that way. It was their thing as best friends of thirty-odd years. Something they had always done, once mobile phones had come into play anyway, in between endless text and WhatsApp messages.

They had been best friends for what seemed like their whole lives, meeting on their first day of primary school, aged just five. Jane had even named Robbie after Sarah's surname, Roberts. She had been through everything with her, including Sarah being her bridesmaid at their wedding, buying the pregnancy test, and even waiting outside the labour room when the twins had started arriving. She had gone to some of her doctor's appointments during the pregnancy if Karl hadn't been able to make it and sometimes even when he had; they were inseparable.

The two of them had a close bond and were more like sisters than friends, borrowing each other's clothes, shoes, makeup, pairing up with boyfriends to double date, and sharing each other's hopes and dreams for the future, even down to planning their weddings for one another. They'd had their ups and downs, as all friendships do, petty arguments and teasing, but never anything major and always resolved within a few hours. They'd never gone a day without being good friends.

Sarah had trained to become a beautician once they'd left high school and used to practise the techniques and treatments on Jane, which Jane hadn't minded in the least.

She loved a good pampering session and enjoyed helping Sarah progress in her career. She had worked hard at achieving the highest grades in beauty, specialising in acrylic nails and high-definition eyebrows. Her talents showed through her large and very loyal client base and word-of-mouth recommendations that she had coming in all the time. She had moved nearer to Jane and had managed to lease a salon in the heart of Cambridge. Jane had helped her to decorate it in the weeks leading up to her grand opening, which was a great success and made it into the local papers giving her that extra boost to start the business. 'Beauty By Sarah' had become the go-to salon in town, and Sarah had employed three more beauticians to keep up with the workload that kept increasing on a weekly basis. Jane took care of her accounts for her, so they benefited from each other one way or another.

Jane gathered herself together again, and a few minutes later, she arrived in the street of the clinic. She double-checked her phone to see which building number it was. She'd taken a screenshot of it after getting the email from Paula earlier in the day.

"Number fifty-four," she mouthed as she placed the phone back in the pocket of her trousers.

Taking the last swig of her bottle of water and putting all her rubbish in the bin close by, she glanced up at the entrance to the huge building towering in front of her.

It was a beautiful Victorian-style structure with black framed windows, wrought iron black fencing with painted gold tips, and a massive front door. They had gone all out on the enormous hanging baskets which were stunning and filled with yellow and red flowers and hints of green ivy trailing delicately over the sides.

She walked up the wide concrete steps to the front door where there was a gold sign with 'Spiral Care' etched on it. Finding the appropriate bell to ring on the wall, she pressed the button.

"Hello, Spiral Care, how can I help you?" a voice answered.

"Oh, hi. I'm here to see Nurse Paula. It's Jane Walden. I have an appointment at one o'clock."

"Okay. Come on in, Mrs Walden," replied the friendly female as the door buzzed open.

The inside was pretty and stylish too. It was a listed building in the centre of Cambridge and had pictures on the walls as you went in of how the building had been in past decades. Some of them were in black and white as it was so long ago. It hadn't changed that much, being preserved brilliantly over the years; it looked gorgeous and vintage in every way that Jane adored.

Bright, fresh flowers adorned the foyer desk, standing in a tall vase with pretty glass pebbles in the base. Jane took a second to sniff them as she passed by. She loved the fragrance of flowers, and these were beyond beautiful in scent.

As she reached the desk, a blonde-haired lady with moon-rimmed glasses sat behind the desk just finishing a phone call on the switchboard. She gestured with her finger as if to say she would be a minute. Jane smiled and nodded in acknowledgement and waited by the desk, still looking around at the features of the ceiling and walls. It was so decorative. She'd never quite seen a building in the city like it before. The ceilings were extraordinarily high and ornate with more vintage decor.

"Sorry about that. Was it Jane Walden?" the lady asked.

"That's okay. Yes, it is. I'm here to see the nurse, Paula I think," Jane replied, turning to face the desk once more.

"Yes, that's right. I have you on our list here. You are seeing the doctor too." She ticked in pencil next to Jane's name in the appointment book "If you'd like to take a seat in the waiting room, Paula will be with you shortly. Would you like something to drink?"

The lady, named Karen (Jane had read her name badge), pointed to the small room opposite.

"No, thank you," she replied and made her way to the waiting area. She sat down on a soft, blue fabric chair, placing her handbag on the seat next to her. There was no one else there, and it was strangely quiet apart from a slight hum of relaxing music playing at a low volume from a nearby CD player on the shelf. Jane couldn't remember the last time she had played a CD, let alone seen a player itself. The family had their music on iPods and phones now although they had recently ordered an Amazon Echo Dot for the kitchen so that music was playing quietly in the background. The kids enjoyed getting it to tell them jokes during dinner times or helping with their homework so it had become a useful addition to the household gadgets.

There was a small black coffee table in the middle of the room with some of the usual celebrity gossip magazines, as well as a few informational leaflets in clear Perspex stands about the clinic itself and all the various services and treatments available there. Posters were attached to the walls about different types of cancer and various support groups in the area. It brought back sad memories of her father; he hadn't had time to read information, and even if he had, Jane doubted he would've spent his days reading them anyway. He wasn't a lover of instructions or informative leaflets when it came to building furniture, toys, or anything else. He liked to work things out for himself, something Jane had inherited. She used to love to watch him figuring things out when she was a child and would always be on hand to pass him the tools that he thought he needed for each job. Most of the time, it all worked out, and even if it had taken a little longer than the instructions said it would, he got things done in the end.

She missed him so much and thought about him every day. He had been the best father to her and an amazing granddad for the short time that he'd been alive to enjoy the twins. He had been a twin too but lost his brother when they were just three years old in a boating accident, so the feelings he had for the two of them and the excitement he felt for their relationship was strong. He knew they would have a unique bond together that would always be solid, and he reminded them of that as soon as they understood.

Noticing a mobile phone sign on the wall, she grabbed her phone from her pocket and switched it to silent. Her phone was never off unless the battery had given up. It was her lifeline to everyone; every appointment and detail of her life was stored on there and hundreds of photos that she kept meaning to get printed out or stored in the cloud in organised files. She really didn't know how she would cope without it now or how she had coped before the madness of mobile phones. The only time it wasn't near her was when she was asleep, although it was still used as an alarm clock on the dressing table in the bedroom at home.

Just as she chucked the phone into her handbag, Paula came into the room. "Hi, Jane, thanks for coming in at such short notice."

Jane stood up to greet her, grabbing hold of her bag from the chair. "Oh, that's okay. The office is only up the road, as you know, so it didn't take too long. I even managed to grab a bit of lunch."

"That's great, lunchtimes fly by, don't they? Anyway, do come this way." Paula led the way down the long corridor to a consulting room, which was just as beautiful as the rest of the building with more fresh flowers adorning a little corner table.

"Wow, the flowers here are amazing," Jane commented as she caught a whiff of their strong scent as she passed.

"Yes, they are aren't they," Paula agreed. "The florist on the high street is amazing, we have a delivery every week. It keeps the place smelling fresh," she continued as she directed Jane into the room. "Plus, they look fabulous and smell delightful, don't they?"

Jane nodded in agreement as she entered the room and saw a lady sitting at a desk, reading some notes and examining some medical scans in front of her.

"Jane, this is Doctor Ramsey, she is one of our breast cancer specialists." Paula gestured towards the desk.

The lady stood up and reached out her hand to meet Jane's, taking her glasses off which then hung around her neck.

"Hi, Jane, please call me Mary. I do hate that doctor label. How are you?" Doctor Mary Ramsey was around fifty with a short bob haircut in a rich mahogany shade. Her dark blue skirt suit was flawless, and she looked very smart and professional.

"Hi… yes, I'm good, thank you," Jane replied as she shook her hand.

"Take a seat, please," said Mary as they both sat down facing each other. "Now, Paula tells me that you have felt a little lump for a few months, and after having a look herself, she has suggested that I take a closer look for you. Would that be okay to do today while you are with us?"

Jane replied, "Yes, no problem at all. I think it's just scar tissue from a breast operation I had to have a few years back. Maybe it just needs more time to settle down or something? It was a breast reduction procedure."

"Okay, well, let's take a look and go from there," said Doctor Ramsey. "Paula, could you show Jane to the examination room, and I will be there shortly when she's ready. You just need to remove your top and bra, okay?"

"Jane, this way please." Paula gestured to a door.

Leaving her handbag on the chair in the main consulting room, Jane followed.

The examination room was light and airy with a small window and cream roller blind dressed again by a pretty wicker basket of flowers on the windowsill. It had an examination couch and a few medical supplies on a silver trolley nearby with a tiny sink and all the necessary cleaning soaps and tissues.

Paula pulled down the roll of paper to cover the couch and asked Jane to pop herself onto it and remove her top clothing. She gave her a white towel to cover herself and then went to let the doctor know they were ready for her.

As Jane sat there, she thought about what the family should have for dinner that night, whether the kids had any after-school clubs, and when did dance class start for Cassie this evening. Glancing at her watch for no apparent reason as you do sometimes when thinking of times, she remembered dance was at five o'clock and Karl was collecting her tonight as he was finishing a little bit earlier than usual. She was sure that Robbie had football training at half seven, so dinner had to be on time for the boys to get to the football training field ten minutes from their house. Her mind was wandering and furiously busy as usual, but it was interrupted by the doctor and Paula entering the room.

Chapter Four

"Okay, Jane, lay back now and try to relax as much as you can. I'm just going to do a quick physical examination of both of your breasts and then we will see where we need to go from there regarding any further investigations or scans that may be needed, is that okay?"

Jane nodded a little nervously in agreement, laid back on the couch and removed the towel from her chest area as the doctor stood closely beside the couch putting some blue sterile gloves on.

It was a little uncomfortable for Jane as Doctor Ramsey pressed into the lump and prodded and rubbed the surrounding tissue. She also began to feel the other breast for comparison as Paula had done at the previous, less formal consultation at her work the previous day.

Everything seemed a bit tense and it was eerily quiet as the doctor concentrated.

"What's the damage then?" Jane jokingly asked as she

glanced up at the doctor and then over to Paula.

"Well… I can feel the scar tissue that you have mentioned but the lump that you have also felt is located slightly off to the left of that mass of tissue. I would like to take a biopsy from it if that is alright. We will send it off to our local lab to get things checked just to make sure there's nothing sinister going on. Would you be able to stay a bit longer today so that I can do that and get it sent off immediately? It doesn't take too long to come back, usually a few days at most and the sooner we can get it sent, the sooner we can give you your results."

"Erm, I guess that makes sense, yes, that's fine, but I would need to ring my work just to let them know I'll be a bit later than I originally thought."

"Certainly, pop the towel over yourself again for now, and we will leave you to make your call. It should only take around half an hour. Give us a shout when you are done with your call. We'll get all the necessary equipment ready, and I'll take another look at the mammogram screening images that you had yesterday from the mobile unit."

"I'll get your handbag for you," Paula went and collected Jane's bag from the other room where she had left it earlier.

"Thank you, I won't be a minute, they try to answer pretty quickly," Jane replied, smiling, and quickly rummaged into the bottom of her bag to reach the phone as Paula left the room once again.

It rang a couple of times but then the office answer machine kicked in, so she quickly left a message. "Hi, it's Jane, could you let Carol know that I will be late back from lunch, my appointment has overrun, but I'll be there as soon as I can. Thanks, speak later." She hated talking to the machine but knew the office may have been busy with client phone calls and the lack of staff who were also on their own lunchbreaks.

Placing her phone back in the bag, again making sure it was switched to silent, Jane popped her head around the doorway of the small room to let the doctor and Paula know she had finished her call.

Paula then wheeled another one of the silver trolleys into the room with lots of stainless steel, sterilized equipment and oversized needles, strategically placed in order on a large piece of blue tissue.

"Wow, that all looks a bit scary and serious," Jane commented, glancing at the trolley, eyes widened.

"It's not as bad as it looks, Jane, honestly. Try not to worry too much. It doesn't hurt. I've had it done myself and it's not painful at all, just more of a stinging sensation than anything else." Paula gave a reassuring smile as the doctor followed her in a few seconds later and Jane lay back down.

"So, what we're going to do is take a sample of fluid from the lump itself and the lymph nodes with a small needle. It might sting a little bit, but I'll be as gentle as I can, okay?"

Jane nodded, acknowledging the instructions.

"Okay, just relax, just a tiny scratch now, Jane." Doctor Ramsey slightly lifted Jane's breast to make sure that she could see the entire lump, inserted the needle, and slowly drew some fluid out before taking a sample from her lymph nodes area too. "There you go. All done," she said as she placed the needles onto the sterilized tray. "Let's get that over to the lab asap please, Paula. I've labelled it all up so it's ready to go straight off, if you could just mark the envelope as urgent for me, please?"

"I didn't feel a thing. You certainly know how to do that alright," said Jane, smiling as she sat up and fastened her bra.

"I do try to make it as comfortable a procedure as I possibly can. I've had over twelve years' practice now. I know it's not a pleasant thing to have but you did brilliantly, Jane, well done." Mary smiled at her and continued, "We would also like to carry out a second mammogram and maybe get an ultrasound scan done while you are here if you have the time? It's best to get everything done sooner rather than later and while you are here, we may as well get all the tests done in one go."

"Oh alright, yes, that's fine," replied Jane as she grabbed the rest of her clothes from the chair next to her.

The doctor finished by washing her hands and drying them on the tissues by the door to the other room. "Come back in when you're all decent, Jane, and we can get the other scans done." She walked off back into the main consultation room.

"Are you alright, Jane? Do you need any help with anything or have any questions for me?" asked Paula as she finished labelling up the padded envelope.

"No, I'm fine. She's lovely, isn't she?" she whispered, nodding her head in the direction of the other room.

"Yes…she is, she's a very good doctor too, really knows her stuff, you're in good hands with her. See you in a minute, take your time and come through when you're ready." She patted Jane's knee as she left.

Just as she was fastening the first button on her blouse, her phone began noisily vibrating. Having forgotten that even when it was on silent it would still vibrate noisily, she rummaged to locate it as quickly as she could.

"Hi, honey. You okay?" said the familiar voice on the other end of the phone; it was Karl.

"Hi, babe. Yes, I'm fine, you?" She held the phone with her shoulder as she continued buttoning her blouse and straightening her clothes, feeling herself heat up with embarrassment.

"Yeah, all good here, darling. Just catching up with you while I have a coffee break. What are you up to? On lunch?" he asked as she heard him slurp his drink.

"Yes, a spot of late lunch actually, nothing exciting going on here, you know, the usual. I'm just grabbing a coffee up the road from the office. I needed to get out for a bit, it's crazy manic in there today so I took a later lunch break for a change," she lied.

"Cool. Okay, enjoy. Remember I'm finishing a bit earlier tonight, so I'll see you at home about five fifteen-ish after dropping Cassie to dance. Then I'll take Robbie to footy after dinner."

"Oh, yes. No worries. See you then, love you. Bye." Jane mimicked a kiss over the phone and hung up, just hearing him mutter, *'I love you'* back.

"Sorry about that. It was my husband," she apologised as she went into the other room where the doctor and Paula were waiting, writing up some more notes in her file. "The phone still vibrates for certain people even when it's on silent, I should've just turned it off, sorry."

"No problem at all, Jane. We are all tied to our mobiles these days, there's no escape at times, hey." She smiled back sweetly at her and continued, "Right…we will get those samples sent off today, a courier will collect them within the next hour and should have some news in a few days. Is this the best number to contact you?" Mary closed the file and showed Jane the details on the front of it.

"Yes, that's it. Anytime is fine. It's never off, as you now know." She laughed. "Although I do try to get some rest from it in the evenings. Maybe during my working hours would be best, like, nine until three thirty? I won't miss your call or texts then." Jane didn't have any worries as the doctor and Paula had made her feel completely at ease and relaxed about everything. "I'm just up the road with work as Paula knows, so I can pop down for the results if that would be easier."

"That's great. Now, Paula will take you through and get your second mammogram done. We can decide from there if we need an ultrasound too. There was a small shadow showing on the scan that you had during the mobile clinic yesterday, so we want to double-check everything for you and have another look. Sometimes the machines can show abnormalities that are nothing to worry about, but it is best to check if any abnormal results do show up."

"Okay, and thank you for your time, doctor, I mean… Mary. It's been lovely to meet you."

"This way, Jane," said Paula as she opened the door for her and took the file from the doctor who'd stood up to see them both out.

They walked along the corridor to the scanning rooms, which were just as bright and cold, with the same massive machines that had been on the mobile breast screening lorry at the office and she was soon prepped again for another breast squashing procedure.

Jane winced a little as the machine pressed down on her breasts yet again. Two in one week was enough, and she thought maybe her breasts could be a little bruised or tender from the first time round of squeezing yesterday, but it was soon over, and she was ready to get out of there. She'd never got dressed and undressed so many times in one day.

"Well done today, Jane. You've done ever so well with all the prodding and poking around. We may call you to discuss things or we may need you to come in and get the results in a few days. Please try not to worry, we will let you know as soon as we get the lab results back and they are fairly quick for us." Paula walked back down the corridor with Jane to see her out to the front door. "See you soon."

"I hope not," joked Jane as she shook Paula's hand and opened the front door. "But thanks, it's not been as horrible as I expected it to be." She left feeling confident she wouldn't need to return anytime soon.

She made her way back to the office and couldn't help but begin thinking about her father again. All the information around the clinic had revived the sad memories of how quick his cancer had taken hold of him and how soon he had been gone from their lives.

It had been such a shock to the whole family, but he had

been so determined, having no intention of giving up his fight against it, staying upbeat and strong right to the end. He even sang a favourite song to her with all the strength he could, a few days before he died. That song now meant more to Jane than ever, and whenever she heard it come on the radio or TV, it took her back to that sad day once again. He was still smiling, and she always had that memory of his caring but also, very scared face. He was trying to be strong, not wanting to leave them, but he knew deep down that he was fading too quickly, by the hour almost. Such a brave and courageous man and someone she admired greatly for his courage and determination for life, even in the face of fast-approaching death, he was her hero that's for sure.

She had spent hours sitting with him, recalling childhood memories of what they had been through over the years; learning gardening skills, building sandcastles on holidays on the English coast, the driving lessons he had given her, both trying to keep calm, her first bike that he'd spent weeks holding onto the back of until finally, she rode off by herself and then promptly fell off within minutes, and so many more great family times and events were discussed. It had kept them both strong at the time, and although painful and emotional, it was their special way of keeping each other smiling during such a sad chapter of their lives.

Janice, Jane's mother, had found it much harder to cope, losing her husband of fifty-two years though having Jane, Karl, and the twins did make it a little bit easier, something to keep her mind busy, and Jane had promised her Pops that she would always take care of her mum. She'd made him a secret promise that she would try and make sure that her mum wasn't on her own forever after he was gone. He'd whispered to her in the days before his death, to find his little dancing queen, as he called her, a nice gentleman to grow older with.

Jane had been their only child as Janice had developed post-natal depression soon after the birth, which had taken a long time to get over. For the first two years, Pops had taken the main role of looking after the baby while she got treatment and help, which was hard for all of them. After she had recovered, several years later, when the subject of more children had come up, they decided that Jane was all they needed, so they never attempted to get pregnant again. Jane always envied the other kids at her school who had a big brother or little sister to play with at home, but she never went without fun and games while Pops was around. He'd made sure of it and took her to weekly kids' clubs and fun days out so that she could mix and play with lots of other children.

She remembered making a pact that she and Karl would have more than one child as soon as they'd fallen in love and got married, and when it was announced that they were going to have twins, it was a complete surprise, but a true blessing and something Pops was more than ecstatic about for another reason.

He'd always told Jane that twins were extra special children. He'd sat her down when they'd found out about the pregnancy and showed her the few rare photos that he had of himself with his twin brother before the tragic accident, and he loved the fact that there would be two in one go for them. Jane had been shocked but happy, of course. When they were born, one of each, their family felt complete at that moment so there was no need to think about having anymore. Their pact had come true sooner than they had thought, and things couldn't have been more perfect.

Chapter Five

The next few days were fairly normal for Jane with running the kids around to various classes, football training, dance activities and sleepovers at their friends' houses, working, meeting up with Sarah, shopping with Janice and spending time in the evenings catching up with Karl and his work tales.

She hadn't given the biopsy or the new round of tests and scans a second thought and wasn't expecting the clinic to call any time soon. She had a big meeting coming up at work, which was all she could focus her attention on over the next week so she had to try and remain calm, collected and in control of any situation that may arise.

The journey to work that day though was unusually stressful and it was really getting to her. It was chucking it down with some seriously heavy rain and seeing through the car wipers rapidly swishing away from side to side was proving extremely difficult. The wind was also picking up, and cars were tooting their horns a lot more than usual and for what seemed much longer than usual too. Everyone was rushing around with their blown inside out umbrellas, crashing into one another or poking people with the spikes unknowingly. The puddles even seemed deeper than normal too, and this meant soaking wet shoes by the time she got to work. Why had she chosen to wear her small ballet pumps today of all days, she thought, looking down at the third puddle she had managed to step in since getting out of the car.

On arriving at the office block, her feet were sodden, so she quickly went to the ladies' room, removed and chucked her tights, then tried to dry out her shoes a bit under the hand dryers. With no success on that front, she carried them upstairs and then relaxed back in her office chair, barefoot, with a huge sigh of relief that she'd made it to the office in one piece before the big meeting, sort of. From then on, everything seemed to calm down a little bit. The rain cleared over the next half an hour or so, and the sun shone through the windows with a double rainbow appearing in the distance, gliding beautifully over the high buildings. Jane was ready to go home already, but a long day ahead was in store, so she set to it, delving into the files on her computer with intense scrutiny to ensure she got everything perfected in time. Before long, it was three o'clock and her big meeting was over, so she was looking forward to finishing on time and getting home for a nice warm bubble bath and glass of wine.

As she was clearing away her files and folders, and packing up her laptop, her mobile began to ring so she grabbed it off her desk and answered, "Hello?"

"Hi, Jane...it's Paula here, from Spiral Care clinic."

"Oh, hi..." Jane stopped what she was doing with a puzzled look on her face. She hadn't expected to hear from them as it had been a few days and she had forgotten about it, if she was honest, what with the busy workload she had on.

"Hi, sorry to bother you but we need you to pop in and see us for another chat about your results from the tests that we did. Is it possible for you to make it this afternoon or early evening?"

"Erm...yes, I guess so. I'm just finishing up at work for the day, I could be over in about twenty minutes to half an hour, is that convenient?"

"That would be great. Do you have anyone you could bring with you, a friend, your husband?"

"Do I need to have someone with me?" Jane replied, worried.

"No, you don't have to, it's just that sometimes people like to have a family member or friend with them for any test results, but it's absolutely fine to come alone if you would rather do that."

"Yes, I'll be fine coming by myself. My husband is busy with work anyway, so no need to worry him or anyone else really, it's just a few test results after all," Jane replied honestly. She *didn't* like to worry Karl at the best of times, let alone randomly asking him or anyone else to come to a cancer clinic with her.

"Okay, Jane, we'll see you soon then," replied Paula.

"Yes, I'll see you as soon as I can get out of here, thank

you." Jane hung up the phone, wondering why Paula had asked that question. Why would she need someone there with her? It's just a lump of scar tissue, after all, she thought, and she much preferred to go to appointments alone these days anyway. There was no need to cause any unnecessary worry to other people for a routine follow-up, something they'd not even known about her going to in the first place. Maybe she was just overthinking the question and being paranoid. She carried on getting her bag ready and collected her shoes from near the window where the sun had dried them out finally.

Carol popped her head into Jane's office wearing a big smile. "Hey, lovely. Some of us are mooching over to the little wine bar on the corner for an hour to celebrate today's events. Do you want to come along, seeing as it's, well, Thursday?" She giggled cheekily.

"Erm, no sorry, I just had a call...I've got to pop and see someone quickly. I'll come along after if it doesn't go on too late. Have fun and have a glass for me if I don't make it over in time."

"Okay, my lovely. Are you alright though? You look a little flushed in the cheeks."

"Yeah, I think so. Just tired, I guess. It's been a really long day, hasn't it?" She smiled, forcing some false cheerfulness into her face. "See you later, maybe? I'll try and get there if I can."

"Okay, hope to see you a bit later then, and well done in there today...you were brilliant, even with your wet, soggy shoes on. I don't know how you do it, my darling, you're just fabulous." She winked as she left, waving her arms around, gathering everyone up.

Jane had been one of the main speakers in the meeting with another firm who were interested in co-working with their company. Carol's idea was that joining forces would help them grow the business faster and she had put Jane forward to pitch them with the idea. She always put more than a hundred per cent into her work, and when it came to big meetings, co-working projects, or presentations, Jane was the best woman for the job. She knew the right things to say and how to get around or answer any awkward questions. This was something that Carol loved about her and encouraged routinely with any further advanced training that was on offer.

Leaving the office, Jane made her way to the clinic once again, thinking about what they were going to say when she arrived. Maybe they could refer her to have the scar tissue looked at. She hadn't liked the feel of it for some time and was always overly conscious that Karl could feel it when they were intimate. Hopefully, it would get sorted now that someone, an expert, had looked at it. Surely it would be just a simple operation to flatten it out or something like that. She hoped for that outcome anyway and then she could relax and stop being so body conscious.

Arrived and checked-in, it wasn't long before she was directed into the consultation room. "Hi, Jane, thank you for coming in so soon. Do take a seat." Doctor Ramsey and Paula were waiting in the office that she had been in a few days earlier, so she sat down and placed her handbag on her lap, relaxed and not expecting the meeting to take more than ten minutes or so.

"Okay, right. Here we are," Dr Ramsey continued as she rustled some files and papers together. "Jane, we sent off the biopsy samples from the breast tissue and we also had another good look and compared the mammograms that you had carried out here and at the mobile unit." There then seemed to be an unusually long pause before she continued. "The shadow that we mentioned before was on the second scan too. It's an abnormality in the breast tissue where you have felt the lump." Another pause ensued as the doctor removed her glasses and looked up at Jane's bewildered face. "I'm afraid it's not the news we were hoping to get back, Jane."

"Oh…so what is the news?" Jane asked, anxiously, leaning forward to try and view the scans on the desk in front of the doctor.

"The results show a very large tumour in the left breast, which is malignant. I'm afraid that it's quite aggressive and has spread to a wider area in your chest. It's treatable but, it's one that is inoperable. I'm so sorry, Mrs Walden."

Jane was stunned and slightly puzzled. Her eyes glossed over as Paula came and sat down next to her, gently placing her hand on Jane's. Her eyes frantically turned to look at Paula and then back to the doctor once again.

"Aggressive? You mean just large, removable? Is it treatable, or what, sorry, I'm confused?" She remembered back when her Pops' doctor had used these types of words when they had given him his diagnosis and discussed treatments with him. She had been with her parents when they had found out the news and they weren't words that she wanted to hear again so soon. Especially directed to her this time.

Doctor Ramsey continued, "It's treatable, yes, as I said, but not curable, it has spread too far. It's malignant, Jane, do you understand what that means?"

The silent pause in the room felt like forever. All she could hear was the ticking of the clock on the wall which seemed to be getting louder by the second. Her eyes moved from side to side, trying to figure out the words that were being spoken to her. What was happening here exactly, what was she being told?

"So, I have cancer, is that what you're saying, and it's not going to go away?" she gasped as a single tear trickled down her cheek.

"Yes, I'm afraid it is breast cancer. We have various treatments that we can offer to help you, such as drugs and chemotherapy, but I'm afraid it's gone too far to cure, your medication needs to be started straight away, and we can go from there as to whether we can look at removing the breast at a later stage to stop it spreading any further if this is something you'd want to look into."

"Okay." Jane nodded her head, agreeing with the doctor but not really hearing everything. "I, erm… I've got to go… I need to… sorry, I just have to get out of here," she stammered as she stood up suddenly, dropping her bag upside down; she'd forgotten to take hold of it as she rose from the chair, and all her things fell noisily onto the floor but in an unreal kind of silence.

Everything was moving in slow motion; she saw the items falling, hitting the floor, and the room seemed to start spinning as if she had drunk too much. Gathering her things as quickly as she could, she reached for the door handle of the office but everything started to appear blurred. She could hardly see through the tears in her eyes. The ticking of the clock got even louder, pounding through her head. Her words became slurred, her legs trembled, and heat flooded through her, sweat breaking out on her brow… then all of a sudden, there was nothing but silence and blackness.

~

"Hey, how are you feeling?" Paula was looking at Jane as she lay on the couch rather pale and disorientated.

Looking around, Jane was confused for a moment as to where she was.

"What… what happened?" she asked, wiping her forehead briskly with the palm of her hand.

"You fainted, Jane," replied Paula softly.

"Oh, God…I didn't?" She placed her hand over her mouth in embarrassment as she sat up, slowly moving her legs around to reach the floor.

"Take it easy now, you've had a shock. Here, drink some water before you try and stand up." Paula passed her a glass of water from the table in front of them.

"Thanks…" She sipped the ice-cool liquid and took a deep breath. "I guess this wasn't a bad dream then?"

Paula just shook her head slowly, "We will do everything we can for you, Jane. I know this must be the last thing you expected to hear, and we hate giving news like that. Do you have anyone you could call to come and collect you?"

"No… no, I just need a few minutes. I'll be okay. I don't

need anyone to come, honestly."

"How is our patient?" Doctor Ramsey asked, walking back into the room.

"She's okay, just a bit shocked I think, understandably," answered Paula taking the glass.

"Doctor…Mary…" Jane glanced up. "Are the results pretty final? Is there any chance of a mistake, any other tests or something else you could do for me because I can stay longer if you need me to?" Her voice trembled as she remembered the words again, *'cancer, no cure, it's spread, inoperable, treatments, chemo, malignant.'*

"The tests that we have run are conclusive, I'm afraid. We've not had any come back inaccurate in all the years we have been running, and we use only the best laboratories to provide the results for us. We can clearly see it on the second scan that you had here with us. Would you like to discuss the options of where we go from here?"

"I think I just need some time to myself now, to be honest. I just thought it was some scar tissue, that you'd send me packing to some other hospital or clinic to get it fixed, removed, or something along those lines." She tried a slight smile and hint of a laugh, but it was hard, and nothing came as she stood up.

"Again, we are so very sorry but please pop back tomorrow. We can begin treatment and, in the meantime, here's some medication that we suggest you start taking straight away. They are chemotherapy drugs and also some anti-sickness tablets to take alongside. The chemo drugs can sometimes make you feel queasy."

"Right. Okay, thanks." Jane looked at the two pill

bottles, still feeling overwhelmed and shocked about the whole situation that had confronted her.

Gathering her things together and wiping her eyes dry, she took the tablets and left the clinic, traipsing up the street without knowing where she was heading or what to think or do. The usual buzz of the streets seemed eerily quiet in some way or maybe she had just switched off to the outside world right now.

What the hell just happened? Her world had been shaken to the very core, and she didn't know how to react to this news. It couldn't be real, and she hoped she would wake up from this nightmare soon.

Before she knew it, she had started running and only stopped when she reached the cemetery gates down the road. How did she end up there and why was she here right now? Coincidence? Maybe she needed to talk to her pops, and he'd brought her here? Everything seemed to be a muffled string of questions running through her mind at nineteen to the dozen, and she was totally confused about it all.

Whatever the reason she was here, it seemed like the best place to be alone and gather her thoughts before she had to make her way home. Maybe it would help her come to grips with this awful chapter in her life.

Slowly walking up to her father's gravestone, she noticed how it was still shiny and looked like new. Jane knew that her mum visited regularly and always polished the headstone and replaced the flowers. There were white lilies laid down in front of the headstone. She ran her hand over the top of it and knelt down, feeling the prickly grass through her trousers.

"Hey, you," she said, her voice breaking slightly as she swallowed hard. "Guess what?" Heavy tears now rolled down her face, and she hung her head down. "We'll be together sooner than we thought, Pops." Gasping for breath, she broke down sobbing at the reality of the situation with her hand still clasped hard on his headstone.

Chapter Six

This all seemed insane, a bad dream, or more like a terrible nightmare. She hoped again that she would wake up any minute, and this tragic day would be over and out of her head. The day had gone from bad to worse to downright awful and she felt like everything was stacked against her now. How was she going to get through this?

"Are you okay?" came a calming male voice from behind her.

Jane wiped her eyes and turned around to see a male silhouette as the sun was shining behind him. "I'm a good listener if that would help?" He shrugged his shoulders and smiled sweetly at her as he moved and came into view.

She looked up into his dark brown eyes. He looked sad too, but friendly with it. She pushed herself up from the floor and dusted off the grass from her knees.

He pointed over to a bench nearby that had two beautiful cherry blossom trees arched over it, just like the trees in her street at home, although they weren't in full bloom at the moment being late June. They slowly walked together in silence, then sat down with a short pause as she gathered herself together and wiped her tears clear.

"Your father?" he asked, pointing at the gravestone where he had found her.

"Yes, my Pops." She sniffed. "Sorry, I'm Jane, Jane Walden."

"James," he replied. "I visit my mum every few days here too. She went off about six years ago now, but it doesn't get any easier. They say time heals, but I don't know, maybe it will one day. Just not right now for me. How about you, how long has it been?" He had a lovely calming voice, well-spoken but with a slight cockney accent to it.

"Ten years nearly. I don't visit Pops nearly enough really. My mum does. She comes here monthly with her special polish and cloth, always has a bunch of fresh flowers for him. He loved lilies, white ones mostly, but she can't get them all year, so any sort will do really…not that he would mind…" There was a moment of silence again as she caught her breath and turned to face him. "Do you mind me asking how your mum… you know…?"

"Died? No, not at all. It was the big C, melanoma, bloody evil thing that it is, took hold of her so rapidly like you wouldn't believe. Killed her other organs and her body so quickly. She fought it for over two years, did well bless her, but hey…once it's decided, that's basically it, isn't it?" He sounded angry still but had so much love and affection in his voice for this lady he called mum.

"It took my Pops too, bladder cancer for him," she

replied. "Within months…just two months he had with us after finding out."

"Bloody hell, no time to think about it then? I'm sorry, Jane. It's a shitty thing for anyone to have, and it's so hard for those left behind too. I just wish it would do us all a favour and leave everyone alone, it's so unfair."

"Yes, I agree totally. The funny thing is…" she paused trying not to cry again, "Well, it's not funny but, they've just told me…that I have it. Mine's breast cancer." It was no good, her eyes filled with tears yet again. She brushed them away as they fell hard down her flushed cheeks, sniffing back loudly, she sarcastically blubbered, "What a joke, hey? Although I'm finding it very hard to laugh about the whole bloody thing."

"Oh shit, I feel like a right prick now with what I just said about mum."

"Don't worry, James, you weren't to know," she answered, wiping away another escaping tear or two.

"As I said…I'm a good listener. I know you don't know me from Adam, but I'm here quite often, and it's good to get out and have a chat sometimes."

Jane continued, "It was literally like half an hour or so ago… I fainted when they told me the diagnosis. What an absolute idiot. And something then brought me here. I guess Pops was calling me to help make me strong, to make me think about it all with him. I don't know…I just don't know…" she flustered. "I was supposed to be going straight home tonight, but…I can't face it, I just don't know how to be with everyone and what to say." Jane shook in sorrow with her hands holding her head as she bent over to lean on her trembling knees.

"Look, Jane, as I said, I'm here most days for an hour or more sometimes. Sad, I know but, well, it just feels better being here with Mum, you know. I sort of feel close to her again… so if you ever need a chat, a cry, a rant or just want someone to sit with in silence," he offered kindly, placing his hand on her shoulder. "Sometimes you just need someone there to let off steam, someone who's not directly involved with it all. I only have my brother but it's hard to talk about Mum with him."

"Thank you. I just don't know what to say at the minute, to be honest. I'm confused. I just thought it was nothing, and now, all of a sudden, I'm dying."

"Okay. Look, it's cool, I understand. Let's change the subject, eh? Why not start by telling me a bit about yourself, married? Kids? Your job? Tell me everything."

He had such a kind voice. She thought that he must be around the same age as her as she watched him talking. He had dark hair to match his dark eyes and was dressed casually in a polo shirt, blue jeans, and trainers. He was getting off the cancer subject to try and stop her from being upset and crying; to help calm her down a little, and it was actually working, so she didn't mind opening up.

She took a deep breath and began. "I'm married to Karl, my college sweetheart." She grinned, glancing at him briefly. "We have two children; twins actually, a boy and a girl. They're my whole life, my absolute world… they've just turned thirteen and are in high school already. I don't know where the time has gone, they were babies one minute and then stroppy teenagers the next, but I love them dearly." She smiled again as she thought of the children and how beautiful they both were, then carried on. "I work in the city, not far from here. I'm an accountant…a bit boring, I know, but I like it, and it's something I trained hard for…" She paused. "Sorry, I'm going on a bit, aren't I?"

"Nope, twins, wow. That must be hard work?"

"It was when they were first born, but it's got easier as they've grown. Once they were feeding and sleeping at the same time anyway." She managed a slight snigger of a laugh. "Cassie and Robbie, my little darlings." She paused again as she thought of them as babies and how quickly they had grown up. How long would she have left with them? The unknown timeline was unbearable. Her thoughts turned to her new confidant, James, as she asked, "What about you? Are you married or have any children?" She looked down at his hands and noticed there were no rings, no wedding band.

James stood up and stretched his arms up high above his head, his T-shirt slightly lifted, showing his bronzed and very toned abs for a fleeting second. "Not anymore, I'm afraid, the married part anyhow. We broke up about two years ago. She, er…went for a younger model…"

"Oh, sorry. What was he, eighteen?" she joked.

He laughed back. "Haha, no, it's cool, she decided that she preferred dresses instead of trousers if you know what I mean?" He looked down at her and raised his eyebrows.

They both broke off and laughed as Jane held her hand to her mouth in shock. "Crikey, really? That must've been terrible."

"To be honest, Jane, I had sort of expected it. She'd

asked me about…well, you know…getting another woman involved in our relationship, as in three of us having a thing and getting someone else to move in." Jane's eyebrows rose in shock again and her eyes widened as she listened. "Not my thing though, not the permanent way anyway," he said, winking cheekily. "I said that if she needed to get it out of her system, maybe she should try it by herself, tried to be the 'open relationship guy' but, that was that. The nail in the coffin, excuse the pun." He pointed to their surroundings.

"Jesus!" Jane exclaimed. "Really?"

"Yep. We never really thought about kids either, we enjoyed the long off the cuff, spontaneous 18-30 club-style holidays in Ibiza and that, going out partying too much, I guess. Just left it a bit late to get into all that baby stuff and then she was gone so that was that basically."

"Me and Karl got all the partying done before the twins came along and no, we enjoy a holiday together as a family once or twice a year if we're lucky. Mum comes with us sometimes too," she replied as she glanced down at her watch. "Shoot, look at the time. I need to go… it's been really nice to talk to you. Would you mind meeting me again? Say no if I'm being too much?"

"Of course not. Same time tomorrow?" He smiled at her sweetly as she stood up in front of the bench.

"Yes… I'll be here after work, around three thirty, and James…" She turned back around to face him. "Thank you. You've made a very difficult day a bit easier to deal with, just by chatting."

They smiled at each other briefly before she turned and

walked away. She now felt much better than when she had arrived and that was all thanks to this complete stranger she had just met under very strained and upsetting circumstances. James had been just what she had needed at that precise time and she felt lucky to have met him when she did.

On her way back to collect her car from work, she thought about what she was going to say to Karl about why she was so late back. She wasn't ready to tell him the awful news when she hadn't begun to come to terms with it herself, so she had to think of something to cover her tracks.

She parked up in the driveway and looked at her eyes in the rear-view mirror. They looked puffy and red. She would have to make something up about why she looked so terrible. He'd know she'd been crying if she didn't come up with a story of some kind. Nervously thinking all the way to the front door and taking a deep breath, she put the key in the door and stepped in quietly.

"Hello…" she called down the hallway, placing her keys on the sideboard in the hall.

"Hello, babe," Karl's voice called back. "I'm in the kitchen, darling."

She made her way through to where he was busy preparing dinner. "Sorry I'm late, babe. Thank you for starting dinner. I had to visit the doctor quickly after work, got something in my eye at lunchtime, just after I spoke to you actually, it was so sore, but it's all sorted now, thank goodness."

"That's alright, my darling, you sure it's okay now though?" he asked, turning to face her. "Oh, they both look a bit red," he said as he looked into her normally sparkling, clear eyes.

"Yeah, all good now, don't worry. They had to put some eye drops in both of them, and you know how I love having liquid in my eyes. Do you want me to finish up here?" She hung her bag over the back of one of the dining chairs and began rolling her sleeves up.

"No, it's all under control here. You go put your feet up. I'll give you a shout when it's ready."

It was as if he knew how much she needed to put her feet up and rest tonight. She glanced back at him as she left the kitchen and smiled to herself. He'd put on her favourite sausage dog clad, cooking apron, making him look silly but it also made him look cute. He seemed to use absolutely everything when he cooked, and the washing up was as though he had catered for thirty or more people, not just the four of them. She had always found this hilarious about him, but she loved his cooking when he did do it, so she never moaned or made fun of him, even when their dishwasher had broken, and she and the kids spent the next hour washing up all the pots and pans and every utensil they had. His father had been a head chef in the centre of London working in some of the biggest hotels in the city, so he'd learned most of his culinary skills from him but enjoyed adventuring into new recipes and food concoctions which explained the copious amounts of kitchen utensils, pots and pans.

Jane went upstairs to change into something a bit more comfortable than her work clothes, some jersey joggers and a baggy T-shirt sounded good right now as she rummaged through her drawers and undressed, chucking her work clothes into the washing basket.

Sitting on the edge of the bed, she caught her reflection in the mirror and took her hair down; it fell gently onto her bare shoulders. She had always had amazing hair, long and with a natural wave to it. Apart from her smile, her hair was another one of her defining features. As she tousled it with her fingers and stared at her reflection sighing to herself, she began wondering if she would lose some or all of her locks from the chemo drugs or treatments that they were suggesting she underwent. What was she going to look like in a few months if that's the amount of time she had left? For now, she didn't know any timescales and didn't want to think about it tonight. She just wanted to be with her gorgeous family, the ones she loved so much and try to forget about the shocking events that had just happened in her, before today, 'normal' life.

That evening after dinner, the twins were watching TV in their rooms so Jane just looked in on them and whispered her usual, "Love you," to them, blowing them a kiss, before going to her bedroom.

The day had been intense, and she didn't know where to go next. All she knew was that she couldn't tell anyone her news just yet. She had a new friend in James to confide in, and that was enough for now. That was until such a time that she felt strong enough to cope with it herself and begin to reveal the secret. She needed to get all the information possible and all the facts regarding her treatments, so decided that she would contact the clinic again the next day and find out everything that needed to be done and get it all arranged as soon as possible. She needed to have the time to sort this all out in her own head so decided she would quickly send Carol a text message to request the morning off.

Hi Carol. Sorry it's late, but could I get the morning off tomorrow? Something has come up that I need to sort out before the weekend.

Carol, as always, texted back straight away; whatever the time, her phone didn't leave her side.

Yes, of course, my lovely. I hope everything's alright, let me know if you need anything. I'll tell you what, take the whole day off. You've earned it this week with all your hard work. See you on Monday. Have a great weekend.'

Jane replied, *Great, thanks, and you, speak soon.*

She then got into bed and pulled the quilt over her, waiting for Karl to finish his shower and embrace her as he did each evening when they curled up together in bed.

Her mind wandered frantically again as she lay waiting, thinking about her father and how strong he'd been dealing with his cancer. She decided that she would be just like him – she would fight this thing as hard as she could too. The determination became even stronger as Karl emerged in just his boxer shorts, climbed into bed, and wrapped his body around hers. She wanted this feeling of closeness for as long as possible so she had to fight. She held him tight as they both fell asleep.

~

The next morning, after the twins had set off to school and Karl had left for work, she rang the clinic. "Hi, it's Jane Walden. Could I speak to Paula or Doctor Ramsey this morning please?"

"One moment please, Mrs Walden. I'll just put you through to Doctor Ramsey's office."

Jane was pacing the floor of the kitchen, and after a short pause, a voice spoke. It was Paula. "Hi, Jane, it's good to hear from you so soon. How can I help?"

"I need more information, Paula, I need to know what is next for me and what we can do to fight this thing. Could I come in today, I've got the day off so can be there anytime, I just need to get my head around it a bit more and get a few more facts straight." She rushed her words and apologised again for that.

"Of course. Give it say, half an hour, we are just with another patient but have had a cancellation for the next one, so if you could pop in then that would be perfect, is that okay for you?"

"That's great, thank you, see you soon." Grabbing her bag and the slice of toast she had made while waiting on the phone, she left the house and began the short drive to the clinic.

As she arrived in their private off-road car park, she stopped for a moment before opening the car door, and looked in the rear-view mirror at herself, thinking that she must stay strong this time around. She took a deep breath and made her way into the building across the road.

"Come on in," Paula called into the waiting room where Jane was waiting patiently but anxiously.

"Thank you and look…I'm sorry about yesterday. For rushing off, and well, for fainting too. How embarrassing. I don't know what happened, I'm not usually a fainting sort of person." She laughed nervously.

"Please don't feel the need to apologise, Jane. We completely understand your reaction to the news we gave you. Everyone copes differently, and we often get fainters. So please, don't worry yourself. It's fine."

"I simply need to try and understand what has happened and why. I just thought it was some bad scar tissue that could be operated on, removed or lasered out, never…ever…this news, the dreaded 'that's it' diagnosis, you know, I'm dying, and that's that, nothing we can do scenario." Her words were almost incoherent and muddled, so Paula called through to reception for some strong coffee and began calming her down by firmly but gently holding her hands and giving reassurance.

"Look, Jane, we have treatments available. The drugs now are very good at helping with any pain, sickness or tiredness, and we also have places for you to go, to help you cope, support groups can be helpful too if you wanted to talk to others about your experiences. We work very closely with a new hospice about five miles away. It's tucked away in a peaceful part of the city. I can go there with you if you like, just to show you that it's not like a normal hospital or as you might imagine it. It has a day club where people meet up to discuss their illnesses, children go there to chat, and this can really help them understand the problems and stresses with whoever is ill. They are a fabulous, friendly bunch of people. Some of the patients even volunteer there while they are able to."

"I don't think I'm ready to visit a hospice just yet but treatments, drugs… yes, I'm ready to attack this thing head-on. I need as much time as possible before… well, you know, before the obvious happens." She sipped her coffee and only glanced at the biscuits on a side plate, as she didn't have an appetite right now.

They spent the next hour discussing all the treatments available and decided to start on the chemotherapy as soon as possible.

"Will I lose my hair?" she asked, wincing at the thought of going bald.

"It is very likely, yes. People with your stage of cancer usually do lose most of their hair, due to the chemo, but we also have a great wig lady who can visit you at home and help with that side of things when you need it."

"Oh, crikey. Right… let's do this. Let's fight this bloody thing. When can I start?" Jane was determined to have the same attitude as her pops had when he was poorly and fight it for as long as she could, as hard as she could. She would not give up the fight against this. She just couldn't give up. Karl and the twins needed her for as long as possible, and she would battle this to the very end.

"I'm not telling anyone yet either, so I will have to fit in the chemo as best I can. Will that be possible?" she asked Paula and Doctor Ramsey who had now joined them.

"Yes, we can sort that out for you. It is often nice to have someone who can sit with you though, during the sessions especially. Are you sure there isn't anyone who could come along? Your husband, a friend?"

"No, honestly, I'll be much better by myself. I'll just bring a good book to read or listen to some music on my old iPod. I'm not ready to tell the family yet. I need to be able to cope with this myself first and confront that issue later when I'm strong enough."

"Right. Well, we'll see you Monday at four o'clock and get you started. Do make sure you start taking the tablets we gave you, as they will kick in within the next few days. You may feel a bit nauseous, but that only usually lasts about a week, or less than that for some people."

Gathering her things together including the minefield of information that she had been given, she said her goodbyes and left feeling just a tad stronger.

Before she drove home, she decided to pop in at the cemetery to see if James was there, and he was just walking out of the shed near the bench they'd sat on under the trees the day before.

"You will be alright, Jane. I get the feeling you are a resilient woman who will fight this thing as much as possible, you've got this," he reassured her with a massive smile as they sat next to each other.

"But I'm not going to see fifty, am I? I'll be lucky to get to my big four zero at this rate," she answered woefully.

"Well… maybe not, but the time you do have left… you have to try and enjoy it as best you can. You never know when the time is going to come, but you have your husband Karl, your beautiful twins, your mother, and now you even have me, if that's any help." He chuckled. "And I will be here whenever I can, I promise."

This wonderful stranger was quickly becoming a good friend, and now he was turning into a true confidant for Jane. She was so grateful for the short but sweet chats they had already experienced together. It did make her feel better to have someone there who wasn't directly involved, someone who had also been through it and understood the pain and stresses that came with the illness itself.

Smiling back at him, she felt relieved to see his kind and caring face beaming back at her and they enjoyed an hour talking together before she made her way home, rather exhausted after another eventful but now, more progressive day.

Chapter Seven

The chemo sessions began the following Monday as planned, and it was a tough start.

They struggled to get the line into a vein at first, so it took longer than normal. Jane became very upset and anxious about the whole process as she just wanted to get going on this treatment as soon as possible, and her silly nerves were making it harder. Her inner self was almost beating her with a cane, trying to stop the treatment from getting inside her, like some sort of barrier, but she wasn't having any of it and managed to calm herself down by taking some deep breaths. This had to happen now.

All the staff had been amazing and made her feel much better during the whole ordeal. She couldn't fault the work and effort and, most of all, the care that these people showed her and every other person attending the chemo sessions. There were around eight people in the session, but weirdly, no one really spoke to one another, even those who had companions with them. Reading books and listening to music was the order of the day for all of them, including Jane, and it seemed to work. Almost like it was their own time out from the illness that they were dealing with, time to ignore it, time to themselves while getting the treatment they all needed so badly to try and fend off this horrible disease or give them a bit more time anyway. A few people had someone to sit with them, but again, very much in solitude as they would also sit and read or listen to music while sometimes holding the patient's hand. It was quite moving to watch loved ones trying to hold on to every single moment they had left with that one special person in the room and Jane often thought about Karl and how he would be if he were here with her. She knew deep down in her heart that he would want to be there if he knew, but she couldn't have it that way just yet. She wasn't ready to see his heart-breaking even if it meant she had the support of her husband for this.

They had been able to fit Jane into her sessions after work hours so that she didn't need to take any time off, and no one would suspect anything.

She'd decided to tell Karl that she had extended her working day until five o'clock instead so that he wouldn't ask each day where she was or suspect anything was going on. That was an easy lie to adhere to, day in, day out and it was working, for now, so she stuck with it and the weeks of chemo soon flew by.

It was hard getting there in time, having the procedure, working and getting home, but she was determined that this wouldn't affect her normal day to day life. Well, for now, it wouldn't anyway.

~

"How was your day today, honey?" Karl asked as he emerged from the shower with a short blue towel wrapped around his slender waist and another one in his hand, rubbing at his dripping wet hair. He looked so handsome, and she paused for a moment to take in the stature and toned build of her husband.

"Oh, it was okay, a little quiet to be honest. How about you?" She leaned forward and kissed his lips, touching his moist chest with her hand. He was warm from the shower and smelt fresh. He'd always kept fit and healthy by running every morning, usually before work while she and the kids were still sleeping.

She remembered watching him play in the rugby team when they were at college. He was only in a friendly team that met up once a week to play on the local field, but he was very good at it. He was no Johnny Wilkinson, though he would score occasionally. He still met up with some of the guys from the team, but it was now mostly to meet at the pub or have a quick match of squash or badminton these days. They were all very competitive and even went to the extreme of making bets on who would win the next match. Even with the regular pub jaunts, he'd managed to keep his six-pack, and she loved it.

"Yeah, all good in the hood. We had a new case come in, so everyone's pumped up about that. It should be a good earner for all of us actually. Hopefully, me and Scotty will front it, so I may get a bonus at the end of the year. You never know, we could get a little holiday in maybe?"

She hadn't told him that she'd taken another day off. He didn't need to know and would only ask questions that she wasn't willing to answer.

Jane tried hard to concentrate on what he was saying, but she wasn't really hearing him. She nodded and smiled as he went on to tell her all about the new project, as she sat on the edge of the bed watching him dress in casual jersey shorts and a t-shirt. She felt really tired today and was looking forward to getting into her warm bed with her man, feeling his gorgeous body against hers for another night.

This evening felt just as special as every other night, but, due to the tiring day she'd had, it didn't take long for her to fall asleep in his arms as he read an eBook about fitness on his Kindle.

~

Morning came, and Jane awoke to find a Post-it note on Karl's pillow written in his funny scrawled scribble. *Love you, sweetheart, see you tonight.* with a big heart drawn underneath. She smiled as she read it and held it close to her chest. He was so sweet sometimes, trying to be romantic with his little gestures of love and affection, but he didn't know how that note meant so much more right now with the way she was feeling and the secrets she was hiding from him.

Glancing up at the clock, she realised that she had slept through the alarm. "Oh shit," she gasped sitting upright and throwing off the quilt. It was gone ten o'clock, and she still had to get dressed to see James before her chemo session at midday. Being a Saturday meant she could have it done at a different time and Karl had been called into work for a bit of overtime.

She chucked on some casual trousers and a baggy jumper, not feeling too bothered with her outfit today for some reason. She just wanted to see James for a chat and get the chemo done and dusted for another day, so she set off quickly.

~

As she was laying some new flowers on Pops' grave that she had purchased from the florist opposite, James came jauntily walking up the path and she beamed a big smile at him. "Hey, you." She stood up carefully and sat on the bench, which he had since moved, so they were closer to Pops' grave while they chatted. "I thought I might have missed you today."

"Missed me? Ah, as if," he joked back, waving his hand in jest. "No chance, Mrs." He grinned.

"I'm having some more chemo today, so I thought I'd pop in quick to see you beforehand."

"How's that going for you?" He held flowers that he'd picked to place on his mother's gravestone.

"It's okay, actually, not as bad as I thought. I've been a bit sicky and so tired. Apparently, it gets worse, and my hair will probably start to go soon, which I'm not looking forward to one bit, I tell you that."

"I'm sure you'll still look beautiful, Jane." He nudged her arm and gave her a cheeky wink. "You know what you need? A good book to keep you company. Mum used to find chemo so boring but having a book helped her get through the hours she spent there. You need a nice romance or something to lift your spirits, keep that beautiful smile of yours going. Here, take this, it was one of my mum's faves. I kept them all, don't know why, just more memories I guess." James passed her a well-thumbed book, with a portrait of a lady on a beach, walking off into the distance on the front cover, and the title, 'A Secret Moment'.

"Oh, good idea, thanks. A lot of the other patients have books, but I've been taking my iPod and listening to music most of the sessions. I'll start this today… actually, I best go, got to be there by twelve. I can't make it tomorrow, being a Sunday, I need to be at home with the kids and Karl. Robbie has a footy match too which I want to watch. See you Monday afternoon around four?"

"Sure, see you then. Enjoy the book and I hope Robbie's match goes well," he happily replied as he walked back into the shed, waving at Jane.

~

The chemo was boring as usual, but she now had a new book to read and began as soon as she was wired up to the machines once more. There were only four people in today, and it seemed eerily quiet. Everyone was alone today too.

"Are you comfortable, Jane, do you need anything else?" asked the nurse, coming over to check the machines.

"No, I'm fine, thank you, Anna. I have a new book to read actually, a friend lent it to me earlier." Jane smiled up at her, showing the cover of the book.

Anna was only in her early twenties and extremely pretty with red-rimmed glasses that were very on trend. They had chatted before, discussing her upcoming wedding, which was planned for the following year over in St Lucia. Jane had told her that she would make a beautiful bride which had made her blush, but they got on well, and Anna had taken in all the advice about planning a wedding from Jane, even to the point of making notes in her phone using the wedding app she had downloaded.

"Oh, that's a great book. I read it a few years back, it's very romantic. A lady who used to come here lent it to me actually, she was so lovely, an elderly lady but so young in herself, if you know what I mean. Her son was rather gorgeous too." She smirked. "Anyway, just shout if you need anything. There's the bell to call one of us if you do need anything okay?" Handing Jane the alarm button attached to the wall, she moved on to the patient next to the doorway who was just finishing up for the day. The man looked very weak and tired which saddened Jane. A few people hadn't been for around a week or so and that hit home to her too. She hoped they had just changed their times for chemo but knew deep down, it was probably for another reason. That they probably wouldn't return.

As Jane opened the book and began reading, she was hooked within the first few pages. She loved a good romance story, and this had it right from the start, grabbing her attention straight away. She wondered too if it had been James' mother who Anna had been talking about and the rather gorgeous son. *Could* it have been James that she was talking about with his mum? He was pretty handsome, too much coincidence?

Her mind wandered back into the story and before she knew it, she had managed to get through a third of the book, and chemo was finished for another day, until the next one of course. She made her way out, saying goodbye to the nurses who made the ordeal just that little bit easier with their kindness and caring smiles.

The chemo days went on and on over the weeks and she began feeling more exhausted after each session. As the nights began to get lighter, as summer went on, it was increasingly hard to stay awake at times.

Today was one of those days, and because she felt so tired, she had forgotten to switch her phone on silent. Ten minutes into chemo, her phone began to ring.

"Sorry," mouthed Jane as she looked around at the other three ladies in the room, smiling apologetically. They just chuckled, smiled back, and continued reading their books.

The duty nurse looked over and Jane felt like a naughty schoolgirl, but none of the staff there were cross. They understood people were human and forgetful sometimes, especially those under increased pressure and stress from these rooms and the treatment they were all going through.

Seeing who it was calling, she whispered into the phone, "Hey, trouble." It was Sarah.

"Hey, why the whispering, you in the library or something?" came a whisper back, and then some loud chuckling down the phone.

"Actually…" Jane thought for a second; Sarah had solved the problem of making something up. "Yes, I am actually, can I call you back later, say about half an hour?"

"Sure." Sarah laughed. "Enjoy your reading, funny little bookworm," she whispered and ended the call.

Jane made sure the phone was on silent this time as the call finished, feeling embarrassed, but it had happened to others. "It's just one of those things," the nurses had said to them. "You can't get away from phones and texts these days, can you, don't worry yourself."

After her session, she decided to see if James was at the cemetery. He was sitting on the bench reading an old book when she arrived.

"How was it today then?" he asked, placing the book on the bench beside him.

"Oh, you'll never guess what happened, James, my bloody phone rang in the middle of it. I was so embarrassed, but do you know what, they were all so lovely. They didn't moan about it or anything, the nurses or the other patients in there."

"Haha, that's funny. I guess they realise there are more important things to moan about, eh?" He always knew what to say but he was right too, there were more important things to worry about.

"Yes, I guess so. Oh, damn it. I was supposed to call Sarah back." She rummaged for her phone in her pocket and began dialling.

"Well, that was a long half hour," Sarah exclaimed when she finally answered. "Get stuck in a bookshelf or something?"

"No, sorry, I got held up chatting to someone from the kids' primary school. Are you okay?"

"Yes, I'm fine, honey. I just wanted to make sure we are still on for next week?"

"Next week? Oh, the hen weekend, yes…I can't wait for it. It's going to be great, and it will be nice to have a few days away with you. It seems like ages since we've been away together, doesn't it?"

"Yeah, it does. Okay, cool. Is there anything you need? I'm popping to town in the week to grab some new travel-size toiletries and stuff."

"No, think I'm all good, thanks, see you soon." Mimicking their virtual air kisses, she put the phone back into her bag.

"You going away somewhere?" James asked when she had finished rummaging in her bag.

"Yes, we've got a friend's hen weekend in Norfolk. It's just a few girls having some fun. It will be a nice break, and we've not been away together for such a long while. Me and Sarah I mean."

"Oh, lovely. Yes, it will be nice for you to do something a little bit different. What about the chemo?"

"They've sorted some higher-dose tablets for me to cover those few days not going in."

"That's great. I'm off to do a bit of weeding now on mum's plot. You coming with?"

"I need to go, I'm afraid. I promised Karl I'd meet him at the shops to get some dinner sorted. I'll see you tomorrow, but it will be more like four-ish as I've got an appointment straight after work and before the chemo session."

"No problemo, JW…" he joked, smiling. "That suits me fine. See you then."

He waved as he walked off up the gravel path towards his mum's grave. How had Jane been so lucky to meet this wonderful guy? It was like they'd always known each other. He was slowly becoming like her male best friend, and she felt blessed. She'd always wondered what it would be like to have a brother, and now she had found one, in some form or another. He would make someone a lovely husband, she thought as she walked to the shops to meet Karl. Then her mind raced for a few minutes, maybe, just maybe, she could set him up with Sarah? She needed someone like him in her life. Her mind wandered frantically, thinking about how she could set them up and what she could plan for them.

The next few days flew past, and it was soon the weekend and time to get away for their girls' weekend. Jane had to get her tablets in order so that she was still taking some chemotherapy medicine in place of the actual sessions. She had gone through the whole process in her mind of taking them while sneaking off to the toilet each time, buying herself a small reusable bottle to fill with water and she had even thought about disguising the pills in a vitamin container. Too far maybe? What a performance, all these lies she had to keep making up. And the worst thing of all was that it was to the people that mattered most in her life. What was she doing? Protecting them was her thought process, or at least that's what she was trying to do anyway.

~

"So, you take these four times a day while you are away, but make sure you are back in with us here as soon as you get back, so you don't miss any more sessions," said nurse Anna as she handed over two bottles of pills to Jane after her last day of chemo before the weekend break.

"Will do, and thanks so much for sorting them out. I really appreciate your help in all this."

"No problem at all. Just try and enjoy yourself. Having

a few days away from this place will be nice for you and your friends."

"Yes, it will be nice to spend some time with the girls and relax a bit, be 'normal' for a few days anyway."

"If there are any problems, or if you need us for anything while you are away, just call." She passed Jane the clinic card info again. "Just in case."

"Thank you." Jane gave her a gentle hug. They were all just brilliant, and she was thankful that she had them to call on as their constant support meant so much. What an amazing but tough job they had to do every day. Dealing with so much sadness but still keeping their wonderful smiles on their faces, making all the patients smile each time too.

Jane made her way home to pack the last of her things and, of course, to make sure her pills were safely tucked away in the handbag that she was taking with her.

"Will you bring us back a present?" asked Cassie as she hugged her mum goodbye before school that morning.

"Of course I will, sweetheart. When have I ever been away and not got you two anything?" They laughed.

"I'll miss you, Mum." Cassie's sweet little blue eyes welled up as she gazed up lovingly at Jane.

"Aww, sweetie. It's only a few days, just till Sunday night, but I'll miss you too. Look after the boys, hey?" They hugged goodbye and Cassie set off with one of her friends to walk to school with Robbie following behind with his mate from a few doors away.

She didn't want to be leaving them for those few days but had to keep up her pretence that everything was fine, and this was no different from any other trip she had been on with Sarah. Deep down, she knew it would do her good too. Clear her head a little bit, to let them in everything on her return, maybe? She just had to remember her simple lies so as not to slip up with Sarah and the girls. Weekend challenge here goes, she thought.

Chapter Eight

"Have a great time, sweetheart, and be good. Especially you, Miss Flirty knickers," joked Karl, pointing at Sarah as he picked up Jane's small overnight bag from the doorway and placed it in the boot of Sarah's convertible mini. He kissed Jane on the cheek, putting his arm around her shoulders as they walked round to the passenger side.

"Be good? I don't know what you mean by that. We are good all the time, Mr Walden. And me, a flirt? I don't know what you mean," Sarah jokingly remarked with a cheeky smile and a wink directed over at Jane who was just getting into the passenger seat.

Laughing along, Jane waved goodbye to him. "I'll try and FaceTime the kids later if the reception is any good there. Love you lots, darling."

She turned in her seat and watched him standing outside the house waving as they drove off up the street, knowing she was going to miss him so much more than normal. But she had to try and enjoy this weekend with Sarah, make it one to remember, for their friendship.

The weekend away was the first time they'd been away for about two years due to both their work commitments, but Sarah had come along on many short breaks with Jane's family. It had been too long since they'd had some quality time away with just the two of them and they were both excited about it.

Sarah had never had any children and it wasn't something that she liked to talk about much. When Jane had become pregnant, she had sort of claimed the twins as her surrogate children. Cassie and Robbie treated her as a second mum most of the time too and loved having 'Auntie Sarah' (as they named her), involved in their lives. She also enjoyed being another mother figure for them, but she was more like the naughty, but fun, big sister than a stand-in parent.

She had an inner child personality and was always the one to clamber on the bouncy castles at parties, jump about like a child on the kids' trampoline in the garden – annoying the neighbours at times – and was the first to ride the most thrilling roller coasters with the twins at various theme parks that they'd visited in the UK. Sometimes, she would stay on the ride for another go while the kids got off, grabbing a crazy ride photo of herself on the way out and making them all fall around with laughter at her funny faces directed at the camera, without fail.

Anytime that she had slept over at the house, she'd always been the one to set up 'camps' in the living room or bring the tent along and stay outside with the kids telling ghost stories and staying up far later than they should have with snacks to boot. Jane and Karl didn't mind at all as they knew how much love there was between the three of them.

"Here we go, babe, woohoo!" Sarah turned the car stereo up louder. "I've got just the tune for us, I dug an old CD out, remember this, from the good old school days?"

Out of the speakers came Cyndi Lauper's 'Girls Just Wanna Have Fun', a classic eighties' tune that they'd danced to at school discos and birthday parties as crazy teenagers. They both laughed and began bellowing along to one of their favourite tunes of all time. As they drove, they were getting some funny looks along the way from people in the streets and passengers in other cars, but they didn't care. They *were* girls just wanting to have fun, and they were certainly achieving this already.

"So, do we have a master plan for the rest of the weekend?" asked Sarah, turning down the music, as they paused for a break from singing.

"Not really," answered Jane, searching the CD cover for a new tune to play. "Shopping, eating…just chilling out a bit will be enough for me to be honest."

"Sounds perfect to me. Hey, shall we stop off for a bucksie? There's one at these services, I think."

"Yeah, defo. I could do with a coffee fix and a little snack maybe to keep us going on the journey?"

"Yes indeed. Ooh, hello there…" Sarah remarked as a car pulled up beside them. A flash Audi sports convertible with a tanned, hot-looking Latino man, adorned with cool aviator glasses, was in the driver's seat. His hair was perfectly slicked back, and he had a white vest top on showing off his muscular arms that had some Oriental style tattoos inked on them.

"Sarah, behave yourself." Jane playfully slapped Sarah's thigh. "He'd eat you for breakfast."

"Yeah, right… I'd show him a few of my old tricks and maybe teach him some new ones too." She winked at him seductively, and he smiled back almost nervously as she pulled away laughing, her strawberry blonde hair flowing back in the wind.

"Can't take you anywhere can I, you little minx? Jesus, he looked as scared a mouse. Poor thing." They couldn't help but laugh hysterically as they made their way into the left lane for the services.

Sarah had been single for a few years now, only having one or two serious boyfriends during her nearly forty years. She didn't really care, and she'd always said that she never wanted to marry and settle down. It was boring. Not the life for her to be tied down to one person. She was so independent, a free spirit, and also overly OCD sensitive with her home. To have someone bring their belongings into her space, she'd always thought would stress her out too much. She'd tried it a few times but failed miserably at having male items in her bathroom cupboard and men's clothes in her drawers.

Jane had often thought it was a shame that she had never found someone to make her completely happy. She was such a loving person and so much fun to be around. Maybe in a few years, she would change her mind. Someone would come along when she was least expecting it and change her idea of fun. James came into her mind once again. He could be just the man she needed. A matchmaking session was long overdue now. She then wondered how he was and knew she was going to miss his chats over the next few days. He'd enjoy hearing all about the weekend next week though and she could also mention that Sarah was available.

The roadside services appeared, so Sarah took the turning into the Starbucks outlet. It was a new drive-through, but they decided to pop to the toilets while they were there, so pulled into a parking space, got out of the car, and headed in, grabbing their handbags from the back seats.

Just as they got to the doorway, Jane tripped up the kerb, dropped her handbag onto the floor and almost everything fell out. "Shit," she gasped as she tried to gather it all quickly, laughing at herself for tripping so foolishly.

Sarah crouched down to help her. "Jeez, you drunk already, babe?" she joked, then stood up slowly with something in her hand. "What are these pills for?"

"Oh, erm… just some new supplements I've started taking. You know, it's my age, I'm getting on now." She reached out and swiftly took the small bottle of tablets from Sarah. "Come on, I need coffee."

Jane hurried into the store hoping no more would be said, that no one had seen her trip and, more importantly, that Sarah hadn't seen what the tablets really were. Surely she couldn't have read the label in that short space of time. It was obvious to Jane that the container wasn't that of a usual vitamin or supplement size, and she had forgotten about disguising them with all the rushing around getting packed and ready, but she remained hopeful that Sarah hadn't noticed and wasn't going to talk about it anymore.

"Hi, can we have a one-shot soya cappuccino and a double Americano to go, large please?" asked Jane at the coffee counter, slightly flustered. "Oh, and one of those double chocolate chip cookies too, thank you."

"Cookies, Jane, that's not like you," joked Sarah as she came out of the toilets reaching for her purse.

"Well, it's a treat to share. You know you love them. I'll get these, you can buy a round on the way home," Jane sarcastically replied.

Swiping her card to pay, she took the cookie which had been placed in a brown paper bag and went to the end of the counter to wait for their drinks to arrive.

"The spa will be nice, hey?" Jane commented, hoping to keep the conversation away from the pills.

Sarah glanced up from her phone, tapping away without looking. "Yeah, looking forward to a sauna and steam room. I hope they serve some fizz for us all."

"I'm sure it was a package deal, so we must get at least one bottle to share between us, wouldn't you think so?" They collected their drinks and made their way back to the car. "Maybe we could pick up a few bottles to have back in our room, you know, just in case?" Jane suggested.

"Great idea. I'm looking forward to it."

"We've not been away as much as we should've these past few years, I miss those times."

"Me too. I'll sort some dates out so we can do it again in a few months. Once I get these new girls fully trained up at work, I can take more time off. Now let's get going."

The journey wasn't going to take too long, but they still had time to chat about memories of the friend who was about to get married.

"Never thought she'd marry though, did you?" asked Sarah, sipping her coffee.

"I don't know. People change, don't they? He seems like a nice guy too. I think Karl knows him from the gym or maybe be the pub." She giggled. "He'll look after her well and she seems so much happier with him than the last bloke, so fingers crossed for her."

"Guess so… another one bites the dust," Sarah joked.

"That'll be you one day, Miss Roberts. I'm sure it won't be long till you catch one," exclaimed Jane, breaking a bit of the cookie off to pass to Sarah.

"No friggin' way. You know I'm not the marrying, settling down type. I'm quite happy in my own little world, and I can just borrow your lot when I want to experience family time."

"Ha…it'll happen when you least expect it, Sarah."

"Nope…I won't let that happen, sweetie, I'm a free spirit, and there's no brave soul out there who could handle me anyway."

"Oh, okay, we'll see, we'll see." Jane nodded, smiling knowingly at what she had planned for her with James.

"Yep, you will see, you will see me at your place all the time. Your kids are practically mine anyway. Who needs a man getting in the way of all that fun?" She laughed.

"Oh, Sarah, you are funny," giggled back Jane as they continued their driving and loud singing once again.

Their hotel was right on the seafront with a small car

park around the back. From the website they had seen that it was a cute, family-run little place with only five rooms, and the girls couldn't wait to see the on-site spa area in the back garden including a hot tub, bubbling away each evening under a fairy-lit gazebo.

The cobbled stone walls looked like they had been recently had a fresh coat of paint, and gorgeous wicker hanging baskets in the shape of animals were hung symmetrically along the front fence with bedding plants giving plenty of colour. One was a pig, one a chicken, and there were a few dog shapes. It was quaint, pretty and peaceful. The only sounds were the usual seagull noises and the faint crashing of the waves in the distance from the beach across the road.

"Ladies, ladies, welcome to Norfolk House and Spa. How was your journey?" a lovely elderly lady asked as she came to meet them after they rang the doorbell, which chimed some classical tune for what seemed like a few minutes at least.

"Not too bad actually, thank you," said Sarah, smiling back at her and stepping inside.

"Good, good. Now, let's get you checked in, my dears. This way please." And she showed them to the main reception area then rang a domed silver bell on the desk. A younger guy appeared in a crisp white shirt, a skinny black tie, and rather tight, black trousers. He was tanned and muscular, and Sarah couldn't take her eyes off him, her mouth slightly agape at the sight of this luscious man.

"This is my nephew, Carlos, and he will help you to your room with your luggage, ladies."

"Ooh, lovely. Thank you, Carlos." Sarah commented in her usual flirty manner and turned to Jane with a salacious look on her face.

Jane mouthed, "Stop it," but smiled and raised her eyebrows at her hilarious friend.

They made their way to their sea-view double room, following Carlos closely up the staircase – Sarah checking his rear all the way and glancing cheekily back at Jane.

He unlocked the door and placed their bags onto the bed. "If you need anything, please use the phone just here next to your bed, it will go through to reception. Have a good weekend, ladies." He had an alluring accent, Italian or Spanish. They couldn't quite make it out, but Sarah, for one, didn't mind either. She was hooked on him.

"Thank you so much, Carlos. We will let you know if we need anything," replied Jane as she closed the door behind him and turned to look at Sarah, eyes wide.

"Well, that was the best welcome I've ever had in a hotel. That old lady has this business sorted. When can we come back? Next weekend okay with you J?" Sarah threw herself onto the bed, smiling from ear to ear and doing full-on starfish mode. "Do you think he'd come out with us, Jane? Show us around for the evening…or…maybe he could just stay in with me?"

"You little minx. He's young enough to be your son."

"Oh, *ha ha* … old woman, nothing wrong with a little age gap. What's a number when you look like that."

With a whole lot of laughter, they began to unpack their bags and Jane made coffee for them from the supplies on the sideboard.

As Sarah watched her friend, she thought again about the pill bottle that she had picked up earlier at the drive-through services. "Jane?" she asked.

"Yes, babe?"

"Earlier, when you tripped over."

"Oh, Sarah, don't remind me of that, how embarrassing." She flushed.

"Sorry, but, well…since when do supplements come in those doctor style bottles, with your name printed on them?" Her sudden change of expression could not be ignored as Jane turned to face her with her mug of steaming hot creamy coffee.

"Erm, since the doctor gave them to me," Jane quickly answered and made her way over to the window. "Look at this view, Sarah, you can see the whole stretch of the beach, it's beautiful." But Sarah hadn't moved as Jane turned around to summon her to the window. "Sarah, come and look."

Slowly, and reluctantly, she got up off the bed and made her way over to stand next to Jane. "Yeah, it's nice."

"This is going to be a great weekend, I can feel it. Hey, where shall we get dinner tonight? My treat," Jane continued hastily, knowing deep down that Sarah was not truly convinced by her response. They both knew when the other wasn't telling the truth or trying to keep something back so she desperately tried to get off the subject by talking about dinner options and what they were going to be wearing.

Sarah decided to leave it for now, and they both carried on getting ready for the evening ahead.

They chose to wear summer dresses and flip-flops as it was now early July and the weather had started to warm up a bit more. Jane's dress was a yellow, strapless number, and Sarah's was pale blue with flowers around the bottom and a halter neck.

Jane made her way over to the bathroom, saying, "I just need to use the loo quickly before we leave," and locked the door behind her.

Sarah spotted Jane's handbag on the bedside table. Should she look in it? Yes, she thought, they didn't have any secrets. Or did they? "I'm just going to borrow your lippy, Jane. Mine's not matching with this dress," she called to the bathroom door.

"Okay," Jane called back. "It's on the side by my makeup bag, I think."

"Yep, I found it," Sarah lied, and carefully opened the handbag instead. Spotting the bottle of pills, she quickly took a picture of the label using her phone, popped them back in the bag and went over to grab the lipstick quickly as Jane emerged from the bathroom.

"That colour looks really nice on you, Sarah. Why don't you keep it? I need to get a new shade I think. I'll take this one out tonight." She grabbed hold of another lipstick from her makeup bag and popped it into her clutch purse.

"Thanks. I need the bloody toilet now. Think it's nerves with not being out for so long or maybe the thought of seeing Carlos again." She laughed back.

Sarah then went into the bathroom knowing full well that she didn't really need to go to the toilet. She wanted to look up the name of the pills and frantically searched

Google on her phone to find the name.

"Hurry up, Sarah. I'm starving," Jane called as she took one of her pills and downed it with a glass of water.

"Just coming," she fibbed to kill time and carry on the search. Sarah finally managed to take a screenshot of the page she found and would read it later on another toilet visit or when Jane wasn't looking; just to be sure she was reading it right.

Chapter Nine

"Wow, that was so yummy. Good choice, honey." Jane wiped her mouth with the napkin and sat back in the wicker chair admiring the decor.

They'd chosen a nice little Italian restaurant just off the promenade by the beach. They both had a love for Italian food, and they'd been pizza addicts when they were younger. Something, obviously, that the kids had inherited from Jane.

"Yeah. Mine was okay," replied Sarah, sitting back without much enthusiasm.

Jane frowned, a little puzzled at her reply. "You okay? You don't seem quite yourself tonight."

"Think I'm just tired. Shall we grab a bottle and get back to our room? Get our PJs on and have a chat maybe?" She wasn't tired, she just couldn't think of anything else but the pills and wanted some answers. Maybe getting a few glasses of wine down her friend would bring the truth out, if there was any truth to tell.

"Sounds like a great plan. I'll just go and settle up and we'll get off." Jane went over to the bar to pay the bill as Sarah watched her, wondering what was going on.

Before they left, she nipped to the toilets to read the screenshot that she'd taken a picture of earlier. "This must be wrong. Oh, come on Google, get it together," she whispered to herself as she searched for the medicine's name, trying frantically to get the spelling correct in her panic. Her expression changed as she realised the drugs weren't supplements as Jane had said. She whispered quietly to herself, "cancer drug… chemotherapy treatment."

She hoped she was wrong. Surely Jane would have told her this sort of news? Confused, she returned to the restaurant to meet with Jane by the front door and they strolled back to the hotel, enjoying the picturesque beach views and salty sea air.

They got their special matching 'staying over' PJs on; black polka dot shorts with a pink vest top, which had 'bedtime princess' printed across the front in sparkly diamantes then Jane popped the cork on the bottle of sparkling rosé that they had picked up on their way back, poured two glasses, and they clinked to 'time together'.

They had also brought a box of chocolates, so both sat on the bed leaning on the headboard with the chocolates between them and their glasses of bubbly in hand.

"Mmmmm, caramel…" Jane smiled as she devoured her favourite selection.

"You and your caramel chocs." Sarah giggled as she

took an orange flavoured one.

"You and your crazy flavours," Jane said, flicking through the TV channels. "You've always had weird taste, you have."

"That's why we're friends, Jane."

"Brill! Look, *Dirty Dancing*'s on."

But Sarah just couldn't get the pills out of her mind or why Jane wasn't telling her the truth. Why had she said they were supplements for her age? Why was she taking pills that treat cancer? Had she looked up the wrong thing, spelt it wrong? Was she worrying unnecessarily? Maybe she needed the loo again to check her findings one more time or should she just ask her out straight? So many questions were flying around in her head and she needed to silence them. Using a new tactic, she asked, "So, these supplements you're taking, do you think they'd be any good for me seeing as I'm a few months older?" She had to ask something more to try and get this sorted out.

Jane glanced down trying to think of a reply, but she went blank. "Erm, I... I don't know... erm... maybe? Probably not though."

"Can I have a read of the label then? See what it says they help with?"

"Really? You want to talk about supplements and old age *now*? Let's just enjoy the movie and bubbly, hey?"

"Why not, you never know. What might help you could help me. We're the same age, if it's an age thing you're taking them for?"

"Sarah, I've had some hot flushes and that, so the doctor said these might help reduce them a bit. They're nothing you need to worry about yet. You're still good to go for another few years. It's just my body giving up a bit."

A long awkward pause made Sarah angry. She wanted to know what was going on, and she wanted to know now.

"Jane, for God's sake, do you think I'm stupid? What's going on?" Sarah got up from the bed, switched the TV off, and looked sternly at her best friend. "I know those pills are to treat cancer. I got them from your bag and looked them up on Google earlier. I'm sorry, I didn't mean to snoop but tell me I'm wrong. Please, just tell me I'm wrong, and I'll shut up about them," she cried anxiously, in hope of some good news.

Jane mouthed to try and say that she was wrong, but the words wouldn't come out. She couldn't lie to her now. She just looked into her friend's glazed over, concerned eyes as Sarah lowered her voice and asked quietly, "Jane, please talk to me. What are the pills for, really?"

This was it. Jane couldn't hold back or lie quick enough, maybe the wine was stopping her thinking so easily. "I… I can't… I can't tell you that you're wrong."

Sarah inhaled a deep gulp of air. "What?" she whispered as tears welled up in her eyes and shaking her head in disbelief. "What do you mean?"

Jane took a deep breath and placed her glass on the side table. "That's exactly what they're for, Sarah, I have breast cancer, and it's not going away. They are chemotherapy drugs to help with pain and, hopefully, give me a little bit more time before, well, you know."

The heavy silence in the room was almost deafening for them both. "When… why… why didn't you tell me? I don't… I mean…what?" Her words were crumbling like a biscuit in hot tea. She couldn't speak properly because the words that had just met her ears seemed like a slap across the face, a really hard slap at that.

"This is exactly why, Sarah. Exactly why I didn't want to tell you. Look at you, you're a bloody mess." Jane got up from the bed and stood in front of Sarah, wiping her tears from her cheeks. "Look, I'm sorry. I don't know how to cope with it myself yet, so I didn't want anyone else knowing or having to deal with it."

Sarah shook her head and grabbed her friend as they sobbed in each other's arms for what seemed like an hour.

After they had both calmed down, Jane poured another glass for each of them, and they sat on the small, padded window seat facing each other. Neither spoke for a few minutes, just looked at each other and took it all in.

"I was going to tell you, I promise. You were going to be the only one I did tell, at least for a while anyway."

"Does Karl not even know then, or your mum?"

"I can't bring myself to tell him, Sarah, and definitely not the kids… and my mum… well, she's already been through this with Pops. She just wouldn't cope. It's going to be so awful, Sarah. I just know it, and I feel terrible for putting them, and you, through it all."

"You'll need to tell them at some point. You can't just go through this by yourself. Well, you won't be getting rid of me now. I'm with you all the way. You're going to have to put up with me even more than ever." She gave Jane's ankle a gentle squeeze of reassurance. Jane knew she could rely on her to be there even if she didn't want anyone else hurting the way she was, like she had been on her own.

"Thanks, I do need someone close. It's been so hard to keep it to myself, but the clinic ladies have been amazing. The nurses are just brilliant and always on the end of the phone if I need them. It's literally only just over a month since they told me after the charity screening thing we had at work, remember?" Sarah nodded. "But it's been pretty mental trying to deal with it."

"That's good you have that support, but you have me twenty-four seven now. No questions." She smiled. "Will you get better though? Just need to take these tablets, and it will go away?" She nodded again, hoping she would get a nod back in agreement.

Jane looked at her, pausing before gently shaking her head. "They said probably a year. Maybe two, if I'm lucky."

"Oh shit. What the hell is this all about? Why you?"

Jane sniggered. "Yeah, I know, I've asked myself hundreds of times already and still don't have an answer to that one. Apparently, it's given to the strongest people as they're the ones who can deal with the disease better."

"Seriously? Who made that crap up?" Jane sensed the same anger in Sarah's voice as she had felt when she'd been given the news. It was crap, total hundred percent crap.

"Look, this weekend wasn't supposed to be like this. We need to have fun like we planned. I really need a break from thinking about it, and you're the person I want to concentrate on for the next few days. I know it's hard, but I need you – now that you know the truth – I need you to help me be strong and enjoy any time we have left."

Gulping hard at the massive lump in her throat, Sarah whispered back, "I bloody love you, Jane," and they both leaned forward clinking their wine glasses together once again. "To friendship," they toasted in unison.

They spent the remainder of the evening going through all the crazy times they'd had as children, teenagers, young adults, and now these past few years as grown women which had flown by so rapidly.

"Do you remember those pole dancing lessons we went to, I ended up in A&E with a sprained wrist," said Jane, and Sarah shrieked with laughter as more and more memories came flooding back.

Laughing and rolling around on the floor as if nothing had changed. They also kept re-enacting crazy dance moves that they used to do at the school discos. As the saying goes, 'dance like nobody's watching' – and they did just that – they didn't care in the slightest.

Their lives and their friendship had now changed though, and they knew these moments were more precious than ever. Things would never quite be the same again, but they would enjoy silly times whenever and however they could.

~

The rest of the hen-girls arrived the next morning around eleven, and as the July weather was warm and sunny, they decided to spend most of the day in the spa area within the little hotel. It was really nice for them all to relax and chat about the upcoming nuptials and everyone was impressed with the facilities that were surprisingly good for a back garden home-based spa in rural Norfolk.

In the evening, they met up with another six girlfriends who lived in the area and enjoyed an evening of dancing at a local club after dining at a Mexican restaurant a few hours earlier. The chief bridesmaid had ordered a VIP booth for the group, and the club had designated two buff butlers to serve drinks at the table for the bride-to-be and her guests.

The nightclub was in the middle of the town of Norwich and the décor was full of bling and sparkle. Even the white leather-effect seats had large diamante detailing on them. The tables were round, made of glass, and there was a large silver bucket in the middle which had been filled with ice and eight Prosecco bottles.

Sarah was particularly pleased with the butler addition and began using her usual over-the-top flirting skills to Jane's amusement, but this evening was different, she refused to leave her best friend's side for a man, because of what she now knew. Flirting didn't seem as important to her at the moment, she just wanted to take care of her friend and be there for her.

As they finished another bottle of Prosecco, a Justin Timberlake song came on that they all loved, so they got up onto the dancefloor to show off their moves. For the past few hours, there hadn't been any sadness and no stress, and it was brilliant; just as Jane had wanted the weekend to be.

But then grim reality of her illness took hold as they were dancing to the next song. Jane felt a sudden burst of pain and clenched her side turning away from the other girls, squinting her face in agony. Sarah noticed immediately and whisked her off to sit down. Unknown to Jane, she hadn't taken her eyes off her all night. Overprotective maybe, but she couldn't help it. She was now conscious of Jane's suffering, and her having to do it in silence all this time wasn't going to be acceptable to Sarah. Her moment to step up and take care of her was now, dancing and men didn't matter anymore.

"It's okay, I'm fine. I guess it's the little bleeder grabbing hold of me or the chemo attacking me...or something like that." She breathed deeper, trying to catch her breath through the pain.

"Do you want to make a move? I'll make up some excuse. There's not long left anyway. We can nip off back to the hotel so you can rest."

"No, Sarah, I don't want to spoil the evening. Everyone's having so much fun, I'll just sit down here for a bit. As you said, there's not long left now, only about half an hour isn't it until the place closes?" she replied anxiously as she tried to straighten her body back up.

Sarah wanted her best friend to be resting. She looked suddenly, very tired, and maybe this weekend hadn't been such a good idea. If she'd known Jane's terrible secret, she never would've suggested they still come. Now, knowing the truth, it was her job to take care of her, so she stayed right next to her. "Come on, let's get back to the hotel. I'll let the girls know that we're going. They won't mind, look at them. They'll be fine, I think Steff has hit it off with one of the waiters actually," she chuckled back pointing at one of the girls chatting at the bar. "Come on, I'll text the group once we get you in bed."

As they got back to their room, Jane lay flat out on the bed, absolutely exhausted. The evening had suddenly taken the wind out of her sails. She wasn't used to it, dancing, drinking and having so much fun, and maybe the lead up of chemo sessions or the pills were making her feel extra tired. She had been sick more than a few times too as Paula had mentioned was likely and she would find herself running to the toilet suddenly at work. It wasn't the ideal situation and she felt incredibly nervous about people seeing or hearing her vomiting. A few times, she had managed to turn on the hand drier before locking herself in the cubicle – just to disguise any noise of throwing up. She'd hoped it would lay off while they were away for these few days and at the moment, it was.

Sarah came out of the bathroom. "You okay honey?" she asked, but glancing over to the bed, she noticed Jane already fast asleep. She just smiled at her friend lovingly and grabbed a spare blanket from the wardrobe to place it over her. "Night my darling," she whispered as she kissed her head and stroked her hair back from her face. Jane looked as beautiful as she had ever done. The bestest friend a girl could ask for, and Sarah felt so lucky to have her in her life. No matter how long was left, she would be there for her best friend whatever secrets she had to keep.

On the Sunday afternoon, after all meeting up to say goodbye at breakfast, luggage was packed up and Sarah loaded their things into the car with the help of Carlos. But she didn't show as much interest in him as she had done on arrival as her only focus now was Jane.

The journey home was quieter than on the way; they both felt pretty exhausted from the weekend, especially Jane. As Sarah concentrated on the driving, Jane began to think about the upcoming wedding of their friend which was in a few weeks' time, and then began to think about the important life moments that she would probably never see with her children. She reminisced about how nervous she had felt on her wedding day but as soon as she'd seen Karl waiting at the end of the aisle for her, all her nerves had been washed away. Her mind wandered into thoughts of Cassie and Robbie's weddings and she knew deep down that she wouldn't get to see those special events. The dreams of being mother of the bride, mother of the groom, being able to see her daughter dressing in a beautiful wedding gown, helping Robbie get suited up for his big day, none of these thoughts would become a reality and the whole idea of that was killing her inside right now. She leaned her head on her hand and stared out of the window with her heart aching even more. At least she had her best friend with her now to help her through this awful chapter of her life. It wouldn't be easy for either of them, but they had each other and would work it out, somehow keeping strong, for each other as much as anything.

"You won't forget, will you? Let me know about everything," Sarah said as she grabbed hold of Jane's hand.

"No, I won't forget, I promise." Jane hugged her friend extra close as they reached the door of Jane's house. "But, Sarah, please remember..." she put her finger to her lips, "you know nothing."

They both held their fingers to their lips and smiled as they said their goodbyes then Jane watched her friend drive off feeling even more love for her and knowing she wouldn't let her down.

Chapter Ten

"Hello, gorgeous." Jane hurried into the kitchen where she could hear the clattering of dishes and cutlery. Karl was washing up wearing her favourite apron yet again.

"Hey, you're back. Come here." He turned around quickly to see her standing in the doorway smiling widely at him, so he shook the water and bubbles from his hands, went over to her and swiftly picked her up. "I've missed you so much, darling. How was it?" he asked, kissing her forehead over and over and holding her face gently.

"It was lovely actually. Tiring, but we had a great time together. The hotel was so cute, the spa was lovely, and mainly, spending time with Sarah was the highlight. It's been way too long since the two of us had a weekend away! Look at us here on the beach…"

Jane reached in her pocket to retrieve her phone and began to swipe photo after photo that they had taken while they had been away.

He glanced at them briefly but was more interested in seeing his wife home and in his arms. "Looks great, but…" he tipped her face up toward his, "I'd rather see your beautiful face in the flesh." A long and sumptuous kiss followed, and feeling a burst of energy, she jumped up, wrapping her legs around his waist. He pulled her in close while rubbing his hands down her back.

"The kids are out with your mum," he whispered as he kissed her ear and down her neck. "They won't be back for at least an hour or two…" he continued, a cheeky grin appearing on his face as their eyes met. She responded by kissing him passionately, and he carried her up the stairs to their bedroom, shutting the door firmly behind them with his foot.

"So, did you miss me then?" he asked her as they lay naked on their sides staring at each other with just a thin sheet covering their entwined bodies.

"Of course I did. I always miss you," she said, stroking his dark hair fondly and smiling up at him.

"Good thing too, gallivanting off without me."

She knew he was joking from the way he looked at her. His puppy dog eyes were a real giveaway, and he didn't mind really because he understood how much she loved spending quality time with her best friend. The friendship between the girls had never been an issue and he thought of Sarah as part of the family, like his little sister.

She had missed him though, even more than she'd thought she would. Although it had been a full-on weekend, she hadn't stopped thinking about him and the twins.

"Have the kids been okay, have you lived on pizza and fizzy drinks?" she asked, lying on her back but still admiring him.

"Actually, I've cooked a few meals, and your mum popped in Friday night too. But no, the kids have been fine. They had a few friends come around on Saturday afternoon, watched a movie in the lounge, Robbie and his mate played some new video game, and I managed to get some work done on this new project we have coming up next month."

Jane interrupted him. "Oh, I see, pull in the ranks while I'm gone." They giggled at each other as she climbed out of bed and began dressing back into her jeans and white, off-the-shoulder jumper.

He laughed back watching her. "You look like you've lost a bit of weight," he commented as he lovingly scanned her toned body from behind.

"Do I?" Jane didn't turn around. She really didn't want him noticing the weight change already, but damn it, he had. "Thanks, but I don't think I have. You've just forgotten what I look like, come on, get up. The kids will be back soon, won't they?" She pulled her jumper down and turned to look at him still lying there, then gave the bed sheet a sudden tug to encourage him to get up which he reluctantly did after playfully tugging it back.

"Hey, listen," he said as he pulled his chinos on and began tightening the belt. "I thought we could have a night out, dinner, cinema, or bowling, like we used to. Something fun with just the two of us. It's been a while since we had a date night. What do you think?"

"Sounds like a lovely idea, when were you thinking?"

"Tonight?"

"Wow, Mr Keen. I'd like to see the kids for a bit first though. We could get them pizza as a treat and maybe some popcorn and snacks?" Jane's phone rang, interrupting their conversation. She glanced down at the number saw it was Paula from the clinic. She'd memorised it but decided she should just store it in her phone as Paula so she could pass it off as a friend from work if Karl ever saw it come up.

"Oh, I need to get this, I won't be a second." She went into the spare room so that she was out of his earshot and answered it quietly, "Hello."

"Hi, Jane, I'm sorry to bother you, but we just wanted to let you know that we need to change your next chemo appointment. Can you make tomorrow instead of Wednesday for this week?" Paula had been assigned as Jane's personal nurse, and they'd struck up a real friendship since it all began.

"Yes, that's fine. Could you text it over to me, with the time, etc, I've not got a pen handy?"

"Sure, are you okay? How was your weekend?"

"Great, thank you." She suddenly noticed Karl standing on the landing looking into the room at her, so couldn't say too much back. "Okay, that's fine. Thanks, will do. Bye for now." Jane felt bad speaking so sharply back to Paula, but she didn't want to get into a conversation knowing that he was listening. She would have to make sure she apologised when she saw Paula.

"Who was that?" he asked as he pulled on his grey T-shirt.

"Oh, just work changing an appointment I had in the week."

"Work, on a Sunday?" he questioned.

"You know what Carol's like, always working no matter what day it is. She's such a busy lady," she turned and made her way downstairs, getting off the subject swiftly. "Coffee?"

Karl looked down at her hurrying and felt slightly concerned. He'd noticed for a few weeks that she had been getting a lot more phone calls after work hours lately and texts seemed to come through all the time, which she would quickly delete after reading them. They'd never been secretive with their phones, but for some reason, she was overprotective of it lately, taking it from room to room, and it wasn't something he liked.

"Yes please, I got in a few croissants too if you want to warm one up to share?" he called down looking over the bannister. Maybe he was just overthinking things, he thought. Maybe her work was just busier than usual he considered as he walked back into the bedroom to straighten out the bed, ridding his mind of any doubts.

Jane reached the kitchen and placed both her hands on the worktop, relieved again that she had managed to cover up another phone call. She would have to remind Paula and the nurses not to ring during certain times or just to text her or email her business address from now on. Emailing to her work account was probably best as Karl didn't have any access to that. Her mind was wandering as usual with all the lies that she had to make up each day, almost each hour it seemed. She took a long, deep breath and began filling the kettle to make the coffee as she heard Karl coming down the stairs.

"So, where do you fancy going?" she asked him as she opened up the packet of croissants.

Karl had emerged dressed but without shoes or socks on. He was always walking around the house barefoot; he had done so for as long as she could remember. Another crazy thing she loved about him, although she wasn't a great foot fan, something he joked about often while trying to get her to massage his feet.

"Maybe that new Thai place in the high street. A couple of mates from work went there with their wives last week and said it was really nice. How about that?"

"Yeah. Okay, sounds great." She passed him his cup of coffee as he searched on his phone for the restaurant's number.

"I'll give them a bell and reserve a table for…about eight o'clock?"

She nodded in response, sipping her coffee.

"Mum!" shouted Cassie as the twins let themselves in the front door, noticing their mum's overnight bag in the hallway.

"Hey." Jane quickly put her coffee on the side and went to greet them. "HI, guys. Oh, I missed you so much, come here." She wrapped her arms around both of them and held them tight, kissing their heads over and over.

"Mu-um," Robbie groaned with a little embarrassment at all the kissing.

They all chuckled. "Want your pressies?" Jane reached for a paper carrier bag by the small table near the stairs and they both rummaged in it to find their gifts.

"Hey, you two rug rats. How about having PIZZA tonight?" Karl called from the kitchen door.

"Yes please," they both yelled as they ran up to their bedrooms with their presents.

"Did you have a good time, my dear?" asked Janice as she appeared in the doorway shortly afterwards.

"Hi, Mum. Yes, it was great, thank you. You okay?"

"Oh yes, dear. You know your old mum, always alright." She giggled, and they gave each other a big loving hug. Janice kissed Jane gently on both cheeks. "Well, enjoy your pizzas, my dears. I am off out on the razzle tonight for a change."

"Oh right, another club? I lose track of all your activities, Mum, you're such a busy bee," answered Jane rubbing her mum's arm sweetly.

"Actually, no, Jane, I have a date." A triumphant smirk spread across her face.

"Oh really? Who's this with then?"

"Ha ha, not really. Your face, my dear," she joked. "I am going out but with Rita from bridge club. We've been invited to a little tea party at her sister's house. As if I'd be on a date, Jane darling. What would your Pops say about that nonsense?"

"Oh, Mum…you are a big tease. You got me excited then, and hey, maybe Pops would say it was okay?" Jane said, trying to reassure her mum. It had been nearly ten years since he died. Why spend the rest of her life alone and then Jane remembered the promise she made to her dad; not to let her mum be alone for too long, but she hadn't succeeded in achieving this yet.

"My darling little butterfly," (this was a pet name she had given to Jane as a child when she'd become obsessed with butterflies), "I'm too old for all that dating nonsense now. What a palaver that would be. I'll see you all soon. Glad you and Sarah had a good time. The children missed you, and so did that big guy over there." She pointed to Karl, who was still in the doorway to the kitchen looking on. Giving him a little wink and a smile, she then scuttled off, humming a tune, calling, "Bye now," on her way down the winding path.

"Bless her." Jane shut the door after watching her mum stroll down the road in her spotted flowing skirt and fluffy red coat. She had always dressed in bright clothes, and Jane loved her individuality. It suited her character.

"You'll be old and crazy like her one day, babe, you've got that madness to look forward to," Karl teased her as she turned around to face him.

Jane knew she wouldn't be old like that, but what could she say back to him? Nothing, absolutely nothing at all about that subject, so she just smiled and gave him a nudge in the ribs as she passed him and went upstairs to catch up with the twins, who were busy on their phones as per usual.

As she went into each of their rooms, she chatted to them about how their weekend had been, what they'd watched with their friends and what sort of pizza they both wanted for that night.

"I'm going to ask Aunty Sarah if she wants to come over and sit with you. You know she loves pizza. Oh, Cassie, she has this new beauty face pack she wants you to try out. We had a little go while we were away, but she thinks you would love it, I'll get her to bring some round if she's up for it,"

"Wicked," Cassie called back, briefly glancing up from her phone, yet still tapping away without looking at it.

"Karl, I'm going to give Sarah a call to see if she can come over while we're out," she shouted down the stairs.

"Okay, sweetheart. Let me know, and I'll nip to the shops for some snacks and that for the kids. See what pizza Sarah wants, my treat, tell her." He went off, whistling, into the garden.

Jane went into their bedroom to call Sarah as she looked through her wardrobe for something nice to wear.

"Blimey, you missing me already?" joked Sarah as she answered the phone within seconds.

"All the time, honey. Look, Karl wants to go out this evening, so I wondered if you wanted to come and sit with the kids or if they could come to yours? Karl said he'd treat you to a pizza." Loud giggles came back down the phone.

"Oh, he sure knows how to talk a woman into things, doesn't he? Sure. I'm just putting a wash on, and I can be round yours in half an hour, is that cool? Best for them to be there, so they have all their gadgets around them,"

"Brilliant. Thanks, Sarah. See you then. Oh, and I told Cassie about that face pack we tried, so if you want to bring that along, she's rather excited to try another one of your products for you."

"Oh, bless her. She's such a cutie. Okey-dokey, no problem. See you in a bit."

Jane decided to wear a dress; smart and sexy with some heels seemed appropriate for their first date night in ages. They had both always made an effort on nights like these, and it made the time just a little bit more special for them. This night would be no different, apart from the fact that she was keeping a major secret from him and this could be one of the few date nights that they would have left in their marriage.

Rummaging through her shoe cupboard, she found her favourite black heels that she'd worn to a summer charity ball the previous year for one of Karl's company's new clients. They had crystals around the top of the heel, and she remembered how sparkly they were when she first saw them in the little boutique; one of the things that had made her buy them. She did love a bit of sparkle.

Pulling out a low-cut, deep red dress and a small black clutch bag, she was set for the evening and couldn't wait to start getting ready.

"All good for Sarah," she called down to Karl as she heard him come back in from the garden. "We'll order the pizzas for them when she gets here. I forgot to ask her what she wanted."

"Alright, darling, I'll get the menu out for them," he called back. "I'll be up shortly."

Going back into their room, she sat down at her dressing table, looking at her reflection. Her hair was noticeably thinner, she thought, and it was happening quicker than she'd expected. She decided to try and put it up loosely so that it appeared thicker. Sarah had given her some hairstyling tips while they had been away after discussing how she thought it had gotten thinner.

Her makeup was flawless as usual, and as Karl walked into the room, she was just slipping on the dress over her lacy red lingerie. "Could you zip me up, Karl?" she asked, turning her back to him.

He walked over and caressed her shoulders, then ran his hands down her sides to reach the zip. "If I have to," he joked, securing the zip and moving his lips towards her neck, kissing it gently. "You smell amazing…"

She turned around to face him. "Thanks, it's the one you bought for my birthday. Will I do?" she asked.

He took in the image of his stunning wife for a moment and took a deep breath, answering, "Erm… do we have to go out, you look extra hot tonight."

Jane smiled at him, moved closer, and kissed his cheek. "Come on, get ready, cheeky, I'm hungry."

He hung his head jokingly, made his way to the bed, and began to get dressed in the clothes that she'd picked out for him, a black slim-fitting shirt, smart grey trousers and his favourite brown brogue shoes, and within half an hour, they were ready to go.

"Have fun you two luscious lovebirds," chuckled Sarah as she waved them off at the front door.

"Thanks, Sarah, we won't be too late." Jane gave her best friend a knowing wink and mouthed 'love you' as she got into the taxi and blew a kiss to the kids who had joined Sarah to wave goodbye.

"I've reserved a table, and it's not too far." Karl rested his hand on her knee as they sat close in the back seats. She felt a wave of excitement run through her bones. Although she was tired from the journey back from Norfolk, this evening was going to be extra special and she was determined to savour every minute.

Chapter Eleven

The spicy aromas of the Thai restaurant were amazing as they opened the door and walked in. It was quite busy, but the table Karl had reserved was in a quiet corner and had a candle burning on the table, with a small red rosebud in a little glass vase. Quite romantic but not too over-the-top.

"This reminds me of one of our first ever dates, do you remember?" he asked as he pulled the chair back for her to sit down.

"Was that at that horrendous Indian place just off Oxford Street in London?" replied Jane, thinking back.

"Yeah, that's it. Some back-alley place, but it was awful, wasn't it? Blimey, what were we thinking going in there? Can you even remember what it was called, Spice Up or something terrible like that, wasn't it?"

"Ha ha, yes. Spice It Up? I don't know. I think we both tried to forget the place after that night."

They laughed as they looked into each other's eyes,

holding hands across the table, and began chatting about their dating antics and time at college. Jane's love for him became even stronger, and her heart ached in sudden sadness for a moment, the ache of knowing that she wouldn't be able to enjoy this sort of date in five, ten, or twenty years from now. She would be lucky if she got to a year or months even. They had always enjoyed going out to dinner and had tried every type of food available. What an adventure they'd had so far and how cruel for life to take this away from them so soon. They still had so much left to do together. She held back the tears as she glanced down to see their starters arrive.

"You alright, babe?" Karl asked as he noticed her looking down.

"Yes, fine. Just a bit emotional thinking about the old days." She reached across and rubbed his hand, glugging back the lump in her throat. *'just enjoy it'* she told herself, *'don't spoil it'* and quickly snapped herself out of her melancholy.

~

"This is really nice," she said as they finished their main courses with the waiter swiftly collecting their plates and clearing the table within seconds.

Karl reached over and entwined his fingers into hers, fiddling with her wedding ring. "Yes, it is. We need to do it a bit more often though. It seems like we are both always too busy now. Let's make a promise tonight, shall we? Once a month, just us two, somewhere new?"

If only he knew what he was saying to her. She just nodded in agreement, knowing deep down that there may not be that many months left for them to be able to fulfil his great idea of regular date nights. She became a little tearful, once again.

"What's the matter, Jane?" Karl asked as he noticed her eyes welling up even more than before.

"Oh, nothing, just me being silly again. I really do love you, Karl, and this was such a good idea, thank you," she murmured holding back the tears which wanted to fall. She wasn't going to let them come out, not now, not at this special moment.

As they left the restaurant, it suddenly began to rain heavily, so they ran into a nearby shop doorway, laughing at getting so wet, so quickly. Jane felt a tinge of pain down her side as she had in the club while she was away and grimaced while holding her hip.

"You okay, sweetheart?" Karl looked down at her concerned.

"Yes, just a stitch from all that running, I think. I'm so out of shape." It wasn't a stitch, she knew it wasn't, and it hurt so much, but again she pretended it was nothing as they stood huddled together in the shelter of the shop. She laid her head on his shoulder so he couldn't see the single tear of pain trickle down her face among the raindrops. They waited there holding each other, watching the rain splashing up onto the pavement as cars sped by.

The moment, although standing where they were, in the middle of Cambridge in a shop doorway, was to be another treasured memory for her. If only she could freeze it right now. Feeling the warmth of his body through his jacket, she felt overwhelmed, and a tear ran down her cheek once again. Why was this happening to her? He didn't deserve to be alone. This man she had loved for such a long time was going to be hurting so much soon, and she couldn't stand the thought of it and he didn't have a clue.

"Here, put this on, sweetheart. You're shivering." He rubbed her shoulders and began taking his jacket off to put 'round her. "I'm going to call us a taxi." He got his phone out of his pocket and dialled for an Uber, which arrived about three minutes later and they both climbed into the back seat, not talking, just hugging.

As they passed the cemetery, Jane looked in. She was sure that she saw someone walking in there, but it was dark, so maybe she had imagined it. Her mind would play tricks on her these days. Surely, no one would be in there at this time of night? It was a scary looking place when all was dark and somewhere, she didn't fancy being on a gloomy wet night like tonight.

When they arrived home, it had just turned eleven, the twins were both in their beds, and Sarah had fallen asleep on the sofa in the lounge with the TV still switched on.

"Pass the spare blanket, Karl," Jane whispered and pointed over to the yellow blanket hung over the armchair opposite. Jane placed it over her friend, giving her a gentle kiss on the head, then they crept out, shutting the lounge door, and quietly making their way upstairs to bed switching off the hall lamp on the way.

Slipping into some warm, cosy pyjamas, Jane lay beside Karl, who was in his boxers and nothing else. He didn't seem to feel the cold like she did, whatever the weather.

"Tonight was lovely. Thank you," she whispered,

glancing up at him.

"It was my pleasure, sweetheart. I enjoyed it too. Give us a kiss, Mrs Walden." He leaned on his arm and kissed her slowly on the lips "You looked extra gorgeous tonight too." He stroked her face and chin, touching her gently. His hands felt soft and warm.

"You didn't look too bad yourself, Mr Walden." She smiled and lay her head down on his chest, listening to the sound of his heartbeat as she fell asleep.

~

The next morning, Jane had another burst of energy, so after everyone else had left for the day, she decided to walk into work but pass by the cemetery on her way, leaving home half an hour earlier than normal.

There was a small flower stall just outside full of amazing colours and styles of bouquets. The aroma was so strong, she couldn't resist buying some.

"Could I have a small bunch of lilies, please?" she asked the stallholder. "The white ones would be lovely,"

She then made her way to her usual spot with Pops and placed them on the ground, making a mental note that she must get a nice vase or some sort of pretty container to put them in. Although James always arranged them beautifully, something of a focal point would look nice.

"They are rather lovely, Jane," a voice came from behind her, making her jump. There he was, never failing to be around. Her newfound, secret friend.

"Hey, you. Yes, they are aren't they, there's a small stand outside today. Didn't you see it on your way in?" She pointed to the entrance as she turned to see him smiling away. He was always grinning, always happy to see her, and it made her feel special.

He shook his head. "No, I didn't. It must've set up after I'd arrived. I've been doing a bit of reading to Mum. She loved her books as you know."

Remembering her taxi ride the previous night, she turned and asked, "Oh… silly question, but were you here last night around half past ten-ish?"

"Me…? No, why would I be here at that time of night? I'm not obsessed with graves you know?" he joked back sniggering to himself.

"I know, I know. I think I'm going crazy some days, seeing things, maybe it's the chemo drugs playing tricks on my mind or something. Me and Karl drove past, and I thought I saw someone walking about in here."

"What were you drinking last night, Mrs W?" he laughed. "Maybe it was a ghost… whooooo!" He gestured with his hands, in a weird ghostly movement, laughing joyfully. "Did you have a nice evening, anyway? And how was your girls' trip to Norfolk? Tell all, come on."

"Yes, it was lovely last night. Really lovely. And the girly trip, well, that was fabulous, albeit a little eventful. I'll have to tell you about it later though. I should be at work now, will you be here about four this afternoon?"

"Erm… maybe four thirty today, got an errand to run in town for a friend first, their dog needs to go to the vets, some sort of ear infection and they don't drive so I said I'd run them over there," he replied.

"Okay, see you then?" Jane rushed off down the path, waving behind her.

Arriving at the main reception at work, she glanced at her watch and realised she was already ten minutes late. She'd never been late before. She must get it together; the last thing she needed was to draw attention to herself in any way, so she decided she would continue to visit the cemetery only after work in the future.

Perry was delivering the post to all the offices as she rushed out of the lift, breathless and slightly red in the face. Her fitness levels had plummeted lately, and she thought about walking to work more often or at least part of the way and then getting the bus to help build her stamina up. They had said that the medication might make her a lot more tired, so maybe it was that? She wanted to try and keep her strength up as much as possible, so she decided she would try and do some cardio or maybe yoga in the evenings at home.

"Morning, Jane," Perry handed her some letters from his pile on the trolley.

"Hi, Perry. Sorry, I'm a tad late today. Did anyone notice?"

"I don't think so… you have quite a few today." He nodded towards the letters in her hand. She didn't tend to get much mail, a few letters per week maybe, but they were at a busy time of year and had recently had an influx of smaller business customers enquiring with them.

"How's the baby coming along?" she asked, changing the subject as she noticed a letter from the clinic in amongst the pile of envelopes. She remembered asking them to send correspondence to work instead of the house and moved it to the bottom of the pile before he noticed the clinic name printed on the front. He was a very observant young man and although she knew he probably wouldn't ask, she didn't want to risk him seeing it, nonetheless.

"Oh, it's cooking nicely. We had a scan, and it was all moving around waving at us." He chuckled. "Amazing, isn't it? The way they move around in there so early on. Such a miracle." He pulled out a scan picture from his top pocket and showed her. Jane thought how sweet he was, a first-time excited father exploring all the new adventures that pregnancy brought with it.

"Yes, it's all pretty amazing. Aww, look at that little hand." Jane looked closer at the image of the baby. "Are you going to find out if it's a boy or a girl?"

"No. The doctors offered to tell us, but we decided that we wanted it to be a surprise. As long as the little bean is healthy, that's all we want, and, to be honest, my mum is very traditional. She doesn't believe in all this 'finding out nonsense' as she calls it."

"Lovely, just lovely, Perry. Give my best wishes to your lady and do keep me updated. It's such a special time for you all," Jane replied, handing him back the scan picture.

"I will, Mrs W. See you tomorrow." With that, he was off again on his rounds for the morning, whistling his tunes as he walked.

She glanced at the letters again and picked out the one from the clinic, folding it carefully and sliding it into her skirt pocket. She would read it once she'd set up for the day when no one was around.

"Hey, lovely, meeting at eleven in the Essex room." Carol suddenly popped her head into the office.

"Oh, you made me jump!" Grasping her chest, Jane had just poured a glass of water, about to take her tablets, as Carol startled her, making her drop the tablet bottle on the floor and slightly spill some water on the sideboard.

"Oh, I'm so sorry, Jane. You okay?" Carol apologised noticing the tablets on the floor.

"Yes, yes. Just a headache. I'll be rattling soon with all these headaches I keep getting lately," Jane lied, picking them up and getting two new tablets out of the bottle while hiding it behind her back and grabbing a tissue with her other hand to clean the water up.

Carol looked on, concerned. "Right, well, see you at eleven o'clock then. You sure you're okay to come along?" she asked, turning around to face Jane who was now looking flushed with embarrassment.

"Yes, of course. No problem, Carol. See you then." She screwed the tablet bottle top on angrily and threw them into her handbag with force. She hated them, and she hated the whole annoying task of lying to her friends, and now to her boss; but at the moment, she felt she didn't have a choice but to go along with making up even more stories and all the lies, or so she thought.

"So, we have to let at least four people go?" asked Jane as she sat around the table in the main conference room with eight other members of the management team.

"I'm afraid so. It's not been a great year so far. Although we've had an influx of customers enquiring, they've not led to any big accounts, and, to be honest, what with the rates for the office building going up *again*, we need to downsize for a while and outsource some of the work to a digital company," Carol continued as she sipped on her coffee. "So, what we need to do is draw up a list of the people we select and offer them redundancy. If everyone could have a think about it and meet up later this afternoon to discuss, that would be great. I know it's not an easy task, but needs must be met just now until things improve."

The meeting was over in about twenty minutes, and everybody left the room apart from Jane and Carol as they gathered up the paperwork and tidied the large glass table of mugs and bottles of water.

Jane began thinking about herself and how long she may have left working there. Maybe this would be the time to leave before she was forced out by the illness when it really decided to take hold of her and maybe, her leaving could save someone else the heartbreak of losing their job. It may not be much longer anyway, a few months, if that, by the way she was feeling lately, so this could be the escape plan she needed. But she would need to confess everything to Carol. She couldn't lie to her in return for a favour that could save a lot of future hassle for her and especially for the company.

If it meant saving someone else's job, she had to do it and needed to talk to Carol as soon as possible.

Chapter Twelve

"Carol, could I have a quick word in private?"

"Sure, what's up? Do you have someone in mind for the redundancy?" Carol closed the conference door and sat down again, getting her pen and notepad ready.

"Well, sort of. This redundancy thing… I may have an idea for you…" She paused, thinking of what to say. "But I need to tell you something first, something very private and that needs to stay between us two only." Should she reveal her heart-breaking news and would Carol be able to keep it to herself to help them both out?

"Ooh, sounds intriguing. Go ahead." She beamed at Jane with an excited look on her face, obviously not expecting the news she was about to hear.

"Well… I've had some news recently that is going to affect my working here at some point very soon so…" She paused again to gather her thoughts and work out the right words to say. Don't lose it now, she thought, be brave, be strong. You can do this. She looked intently at her boss, who now looked slightly worried.

"Jane… is everything okay?" Carol leaned forward, placing her hand on Jane's now trembling fingers.

"No. No, I'm afraid it's not, Carol. I've just been told, I mean, I had some news and, well…" She paused, hanging her head down and then looked Carol straight in the eyes once more taking a very deep breath. "You know the screening we had for the breast cancer charity day?" Carol nodded as Jane continued, "Well, they looked at a lump I've had for a while, done some more tests and have since told me…" Another silent pause ensued. "I have a large tumour that has spread too far…" She swallowed hard to keep the tears in. "It's cancer, Carol, and it's not one they can get rid of now. It's too far gone." It was all coming out easier than she'd thought it would as she continued, "I'm on medication, having chemo every other day, and, to be honest, I'm not sure how long I will be able to continue working here. They've given me up to a year, maybe if I'm lucky, so… I was thinking…"

Carol just stared at her in disbelief for a moment, her eyes glazed over. "Oh my God, my darling. I'm so sorry to hear this." She grasped both Jane's hands, which were now stone cold and shaking with nerves. "Why didn't you say something before now? When did you find out? I could've helped, I could've come with you, or something? Given you time off?" She spluttered her words.

"It's okay, I've just about come to terms with it myself, but it's been a struggle with working and treatments. So now that this redundancy thing has come up, I think it could solve a lot of problems for me and obviously now get rid of some issues for you here at work too?" She moved her hands to rest on top of Carol's. "Do you think, maybe, I would be able to put myself forward for the redundancy, or you could suggest that I go? Or maybe tell everyone I'm transferring to the digital side and working from home or something like that?" She continued, "The redundancy money would help us to enjoy what time I have left with Karl and the kids, and my salary would save maybe two or three admin people from losing their jobs, wouldn't it?"

"I guess so but are you sure that's how you want to play it, I mean, you must have years ahead of you yet. You're so young, you're much younger than me."

Jane just shook her head slowly. "I'm afraid it's gone too far now, and they've been honest with me and told me not to expect too long. I am just managing it with the tablets and the chemo to get a few more months, if that, but I'm not expecting long to be honest. I've been feeling terrible, my hair's started thinning and I'm getting more pain each day now so…"

"I can't believe this. I really can't. You're one of the best girls here. This is just awful, but, yes, the number of things you have done for this business over the years, I can sort this out for you if that's what you really want, but only if you are sure. Just let me know which way you want to do it, and I'll support you all the way."

"Thank you, Carol. I really need to do this. It would give us enough money to enjoy the last few months or so that I have, go on holiday with the kids and that. I would really appreciate your help. I've not told anyone else apart from my best friend and that was only at the weekend and I would prefer to keep it that way for now. I can't deal with telling everyone and seeing their faces all worried and sad, I'm not ready for all that emotional stuff just yet."

"No problem at all, Jane. Will Karl be okay with it? I mean, giving up work?"

"I've not told him yet, as I said, so leave Karl to me. I'll make something up. He'll be fine. He's always wanted a dream holiday to Florida, and this is my way of giving it to him before, well, you know… I'll tell him when I need to and just pretend to come to work each day, so he doesn't need to know just yet. This would help me out so much, thank you."

"Jane… the tablets earlier? Were they really headache pills or part of the treatment?"

"They are anti-sickness and chemo drugs that I have to take four times a day. They are helping a little bit. The tablets just give me some more time, so I have to make sure I take them throughout the day."

"Good, you make sure you do." Carol smiled sweetly at her, not wanting to ask anything else. She had never seen Jane taking any sort of tablets before, so it had stuck in her mind when she'd seen her drop them earlier, although she never would've expected the pills to be what they actually were and was shocked but more saddened than anything.

Slowly, Jane rose then pushed her chair back under the table and left the room while Carol slumped back with a dazed expression, trying to comprehend what she had just heard. It wouldn't be the same without Jane there in the office, but she knew she could support her and set to work sorting all the paperwork out immediately, including getting the money arranged and transferred as soon as possible.

Jane began racking her brains about what she would tell Karl about the money. She didn't want to tell him she'd taken redundancy, wanting him to believe that nothing had changed, that she was still going to work each day, to continue the 'normal' life that they both led from day to day, so what would her story be? Time for more secrets and lies but surely it was better than the truth right now.

As she thoughtfully walked past the waiting area in reception, she noticed a daily newspaper on the small coffee table with a huge headline. There was a story on the front cover about someone in North Yorkshire winning the lottery. Her mind suddenly raced with ideas; that was it! She would tell Karl that she'd won a large share of money through the staff lottery syndicate (which didn't exist). There'd always been talk in the offices about starting one up, and she was sure that she had mentioned it to him at some point. If she remembered rightly, he'd thought it was a great idea at the time, so she could configure it to work for this next lie.

The fake story seemed fool proof in her mind, and she began frantically writing notes on her phone when she got back to her office desk. What was the amount going to be, what did she need it to be, who had won and what could they do with the money themselves as a family? She hated the whole deception, but her brain was telling her that this was the way to go for now and why would he find out that she was lying? The plan was now set, and she was finding it much easier than she'd thought she would.

~

Within a few days of their meeting, Carol had arranged the redundancy package and transferred the money into Jane's bank account, and her last day at work came just a few days later which was a sad day for everyone. As she was clearing her desk and the office which she loved working in, she knew she would miss it all so much, but much more than that, she would miss her friends and colleagues there.

Carol passed Jane another book. "I'm going to miss you so much, my darling. You will keep in touch, won't you? Let me know how it's all going?" Her eyebrows raised in concern.

"Of course I will. I'll pop by as much as I can for a coffee and a cake with you. I can text you to let you know how I'm doing if you like?"

"Great. Yes, do let me know, and please… let me know if you need anything. Anything at all. You know, when you can." Carol felt awkward talking about the cancer to her. It wasn't something that she'd ever had to deal with as yet and found it difficult to accept that her colleague and, more importantly, her good friend was going through this awful predicament alone.

Jane hugged her tightly as she got to the door with a box of her things. "Thank you for everything, Carol. It's been great working with you all these years, and I won't forget what you've done for me, especially this plan. I really appreciate it."

"Oh, stop it, you'll start me off again. Look, let me get Perry to help you with your bits and pieces. He's been doing some extra hours handy work today, and you can't manage all this by yourself. Give me five minutes. I think he's in with Sheryl showing her another scan picture."

"Sure, that would be helpful. I'll pop this in the car and meet him out there. He knows where I park."

"Wow, I'm sure going to miss that smile of yours each day, Mrs Walden," exclaimed Perry as he brought down the last box of books to Jane's car and loaded it into the boot.

"Aww, thanks. Sometimes you have to move on in this crazy job world." Carol and Jane had decided to tell everyone else that she was going on to a new job rather than tell everyone about the redundancy and have them ask more questions as to why one of their best team members was being let go. "You take care of that baby when he or she arrives. I'll hear all the gossip and get some updates from Carol, I hope."

"Will do. Goodbye, Mrs Walden." He held out his hand to shake hers formally, but she laughed and pulled him in for a hug instead. His shy little face was slightly crimson and blushing as he waved her off, and she chuckled to herself at his reaction. Such a great guy with so much future happiness ahead of him; a new beginning with his new baby, how exciting.

So now she was on her way home to tell another lie to her husband. The biggest lie to date, and she hated it all with a passion, but what else could she do?

It was a lie, but a reasonable one at that, she thought as she drove, wondering how he would react to the plotted plan of action that she'd dreamt up. For now, life would have to be like this, a life full of lies.

She ran through it in her mind over and over again to try and get the story straight in her head so she wouldn't mess up any details of the plan. When would she start the chain of lies, what was she going to say, how was she going to say it? The production of it all seemed so easy in her mind and she was begging her brain to make it that easy when it came to it. She'd never lied to Karl before in all the years they had been together. This was not something she wanted to do but she was doing it for the best, to avoid any more pain for the family, for now. But first, she needed to stop off somewhere to get some advice before the big lie commenced.

~

"Are you sure that's a good idea, Jane?" asked James as they sat together on 'their' bench.

"Yes… for now anyway. It's the only way I can cope with it. I just can't face telling him the truth that, sorry, darling, I'm dying but this money may help. As they say, live for today, and that's what I'm doing."

"It's your choice, Mrs W, and if that's what you need to do, then so be it. Good luck. I'm sure you will think of the right things to say and remember, you know where I am if you need to chat afterwards."

Smiling at him, she added. "I'll see you tomorrow. I've got to unload my car of office stuff and hide it in the garage before everyone gets home later."

"Oh, don't be silly, why don't you leave it here in the shed? I've put a new padlock on it and it saves you having to bother when you get home. Plus, old muscles here can help with all the heavy lifting." He jokingly raised his arms to flex his muscles, making her giggle.

"That's a good idea actually. It's only a few books and folders, you know. Bits from the office that I don't need at home but don't need to get into explaining why they are there, if you know what I mean?"

"Sure, makes sense, come on then. Let's get to it. You pass me the boxes, and we'll get them loaded into the shed in no time."

The only things she was taking home were the kids' creations from her desk. She would have to make up some other lie like she wanted to see more of them in her house rather than just in the office, so she placed them on the hall side table when she returned home after spending another half hour chatting to James.

That evening, she decided to tell Karl her 'lottery news' while the kids were at their dance and football practices.

"So, how was your day, sweetheart?" Jane felt strangely upbeat to begin telling Karl the story of a lifetime. He wasn't ready to hear the truth right now, she was sure of it, or more like, she wasn't ready to give it to him.

"Oh, it was good. Got that big project secured, and oh, yeah, check this out. Adam had some amazing news to tell us all today. He and his missus are having another baby," Karl emptied the dishwasher and passed Jane the basket of cutlery to put away.

"Oh, wow. That's exciting, when's it due?"

"Erm… February I think he said. Crikey… five kids, one brave guy, eh?" he joked.

"Aren't the other four teenagers now though?" Jane

asked as she grabbed a bottle of water from the fridge.

"Yeah, I don't think it was planned, but hey, he's fit enough to cope with the endless, sleepless nights, nappies, feeding and all that baby stuff."

"Blimey, remember those days, Karl? All those nappies we got through with the twins. How often we used to sit up through the night with them, taking turns sleeping? There seem to be babies everywhere right now. Perry from work is having one too in December. Well, his wife, you know what I mean." She shook her head comically. "Anyway, I have some news of my own. Leave the rest of this, for now, we can clear up a bit more after."

"You're not pregnant, are you?" he teased, winking at her as they sat down at the kitchen table with a slight hint of nervousness in his voice.

"God, no, can you imagine starting all that again? No, listen. We've had some good news at work. Carol got us all to start a lottery syndicate thing a while back, do you remember me telling you?" He nodded, eyes widened as she continued, "Well, it's been going on at work for a few months, and this afternoon, we were all called into Carol's office." She held his hands over the table-top and smiled broadly as he waited patiently. Could she go ahead with this? Should she go ahead? Yes, this was it. She had to, now she'd started this elaborate mess of a lie and by the expression on his face, he was expecting something good to come out of her mouth any minute. The time had come for her biggest lie so far; she looked straight into his eyes and blurted it out, "We won, Karl!" She squeezed his hands hard as she uttered the words with complete and surprising ease.

"What, are you serious? How much are we talking here? How much of a share have you won?"

She reached for the dummy cheque from her trouser pocket and passed it to him, slowly sliding it across the table with a massive grin on her face, hoping he would fall for it, and he did.

Karl stood up in shock as he took hold of the crisp piece of paper. "Wow, this is amazing, why have you waited all day to tell me this? Woohoo!" he squealed and ran to her side of the table, picking her up and swinging her around before setting her down, glancing again at the cheque in disbelief.

"I can't believe this; you never play the lottery!" shrieked Karl excitedly again.

Jane hastily replied, "I know, who would have thought it?" She tried her best to portray a huge smile as he kissed her forehead and held her arms with his strong, yet gentle, trembling hands.

The reasonable lies had begun.

With a deep breath, she continued her story.

"Hey, you know we've always wanted to take the kids on holiday to Florida. Let's do it now, Karl, let's book it today and surprise them. It's nearly the end of term, so it's an ideal time to go. We don't have to worry about taking them out of school, they'll absolutely love it." Jane reached behind her into the kitchen drawer and pulled out a brochure they had picked up a few months back after seeing a programme on television about a family moving to Florida.

They'd discussed how great it would be to have a longer length family holiday there soon, and the kids had already been busy choosing the biggest rides and theme parks that they wanted to experience.

They'd been too busy for the past few months to think about it, and money had been a little bit tight so it had remained just a dream for a while, but now, they could have their dream holiday come true, thanks to this lie.

"YES!" shouted Karl with joy. "Let's get online and book it now. The kids are going to be so stoked." He hurried over to his laptop bag on the kitchen table where he had left it after getting in from work earlier. Jane had called him to come home straight from work as she had this urgent news to tell him.

"We should go for a few weeks, Jane, really have a fantastic holiday to remember," Karl said as he tapped away on his computer finding the best deals for Florida holidays and excursions to go on. "We could even visit Miami like you've always wanted to, if you like?"

His enthusiasm was so cute, and she watched intently as he read out to her about the parks and attractions that they could go and visit. It became a blur to her as she enjoyed watching his fun-filled face, knowing he would be the last person she ever loved. The next few months would be the most special time they would have together; whatever lies she had to tell.

"It's not a fortune, but wow, we can relax a bit at work now and enjoy some family time before the kids are too old to come away with us. I'm sure Adam wouldn't mind letting me have a bit of time off work. He owes me anyway for all those extra hours I put in for the Brews Project this month," Karl continued. "Do you think you will be okay with getting the time off or using up your holiday time?" He didn't glance up once, he was so busy looking at places they could visit.

If only he knew that this was going to be the last holiday they spent together. Times like this would now be precious moments that Jane could treasure more than she ever had before, and all while in secret.

"Yes, I'm sure it will be fine, Karl. Let's not tell the kids until the day we leave though, make it a complete surprise for them like we've always wanted to do; they will love being surprised like that." Jane hugged him from behind the dining chair, watching his computer screen change rapidly as he searched the many theme parks and attractions. Her bronzed arms gently wrapped around his chest. He smelled wonderful. The rich aftershave was intense, manly, and she loved it. She had bought it for him for Christmas the previous year. Before that, he hadn't really liked to wear any sort of aftershave, but this fragrance had grown on him, and he enjoyed the way it made her feel. She thought to herself at that moment that she must remember to get him a new bottle soon as it was getting low.

Jane looked intently at her gorgeous husband as she sat on the chair beside him. He was running his fingers through his black hair in anticipation, overwhelmed with the excitement of what was to come. He was smiling so widely, like a Cheshire cat, as they say, like the cat that got the cream. He was so happy, and Jane knew this was the only thing that she wanted to see over the next few weeks, months, and, hopefully, years; just happiness, smiling, love, and her family close by for the time she had left with them, but without them suffering in the knowledge that only she knew right now.

The holiday would be the start of their lifelong dreams and as much as she could make them happen, she would, no matter what. For no matter how short a time scale, whatever she had to do, she would.

Knowing the truth was heart-breaking enough for her, but she just couldn't face telling her beloved husband of eighteen years and their beautiful teenage twins, Robbie and Cassie, at this time. It didn't make sense to her just yet, so why upset them now? She wanted joy in their house, not pain and broken hearts. This was her time to protect them for as long as possible.

Jane had not known where to turn when she got the news, and this was her only way of coping and keeping her family from months of stress and worry.

The time was now, and she had to do this for them; even if she had to lie to the most important people in her life.

Nothing else mattered from this day forward…

Chapter Thirteen

The school term came at the end of July and Jane and Karl had booked everything for the holiday, including all the amazing outings and adventures that they wanted to experience in the two weeks. Now they just had the amazing task of revealing the surprise to the children and they couldn't wait for the moment to come and watch their faces explode with excitement.

"What's going on?" asked the kids as they returned home from school to find their suitcases all packed and ready in the hallway.

"We are going on a little family trip." Karl had been waiting for this day to arrive. He knew that seeing their faces would be an awesome memory and had set up the GoPro to capture the moment.

Jane looked on as he excitedly began to tell them where they were going and what they were going to get up to in

Florida for the next fortnight.

They were overwhelmed with excitement recalling all the adverts on television that they'd seen numerous times commenting that they'd love to go there one day and do all the crazy roller coaster rides. Now it was actually going to happen, and they began jumping around, ecstatic with joy. As Jane watched them intently, all she could feel was pure love for this beautiful family of hers. What an incredible experience this was and how proud she felt of them all.

She watched Karl's face, grinning massively like he'd done so on their wedding day as he'd seen her walking towards him. All their faces were beaming, and a lump appeared in her throat. Cassie was jumping about and texting her friends at the same time to tell them the news as fast as possible. This in itself was a great memory for Jane, and she felt good about it, even about lying to them all; it was for the best. It was the right thing to do.

"I've packed all the things I thought you might want, but if there's anything else, let me have it, okay, kids? We'll stuff it in," Jane called to them as they rushed upstairs to get changed. They were leaving for the airport in just a few hours.

"Oh, Jane, how awesome was that?" Karl hugged her tightly. "It's going to be a holiday like no other." He went into the lounge to gather up his work things. He'd been working from home that day so that he could see the twins as soon as they came home from school, waiting all day to tell them, and it had been so worth it.

"I'm just going to nip out, Karl. I just remembered I forgot to get a few of the toiletries we need. I won't be too long," Jane said as she looked 'round the doorway to the lounge to see him clearing up.

"Do you want me to come with you?" he offered. "I can run you there in the car."

"No, it's fine. It's only a short walk to the corner shop, won't be long." She waved her hand, grabbed her jacket and door keys and left.

~

"Boo!" She popped her head into the shed where James was reading one of her workbooks that she was storing there.

"Hello there, stranger. Aren't you off on your holiday today?" he asked, smiling up at her and chucking the book back into the box. "This is rather boring stuff, isn't it?"

"Ha ha. Yes, we are. We've just told the twins. They are… well, let's just say rather excited." Her face blossomed today like it hadn't done for a long time. It was full of colour, and no painful grimacing or sadness was in sight. The adrenaline must have taken over.

"That's lovely, I bet they can't wait."

"Oh, James, their faces were adorable. We are off for two weeks. I'm going to miss our chats though." She pouted as she went out of the shed to see the flowers that he had laid that day.

"No, you won't, you'll be having way too much fun to think about old me, here in boring old Blighty."

"I will, I've seen you nearly every day for like… well for what seems ages. I know it has been just weeks but, I love it James, you've helped me so much. I'll bring you a souvenir back. A nice Florida cap or something." They laughed.

She'd never seen him wear a hat, even when it had been hot with the sun beaming down on them. His hair had always been perfect, so she guessed he didn't want to cover it up or maybe he just didn't like hats? She had noticed how he loved to wear a scarf, although it was only a thin type of material; it was a statement piece and it really suited him.

"Just go and enjoy yourself, Mrs W. Don't worry about me," he assured her. "I'll be here when you get back waiting to hear all about it. And, by the way, you look totally awesome today. It's lovely to see that beautiful smile of yours shining through for a change."

She beamed back at him before looking down at her watch. "Oh, blimey! I better go, we're leaving for the airport soon, and I'm supposed to be at the shop buying some essentials. I just wanted to see you before I left."

"Aww, you are such a lovely lady, now, go on, take care and remember, just have fun and stay safe."

Jane scuttled off but quickly stopped by the corner shop to get a few toiletries, so Karl didn't suspect she'd been anywhere else. She didn't really need them of course. She was too organised and had already picked everything up a few days earlier. He didn't know that though, so another lie was yet again, covered well.

She had thought about telling him all about James but just hadn't got 'round to it. There'd never been a moment when she had thought it was the right time, and it was kind of nice that they had this little secret between them. There was nothing in it. No other feelings but companionship, friendship, and support for two souls who needed each other, so it was just like she was meeting up with a friend each time. One only she knew, not a family friend, and not someone directly involved in the life of lies that she had to tell everyone else at this moment in time. She enjoyed the hours spent there with James and this was one person who she didn't have to lie to. It sounded strange in her head, spending time in a cemetery, but it always took her mind off what was actually going on in her life. It helped her deal with it, and she got the feeling that James needed it too. It was also nice to feel close to Pops; now more than ever, she understood exactly what pain and sadness he had endured.

"Jane, we leave in half an hour. Where have you been?" Karl called as he heard the front door close.

"Sorry, darling, I met a friend from the twins' old school and got chatting. You know what it's like," she lied. "Are we all ready to go then?" She was getting good at random stories and surprised herself sometimes.

They travelled to Gatwick airport by taxi where Sarah met them to wave them off as a surprise for the children.

"I just need to use the ladies' room before we go through to board, Karl. I'll be five minutes." She ushered Sarah into the toilets. "Babe, I need you to do me a favour. Could you ring Paula at the clinic and get her to order some new tablets for when I get back? I totally forgot with all the excitement over the past week and will only have a small supply when we fly back." She handed Sarah a Post-it-note with Paula's number on it. "Tell her that if she needs to contact me to text me on this number." She pointed to the number at the bottom of the note. "It's a cheap pay-as-you-go burner, so Karl doesn't see calls and texts from the clinic on my main phone. I think he's been noticing, and I don't want him to ask questions. They know I'm going away for two weeks, but it's just in case they need to tell me anything or change any appointments before we return."

"Yeah, no problem at all, Jane. Hey, I'm going to miss you so much. Two weeks of not seeing you lot is ages." Sarah pulled a sad face at Jane as she took the note from her and put it safely in the zip-up pocket of her jacket.

"I know, I'm going to miss you too, and I will get the kids to FaceTime you. Cassie has already told me she's going to miss you the most. The clinic has arranged for me to meet up with a doctor over there to have a few chemo sessions and chat about some new drugs that they're testing out. I've just got to work out a way to get there without Karl and the kids suspecting anything."

"Crikey, Jane, you are living dangerously. Be careful. The last thing you want is for it to come out over there and ruin the holiday."

"Don't worry about me. I'm getting good at this lying game now. Look, I better go. Oh, and here…" she handed Sarah an envelope with a big heart drawn on the front.

"What's this?" she asked curiously.

Grasping her hand, Jane replied, "Look, I know you booked next week off work, so… it's a ticket to join us. I can't go all the way to bloody Florida and not have you there to experience it with. I've cleared it with Karl, and he loves the idea too."

"Seriously? Are you kidding me?" Sarah gasped, her mouth nearly dropping to the floor.

"Nope, I'm not kidding. Just don't tell the kids now. It will be another fab surprise for them next week. Karl will meet you at the airport and bring you back to the hotel. It's all been arranged. You have your own room next to ours and everything. The children will love having you there, and so will I. So now you only have to miss us for a week."

After a massive hug and a few tears, happy ones, of course, they hurried out of the toilets to meet up with Karl and the kids, said their goodbyes and went to check-in. Jane winked at Sarah as they went through the departure gates to jet off. This was an amazing feeling for Jane, and she couldn't wait for the holiday to begin. As she stepped onto the plane, she felt a sense of enormous relief, knowing she'd been able to sort this all out for her wonderful family and Sarah.

~

"This is awesome, Jane. Look at it!" Karl took off his hat as they finally arrived at the airport in a very hot, and very sunny, Orlando. "Kids, this is going to be wicked, isn't it?" He grinned widely at his beautiful but extremely tired wife, mouthing, 'I love you'.

She smiled back at him and cherished the sight of her beautiful brood once again, even though she was in a degree of pain after the long nine-hour flight. She felt so lucky to have them in her life. It almost eased the cancer agony and stress that was all too real at times. She mouthed back, 'I love you' to him.

Paula texted Jane that evening on her second phone to let her know the times and arrangements for the doctor in Florida. Sarah had worked fast, she thought. Now she had to figure out how to get to the hospital without letting on to Karl. More bloody lies! her brain chastised her.

"Hey… there's a snorkelling trip later this morning, I've booked you and the kids on it for a few hours. I'm going to try out the spa areas, chill for a bit," Jane said as she passed Karl the snorkelling leaflet and booking information.

"That sounds great. Kids? Fancy some snorkelling? Are you sure you don't want to come with us though, darling?"

"Karl, you know I don't like swimming. You three go and spend some time together. I'll be just fine having a massage and getting my nails done. It will be so hard being a mum relaxing in a Florida spa," she bragged.

"Only if you're sure, honey. I don't like the thought of you being here on your own."

"Alone in a spa getting a massage… mmmm… tough times," she joked. "Go on. The kids will love it, and it's only a few hours. I've booked myself in now anyway so… maybe we could go and get something to eat at Citywalk later on this evening? There's a Bob Marley restaurant and bar that looks good."

"Sounds perfect. Okay, kids, let's go get ready, and sweetheart… thanks for this, I think I'm more excited than them right now." Giggling like a schoolboy, he kissed her on the lips gently before rushing off to get them all ready.

After they had collected all they needed and set off, she quickly checked the address of the hospital and called a taxi for the ten-minute drive along the vast highways. She took in all the sights along the way admiring the massive hotels with gigantic signage flashing away and even the landscapes were big but beautiful.

She arrived with plenty of time to spare, thanked and paid the driver, and walked up the pathway to the large glass doors of a tall building, pressing the buzzer. "Hi, it's Jane Walden, I have an appointment with Doctor Michael." She was buzzed in.

There were three main receptionists at the busy welcome desk. It was a lovely, clean, if a bit too clinical-looking building, but everyone was friendly as the Americans always were in the movies.

"Howdy there, Mrs Walden, pleased to meet you. Doctor Michael won't keep you a moment," said the male jet-black haired receptionist, smiling with gleaming white teeth. He was very smartly dressed in a fitted blue shirt and matching hospital tie.

The building was a lot different than the vintage, traditional, clinic back home in England. Everything was super modern and seemed so much bigger in America. The chairs were big; the doors were big; even the vending machines were bigger.

There was a coffee machine on a high table in the corner of the room, so she decided to have a cup while she was waiting. It tasted really strong, and she couldn't manage to drink it all. Maybe her tastebuds were changing, or maybe she just wasn't in the mood for coffee right now. She was exhausted. It had been a busy few days, and it had taken its toll on her body. Already, she was missing Karl and the kids, and she felt a tinge of sadness that she was at the clinic instead of watching them having fun on their dream vacation; a holiday that they had always talked about since having the children. Waiting for them to be big enough, old enough, to really have memories to treasure, and now she was here having treatment for something they knew nothing about. Something she hated more than ever right now. But all she could think of was at least they were in Florida, living their dreams one way or another. There would be plenty of time together over the next couple of weeks and she had to think positive.

Within a few minutes, Jane's name appeared on the screen at the front of the waiting room directing her to the consultation room. She made her way in and knocked on the door where another friendly reply came, "Come in."

Pushing the big white door and entering another massive room, she poked her head around the door and said shyly, "Hi," looking at the doctor at his desk.

Immediately, he stood up and walked over to welcome her. Americans certainly knew how to greet people and make them feel at ease, she thought. "How are you, Jane? Not too tired after your plane journey, I hope?" Funnily enough, he had a very strong British accent.

"Not too bad actually. A little bit tired to be honest, but I think that's just the long flight so maybe a bit of jet lag," she replied, sitting down as he showed her to a seat and returned to his on the other side of the desk.

"Good stuff. It is rather a trek, isn't it? Anyway, you're here now. So, we're going to help you with your chemo sessions and try out our new meds while you're on holiday. Is your husband going to be attending with you?" He looked slightly puzzled that she had come alone, glancing back to the door she'd arrived through.

"No, it's just me. I've told him and the kids to go out and enjoy themselves, there's no need to depress them with all this. It's boring for the children too." Another lie to another person.

"That's a lovely idea, yes, it can be a little tedious for the family members sometimes, especially children." He smiled back, oblivious. "Right, Nurse Loveday will now get you all wired up, so you can get back to your family as soon as possible." He signalled to the nurse, who began getting everything ready as the doctor left them to it.

"So, what are your family up to today?" asked the nurse.

"They've gone snorkelling. The kids have never tried it before, they've dabbled at the beach with toy snorkelling gear, but to do it out here should be amazing. I've set up a swim with dolphins' experience for them all too, which they will find out when they get there. That should keep them busy most of the day."

"Oh, wow, that's awesome. We take our children to the snorkel centre about once a month. They absolutely love it, and I'm sure yours will too. How old are they? Ours are six and eight."

They continued chatting, and it took her mind off what was actually happening. She was thankful that she had something to do other than thinking of her short future and all the drugs that were being pumped into her body once again. Thank goodness for this 'Lottery' money making this treatment available to her.

Chapter Fourteen

Jane made it back to the hotel with ten minutes to spare before Karl and the children returned from their trip. She had decided to try and get a little bit of shopping done after her treatment to chill out a little bit but shopping and sightseeing wasn't that much fun on her own, so she had ended up just sitting and almost watching the world go by enjoying the heat of the sun on her skin. Realising the time, she had rushed back up to the room, slipped into one of the white fluffy dressing gowns that were supplied in the hotel room and tied her hair up quickly and ever so roughly as though she'd been asleep from all the massage.

Lying on the bed, switching the television on, she tried to catch her breath as she heard the door opening. The children came bursting into the room, full of the day's news and events and fighting to tell Jane all about swimming with the dolphins and seeing all the amazing underwater scenes, waving photos of themselves in the water that the centre had taken for them.

"Come on, kids. Let Mum breathe for a minute," Karl entered shortly after, carrying all the swimming stuff and souvenirs they had bought. He smiled at Jane and leaned over to kiss her forehead. "How are you, sweetheart, nice massage?"

"I'm good. Very relaxing, yes." She stretched her arms up and pretended to yawn. "Did you have fun?"

"Oh man, it was amazing. I just wish you could have been there to do it. I'm sure you'd like it; you don't have to go too deep. Wouldn't Mum have loved it, kids?" He went over to the table where they had now plopped themselves with their phones to catch up on their social networking. They both nodded in agreement, and Cassie smiled sweetly over at her mum, looking up briefly from her mobile as she took that all-important selfie to mark the occasion of returning to the hotel after her exciting day.

"Come here, you two. Leave those things alone and come give your mum a cuddle." Jane held her arms out, welcoming them to her, and they both leapt up and bounced onto the bed on either side of her. She smiled up at Karl as he looked on.

"So, dinner?" he asked, rubbing his tummy. "Shall we eat out at Citywalk tonight, or do you want something in the hotel, it's been a long day hasn't it?"

"PIZZA," shouted the kids in unison.

They all laughed, and Karl went to get the menu of the hotel. Staying in was a much better idea for tonight. They all felt exhausted after their busy day and there would be plenty of evenings to eat out.

Jane enjoyed the moment of hugging her kids. How long would she be able to do this? Why did this have to end so soon? She swallowed hard to avoid tears escaping and kissed them both on their heads in turn.

She spent the next few days taking her tablets in private, calling the clinic to let them know how she was feeling, and sneaking off for some stronger chemo while spending as much quality time with Karl and the kids.

Sneaking off wasn't a fun activity, but she had no choice; if it meant a bit longer for her, then that's what she would do and keep doing for as long as was needed. Her heart felt clogged with guilt every time and she detested the lies.

They had booked to visit a few theme parks while they were there, and this was exhausting for Jane. She hid her pain and didn't give away that she couldn't do the things they wanted to do. A couple of times, she had to quickly zoom to the toilets to be sick and she hated that more than anything. Karl would start suspecting she was pregnant if he heard her throwing up so often; she had suffered sickness in the first four months of pregnancy when she was carrying the twins all those years ago. She continued taking the anti-sickness pills in the hope that they would suppress it a bit more and it seemed to ease off as the week went on.

For hours on end, she didn't even think about the horrid cancer and what it was doing to her body. She was just a normal, healthy woman on holiday with her beautiful family and had no worries, no illness and apart from the exhaustion, there was plenty to keep her mind off the dreaded C-word and keep her smiling, plus the sun helped relax her. The warmth of the rays on her tired bones softened the aching and she enjoyed lazing out in it by the pool watching the children splash around and have fun with Karl and other children they'd met already.

She was easily blaming the long, exciting thrill rides and walking for her tiredness. Luckily, the kids and Karl were also exhausted at the end of each day, which made the lying a bit easier to hide.

That evening, the kids had met up with some of their new friends and were playing a game of volleyball in the pool area. Jane and Karl watched on laughing at their water splashing antics and loving the fact that they had made friends so easily and so quickly.

They noticed a man pushing a lady in a wheelchair approaching them. "Hi there," the man said. "Are those your children playing volleyball with our two?" He pointed towards the four children.

"Yes, they belong to us, Robbie and Cassie," replied Karl standing up to shake the man's hand.

"Isn't it great how kids can make friends so easily? Pleased to meet you both, this is my wife, Marie, and I'm Bradley, just call me Brad though if you like."

"Hi. I'm Karl, and this is my wife, Jane."

"Hello, Karl, Jane. Can we get you both a drink, cocktails for the ladies maybe?" Bradley asked, stepping hard onto the brakes of the wheelchair and directing his eyes towards the poolside bar.

"Erm, yes, sure, that would be great, thanks, I'll come give you a hand," replied Karl as they both walked over to the main bar area leaving the two ladies alone.

"How old are yours; they look about the same age?"

asked Marie as she pulled her blanket over her knees.

Jane moved to the lounger nearer to Marie. "Yes, they are twins. Just turned thirteen, yours?"

"Ah, that's divine. Daniel is twelve and Sophie has just turned ten. Little cherubs at the moment but maybe the teenage years will get a bit crazy," she laughed back.

"Ha ha," chuckled Jane. "Yes, we do have the occasional mood swing but they're not too bad, they're good kids most of the time anyway." Jane noticed that Marie had some medical tubes inserted into the back of her hand and frustratingly, was caught looking.

"It's okay, you can ask if you like?" Marie smiled.

"Sorry, I didn't mean to…" Jane apologised, a little flustered and embarrassed.

Marie interrupted her. "Don't worry, honestly, it's fine. I'm used to people staring and I don't mind them asking what it's for either. I've got cancer and that's all my lovely medication going in."

The words hit Jane hard, like a swift punch in the stomach. This woman had cancer too, but she looked so weak and frail. Would that be her in a few months, stuck in a wheelchair being fed drugs through a tube? She couldn't help but think about herself and then felt bad for being so selfish. "I'm so sorry." She moved even closer and held onto Marie's surprisingly cold hand.

"It's cool. I've come to terms with it now, we all have actually. This is our last family holiday together. The kids have been finding it really hard the last few weeks as I've got weaker, but when they said they'd met some friends out here, we just wanted to come and thank you and your little

160

ones for helping them enjoy this time a little bit more. It's been a tough time for them, and us too actually."

"I can imagine. I'm glad they've helped though, in some way." Jane didn't know what to say. She felt sad but encouraged by this lady's strength and extremely positive attitude. "Do you mind me asking what type of cancer it is?"

"Not at all, it's melanoma, stage four, the big one."

For a moment, there was no talking, they just watched the children, smiling at their fun, but Jane felt so deflated and wondered if she could be that strong when the time came.

The guys returned from the bar within a few minutes with some fancy cocktails for the ladies, mocktails for the four kids, a beer each for themselves and a large plate of nachos for the children to share.

They all spent the rest of the evening chatting and getting to know each other, while the kids played happily and later on, watched a poolside movie together.

As everyone laughed at scenes of the film playing, Jane got completely lost in thought and wasn't taking anything in. All the chattering voices, soft playing music, water sounds and chinking of glasses disappeared as though she was the only one existing at this moment.

Looking around at Karl and the kids giggling and smiling and then glancing at the wonderful family they had just met she couldn't help but think about how her time had now been cut so short. There was no sound, she felt completely absent from everyone and everything around her until she suddenly felt Karl touch her knee gently, asking her, "Another drink?"

All the sounds and splashing returned louder, snapping her out of her solitary thoughts. She smiled sweetly up at his gorgeous face and just nodded, trying to yet again, hold back tears for the secret that she was holding in her heart from her wonderful family.

~

"I was thinking we should do something a little bit crazy for ourselves. After meeting Marie and her family, life is too short, hey? I can't imagine going through all that sadness and pain, that poor family, what they must be going through right now." He paused to collect his thoughts. "We do have a bit of spare spending money, so why not?" Karl was pouring a glass of wine the following evening once the kids were in their bedrooms asleep and he passed it to Jane.

If only he knew, but he didn't, and she had to go along with it. "Yes, it's an awful shame for such a lovely family to have to go through, what are you thinking of doing?" She changed the subject. "Please don't say you want to jump out of an aeroplane or something stupid like that, Karl," she replied a little worried at his excited tone of voice.

"No, not jumping out of something but… this." He pulled something from his pocket and showed her a leaflet he had picked up earlier in the hotel reception.

"A helicopter ride," she gasped. "Okay. I've never thought about doing that actually."

"We were going to do it on my stag weekend in France, but the lads decided we should all do a bungee jump instead. I was talking to Brad last night about something special to do and he said they all did it a few days back and

162

Marie especially loved it." He laughed as he knelt on the bed, bouncing like a child. "So, fancy it? Go on… be a devil."

"Oh dear, you men. Yes, let's do it. You only live once, as they say." Jane replied ironically as she stroked his sun-kissed cheek. He went straight down to reception and booked the four of them in for the following day.

~

The first week of the holiday passed way too quickly, for Jane especially. They were having the time of their lives and none of them wanted it to end.

Sarah joined them for the second week as planned, and this made it a little easier for Jane to visit the hospital because they could use shopping trips as an excuse to go out without Karl and the kids.

Although she loved spending time with Sarah, she also hated being away from the children and Karl for even a minute or an hour of the day. Time was running out quicker than she had imagined, and this scared her. She knew that her time was precious and short, and it was so annoying, but Sarah tried her very best to help her deal with it all and keeping the secret.

Three days before they were due to leave, Karl and Jane met with Bradley and Marie to swap addresses and phone numbers. They were leaving the next morning as Marie had taken a turn for the worse and needed to be back in hospital as soon as possible. They were from Miami, so they needed to get going on the four-hour drive down the coast.

As they waved them goodbye, Jane held onto Karl a little bit tighter than normal knowing that this situation would arrive at their door fairly soon. More than ever now she didn't want this holiday to end with the realisation of what was going to come over the next few months; she didn't want to leave her family, not now, not ever!

Reality would soon set in and she despised the cancer for doing this to so many people, and for ruining the lives of so many families that had to deal with it.

As she packed her cosmetics bag up and secretly took the last of her tablets in the bathroom, she looked in the mirror and sighed deeply. This had been the most amazing two weeks, a time she would never forget, but now she had to get back to all the horrible lying again on their return home, for a bit longer anyway. She didn't have a clue when the truth would come out and she wasn't looking forward to it one bit.

"This was the best holiday ever. Thank you so much for bringing us, Mum." Cassie leaned over to hug her mum as they sat in their seats on the plane waiting to take off for the long flight back to England.

"Aww, that's okay, sweetie. I'm glad you enjoyed it. It's been amazing, hasn't it? All those rides and the doughnuts we've eaten, I think I'll need to go on a diet," she chuckled back smiling.

"It was sick," Robbie called over from his seat next to Sarah, wearing his Orlando cap backwards and tapping away on the TV screen in the back of the seat to find a movie to tune into. Sarah smiled knowingly back at Jane as their eyes met.

"Shame we didn't get to Miami. I'll take you there next year for our wedding anniversary." Karl held onto Jane's hand tightly as the plane's engines started up.

If only I had next year, Jane thought, feeling her insides shattering once again. Not knowing what to reply with, she just squeezed his hand gently and smiled.

Those precious moments, those small comments, those times, this family, something Jane would keep close to her heart, now more than ever before.

Chapter Fifteen

September came and the school term started, a few weeks after the family had returned from their dream holiday. The kids were thrilled to be able to tell their friends and teachers all about it. They'd been busy printing photos out and creating their summer break assignment and had so much to write about and so many great pictures that it had taken quite a while. However, they'd enjoyed collating it all and reliving some of the amazing memories, videos and fun adventures that they had had during those two weeks. Sarah had even got involved with some sticking and decorating of a scrapbook with Cassie.

Karl had returned to his work with some brand-new projects lined up, and Jane had begun living the life of pretending to go to work again. She was really looking forward to meeting up with James and relaying all the holiday details in full once 'normal' day-to-day life had returned.

As Karl made a coffee by his machine in his office at work that afternoon, his mobile phone began to ring.

"Hello, Mr Walden, it's Cassie's form tutor, Mrs Daniels, do you have a moment for a chat?" said the voice on the phone.

"Yes, of course. Is everything okay?" Karl replied in a concerned voice, attempting to hold onto the phone with his chin while clutching the steaming hot coffee.

"Cassie is fine, but I do need to speak to you and your wife, today if at all possible. Would you be able to come along after school this afternoon?"

"Sure, that's no problem," he answered. "I'll contact my wife and meet her there."

"Great. We have tried calling Mrs Walden already, but her work said she was in a meeting out of the office," said Mrs Daniels.

"Oh, okay. I'll go and see if I can meet her, then we will come together. See you later." It was nearly two thirty, so Karl gathered his things and went to his boss's office, just up the corridor from his. "Boss, can I have a quick word?" he asked as he gave three short knocks on the open wooden door.

"Yes, of course, mate. Come on in," said Adam as he looked up from his paperwork, chucking his pen onto it. "I could do with five minutes off," he grumped.

The office was incredibly impressive and had a wide view of the Cambridge University buildings and its gorgeous grounds. The huge glass windows went right to the floor and coordinated with the big glass-topped desk that Adam sat at.

"Have a seat, my friend. Is everything okay?" He got up and pointed to the leather chair across from his.

"Yeah, I think so. It's just the school has rung me, and they need to talk to us about Cassie after school. Would it be okay to leave now and pick up Jane on the way? The school can't get hold of her at the moment as she's in a meeting, so I thought I'd go and see if I can find her and go together."

"Of course. No problem, mate," replied Adam.

Adam was a kind, down-to-earth, family man and understood when people needed time off. When any of his staff had problems, he had always lent an ear and endeavoured to help them any way he could. "I hope everything is okay, mate, and do let me know if you or the kids need anything sorting out," Adam said as Karl shook his hand in thanks. "It's probably nothing. You know what these teenage girls are like, and I'm sure the school will have it sorted quickly, whatever it is. They are good there; we always found the teachers to be on the ball with bullying and that. Charlie had some issues when he first started but it was all sorted out very quickly."

"Hopefully, it's nothing, you know, but need to just keep a check on it, I'll be in earlier tomorrow to make up the hours," Karl replied checking his watch.

"Mate don't worry about that, it's cool. See you normal time." And with that, Adam picked up the phone and began dialling.

Karl gave him the thumbs up and swiftly collected his jacket and bags from his office.

As he made his way over to Jane's workplace, he

wondered where she could be. She rarely went out without letting him know where she was going, and he usually knew about meetings out of the office as she'd write them on the wall calendar at home, but he hadn't remembered seeing anything that morning. He'd tried ringing her a few times on the way, but it had gone straight to the answerphone. Very unlike her to not have her phone on either, he thought to himself. Maybe her battery had given up, and she hadn't noticed. He'd soon find out he guessed.

"Hi, Shirley, is Jane in her office?" Karl asked the receptionist as he arrived.

"Just let me check for you, Mr Walden," the lady replied, tapping away on her desk phone to ring out.

While he waited, he looked around the main reception area, and noticing his wife's photo up on the wall, he walked over to it, smiling at her as though she was smiling back at him. The photo had been taken last year just before Christmas. She looked stunning as usual. Her hair was a lot darker, and she'd been wearing one of her favourite pink jumpers with a white collar peeking out. She always looked smart but casual for work, and she knew just how to pull off any type of look. Her mum had always remarked that she could make a bin liner look glamorous.

His thoughts were interrupted as Carol appeared. "Hey, Karl, darling, how are you?" she air-kissed him, holding both his arms. They had met many times at functions that the accountancy firm had held.

"Hi, Carol. I'm good, thanks. I'm just trying to reach Jane. Do you know where she is? The receptionist is calling through I think?"

"Oh, erm…" she nervously answered as she waved to Shirley to put the phone down. "She did say something about a meeting today out of the office. Now, what time did she say?" She thought for a moment trying to think of the best thing to say. "Yes, a two o'clock one. I'm sure that's what she said, about ten minutes from here, but I don't think she'll be back until around half past four-ish, maybe five? We've had a few late appointments just recently for some reason."

"Oh, right. Okay, no problem. I have to go to the kids' school now. They rang earlier. Do you think she'll be popping back in here before she comes home?"

"Yes, she did say she needed to collect some papers to take home for a case we are working on. I'll let her know you came in and get her to call you asap. See you soon. Take care, darling." With that, she gave another quick air kiss and went hurriedly up the glass stairs, tapping away on her phone frantically. She was sending Jane a text to let her know that he had shown up there, hoping that she would receive and see it before Karl saw her back at home. She felt awful lying to him but had promised Jane that she would keep her secret for her. She had no other choice but to go along with the story right then. Glancing back down at Karl, her heart sank a little as she remembered how Jane had shown such bravery that day when she had told her the news. Such a shame that he didn't have a clue what she was going through, but it was understandable for Jane to do it when she was ready. It wasn't right for anyone else to tell him that sort of news.

Karl thanked Shirley, the receptionist, for her time,

made his way back to the car park and proceeded to drive to the school.

"Thanks for coming in, Mr Walden. Will Mrs Walden be joining us?" Mrs Daniels was head of year as well as Cassie's form teacher. She was in her late fifties, well-spoken, smart, and always had her glasses on a chain around her neck. The kids thought this was hilarious, remarking that their grandmas did that with their glasses, but it had always made her laugh, so she played up to it.

"I'm afraid she's out on an appointment. I went by her office quickly before coming, but I don't think she's going to be back in time."

"Not to worry. I'm sure you can fill her in later. I've asked Cassie to come here straight after her last class, so she should be here shortly. Would you like a drink of something? Coffee, tea, water?"

"A coffee would be lovely, thank you. No sugar."

Mrs Daniels showed Karl to a side room that had been set out for their meeting and then went to fetch the refreshments.

Karl quickly sent another text to Jane. *'Hi babe, where are you? I'm at the school if you can get here in the next half hour, no panic, just a quick meeting with the form teacher about Cassie x'*

He kept peeking at the phone, but no reply came back as Mrs Daniels returned with the drinks and Cassie, whom she had met in the corridor.

Placing his phone face down on the table nearby and switching it to silent, he rubbed Cassie's arm as she sat down next to him, staring at her lap. "Hey, trouble," he joked.

"Here's your coffee, Mr Walden. Milk or cream?"

"None, thanks, just black is fine."

Sitting opposite them, Mrs Daniels began. "So, Cassie, would you like to tell Dad what's been going on?" She sipped her tea and looked over her teacup at Cassie. A short silence ensued.

"Well, there's been these girls…" she paused. "They've been making stuff up about Mum…" Cassie then broke down in tears rubbing her eyes frantically.

"Cass, darling… what have they said?" Karl put his cup down on the desk and put his arm around her shoulders as she leaned into his chest. He glanced over at Mrs Daniels who looked upset for them both.

"Oh dear… right. Cassie has been having a few problems with some girls in the year above her, and it seems they have been sending her messages on her Instagram or Snapchat social media accounts, which, let's just say… are not kind and not acceptable in or out of school time. They have been spoken to, and I am ringing their parents after I have had this meeting with you. Cassie wanted me to bring you in as this has been going on for some time, but she was a little worried to tell you, bless her. She was trying to deal with it herself." She leaned over her desk and handed Cassie a tissue from the box behind her.

"Oh, sweetheart. Why? Come here, darling." Karl gave her another comforting hug as she calmed herself down.

"Sorry, Dad. I just didn't want you and Mum to worry. I thought they would just stop."

Mrs Daniels added, "Well, they will stop now. I can assure you, Cassie, dear. I will be on the phone to their parents very shortly after you leave here, and if you get anything after that from any of them, in any way, you need to come straight to my office. Although I will be surprised if they do carry on. I know all the parents very well, and they will not be happy about this form of bullying by their children." Mrs Daniels had handled it great. She had always come across as a no-nonsense kind of teacher but fair with it too. Their first meeting with her when visiting the school had impressed them, and the kids all felt that she was one teacher in particular that they could turn to and get advice or help whenever they needed it.

"Thank you so much, Mrs Daniels. And thank you for calling me. I'll fill Jane in later. We will do all we can to help Cassie and anytime you need us to come in, please don't hesitate to call us."

Mrs Daniels placed her hand on Cassie's shoulder. "Go and wash your face, dear. We can't have you leaving school like that." Collecting the cups, she turned to reassure Karl. "Look, this happens all the time, especially with the different year groups. They are trying to find their feet and be 'top dog' of the school. We get it every year, especially in the year seven intake. That's the worst year for it actually, they are coming from being top of the school in primary to being at the bottom in high school, it's hard for some of them to grasp, but that doesn't mean that we will not deal with every single child who does this sort of thing. The school will not tolerate that behaviour or upsetting treatment to any of our students. You can be assured that this will be dealt with and that it will be the end of it." With that, she shook his hand and escorted him to the main reception to meet with Cassie who was just coming out of the girls' toilets in the main corridor.

"I'm so sorry, Dad," Cassie said quietly as they walked to the car park.

"Sweetheart, it's okay. I understand what it's like, and we all have to go through this stuff to make us stronger. Mrs Daniels will sort it out, but promise me you will talk to us if anything like this happens again before it gets to be too much?"

"Okay, Dad, I will. I promise."

"Do you want to tell me what they've been saying to you about Mum, Cassie?" he asked, scrambling in his pocket for the car keys.

"No not really, Dad, I'd rather not talk about it anymore, can we just leave it?" Cassie replied looking down at her feet once more woefully kicking a stone.

"Okay, but if you want to talk, about anything, just let me or your mum know, yeah?"

Just as they approached the car, Karl spotted Jane rushing towards the school reception.

"Jane!" he yelled.

She turned to follow the voice and smiled, slightly out of breath, and made her way over to the car. "Hi, guys. Is everything okay? I've only just got your text, my phone died in a meeting, I got here as soon as I could." Trying to catch her breath again, she put her arm around Cassie and kissed her head asking, "You okay, little one?"

"Yes. I'm fine, Mum. Really, it's nothing. It's sorted now." Cassie jumped quickly into the back of the car and fastened her seatbelt.

Jane made a sad face to Karl, who proceeded to tell her

quietly, "I'll explain when we get home, but it's nothing too serious. Hop in. Let's get her home." He reassured her with a kiss on her cheek.

They both got into the car. Jane had caught a taxi there as she had left her car at home that day. She hadn't expected Karl to be out of his office early. "I had to get a taxi. I left my car at home today. It was making a weird clunking noise, so I thought it best. Maybe it needs a service or something?" she fibbed as they drove home.

"I'll have a listen after Robbie's football training, then ring Steve at the garage to give it a check over."

"Yes, that's a good idea." She was more on the ball than she'd ever imagined she could be with the lies; it was becoming easier each time. But not in her head, she hated it more and more each day and didn't know how long she could keep all this nonsense up.

And not being there today made her feel terrible, the bloody chemo was taking over and she hated it.

Chapter Sixteen

"She's a tough little cookie, isn't she?" Jane said as she sat down on the sofa next to Karl passing him the local paper that he enjoyed reading each week. He'd just got in after football training with Robbie and slumped down looking tired. She kissed his cheek. "Sorry I wasn't there with you both, bloody work. Such a shame she didn't tell us anything earlier. I know a few of the girls' mums in that year, so I could've had a word with them or something. I wonder what they've been saying to her to make her so upset?"

"Who knows with teenage girls? I guess she'll tell us when she's ready. Anyway, Daddy handled it, and I'm sure it'll be fine. As you say, she's a tough cookie." He winked at her and continued, "Mrs Daniels was really nice, and she definitely means business where bullying is concerned doesn't, she? I spoke to Cassie briefly afterwards when we came out of the school and she has promised to let us know if anything else is said or goes on in the future."

"She's growing up so fast, Karl. I guess she just wanted to try and handle it herself. Bless her. I feel bad for not being there today."

He smiled, putting his arm around her. "Don't worry, darling. She is a strong-willed little woman, just like her mother, or should that be stubborn?" He laughed as she nudged him in the side. "Where were you this afternoon anyway? Getting your nails done again?" he joked, holding up her hand to check her manicured nails which were getting a bit worn down.

She hadn't rehearsed any stories, forgetting to set something up in her mind, what with all the worrying about Cassie, so she just quickly replied, "Oh… ha ha… no we er… we have this client who doesn't like heights, so I said I'd go to her instead of her coming to my office. I mean it's only the first floor, but apparently, she has it really bad, and the flight of glass stairs is too much for her." Jane had really been having a round of chemo at the clinic. It sounded very weird as she heard herself speaking. She'd never heard of anyone with a fear of heights like that, and she wondered if he would believe her stupid and rather terrible fib.

He did look a little puzzled as she faced him in hope, but replied, "Whoa, that's some fear of heights. Anyway, do you fancy a glass of the red stuff tonight?" he asked. "I got a new bottle on the way back." He got up from the sofa to walk towards the kitchen.

Thankful that he'd changed the subject so quickly, she replied with a sigh of relief, "No, I'm good. You go ahead, darling. I might go and run a hot bath. My back has been aching so much today, I think the running around didn't help either." Jane knew she shouldn't be drinking alcohol while having chemo and although it was hard to refuse a nice glass or two of an evening, she felt she should miss out tonight.

"Do you want me to run it for you? You got some new candles last week, didn't you?" he kindly asked her, popping his head back in the lounge.

"No. It's fine, Karl. You enjoy your wine. Isn't there some football on for you and Robbie to watch later?"

"Not tonight." He disappeared into the kitchen again, so Jane made her way upstairs and started running the bath sitting on the side rubbing her tired face. She felt very weak and rather nauseous. Maybe all the rushing to get to the school wasn't such a good idea, but she'd been worried after seeing all Karl's missed calls and Carol's texts and wanted to get there as quickly as possible. Sometimes, adrenaline took over but then tended to slap her down with exhaustion when she did finally get a moment to rest. She quickly sent Carol a text to thank her for the warning that Karl had been to the office. She must remember to add made-up appointments to the calendar or at least mention that she had some 'meeting' to cover the deceit of all the fibbing she was continuing on a daily basis about going to work.

As she brushed her hair, she noticed that there was a considerable amount of it coming out onto the brush, more than normal. Already, the treatment was affecting her beautiful locks, how long before she had no hair? She moved it around frantically to check for any patches appearing on her head. Luckily, although it was noticeably thinner to her, there weren't any gaps or bald bits just yet, so she quickly ripped out the excess hair from the brush and put it in the bin under some tissue.

She was then startled as Karl knocked gently on the bathroom door and tried the handle. "Honey, you okay?"

"Yeah, fine." She dropped the brush and as she stood up, caught sight of her arms in the mirror, seeing the bruises that she had from the needles during the day. She needed to get herself some cover-up makeup before they looked so bad that Karl would start asking questions about them next. She'd have to make up some excuses for them too and how the hell would she explain that? All this lying was getting to be hard work, and she didn't know how much longer she could cope with it. How long could she go on before he noticed her weight loss again? The thinning of her hair? The bruises? Her awful brittle nails that were once always manicured and long. Her brain was crushing with the anguish of thinking it all up.

"Shall I come in and keep you company? I poured you a glass anyway. You look like you need a little pick me up tonight." Karl tried to open the door again with no luck.

"I just need a half hour or so to relax, darling. I'll be finished soon, please, have my glass for yourself. I'm okay for wine tonight."

She always used to love him joining her in the bathroom while she soaked any aches and pains away. It was their little time to sit and have a chat about their days and make plans for the coming weekend. They had even purchased a little fabric chair specially to go in there for either of them to sit on while the other was in the tub.

Standing outside with two glasses of wine in his hand,

Karl was bemused by her answers and wondered why she had locked the door, but he replied gently, "Okay… let me know if you change·your mind. Text me. See you in a bit, yeah?" He walked off, thinking it was strange, but maybe she just needed some time to herself tonight as she had said. He'd wait in the bedroom for her and have their daily chat when she was ready. On his way to their room, he placed the glasses on a side table and checked in on Cassie who was already fast asleep, so he pulled the covers over her and crept out of the room, switching her light off and closing the door behind him quietly then checking on Robbie who was just finishing up one of his games, so he left him to it.

Collecting the wine glasses once again, he continued to the bedroom placing each glass on the bedside cabinets.

A pile of Jane's clothes lay neatly on the bed and as he picked them up, a small pink Post-it note fell out of the pocket of her jacket onto the floor. He recognised that it wasn't Jane's writing: *P – 07415 856321 xx Anytime. X,* he read and then shrugged.

He placed it on her dressing table, wondering who 'P' was, but she'd had numbers before on Post-it notes, so he thought no more of it. He sat on the bed to read the daily newspaper which he'd not finished earlier, hoping that Jane wouldn't be too long. He'd really missed her today.

It was late when Jane had finished her bath. She had tried her utmost to prolong the time in there, so she could just go straight to bed afterwards. Karl had fallen asleep on the bed with the paper on his chest, his wine glass empty but hers was still on her side of the bed half full. She would have to tip it away so he would think she had drunk it.

She walked around the bed to collect it and then her heart skipped a beat as she noticed the Post-it on the dresser. Grabbing it, she placed it into her purse pocket which was in the wardrobe nearby. Would she now have to make up some excuse for that? Hopefully, he hadn't taken any notice. She went over to the bed again and looked down at her husband. "Karl," she whispered, "you need to get into bed, sweetheart." She placed her hand gently on his shoulder, moving the newspaper to the bedside table.

A slight mumble of words was all the answer she got, so she decided to take herself into the spare room to sleep instead of disturbing him. She didn't have the strength tonight to move him over anyway and he looked so peaceful. Grabbing a pillow and a blanket from the airing cupboard on the landing, she made her way to the spare bedroom where there was a single bed. It was a bit of a storeroom but had a bookshelf filled to the brim with books in all types of genres, and all the family enjoyed the odd reading hour in there when they could.

As she lay there thinking about the day, thoughts of him finding out her terrible secrets crossed her mind. She needed to be more careful in the future. If she had a clinic appointment for her chemo, then she must make something else up and text him to say she was going to be out of the office before he rang or texted her and started worrying or suspecting anything. He could turn up at her office like that again any time, and if she wasn't careful, he would suspect she was up to something before long, or worse still, find out what was really going on through someone else.

He'd turned up at her office on her thirtieth birthday

with a massive bunch of red roses and her favourite box of chocolates with a red heart-shaped balloon attached to them. He'd arranged with the ladies who worked alongside Jane that he'd whisk her off in a limo, which was parked in the private staff car park, with champagne on board and full of more heart-shaped balloons. He'd carried her out of the office just like the scene in the eighties' movie, *An Officer and a Gentleman*, but without the gorgeous white naval uniform. It had been a dream scene. He did have a beautiful tuxedo on though, and he always looked gorgeous in black. She had been stunned to see him arrive like that and declare his love in front of everyone, both of them blushing like young lovers.

The women in the office had thought it was amazing and enjoyed telling their other halves about it when they had gone home that day. They had all lined up in the corridor to see them off, clapping his efforts and singing Happy Birthday to her as he carried her out.

Inside the car, there was a large white box with a big ribbon 'round it. Inside was a new dress and shoes for her to change into. It was a halter neck, red satin dress with a side split, very glamorous and the shoes were red and full of sparkly diamantes.

"Wow, this is all so beautiful, but where the hell are we going?" she'd said on opening the box. "Oh, what about my hair?" She remembered worrying about that on the way. He'd reached to the back of her head where her hair was lightly pinned up with a clip for work and released it. "It looks beautiful down. You don't need to worry about anything, you look as beautiful as ever, my darling." He'd kissed her softly as her hair had tumbled down naturally. "You'll have to wait and see where we are going, but I think you will like it." With a wink and a kiss to her cheek, he'd put his arm around her, and they'd sat back in the leather seats, sipping champagne and nibbling on some takeaway chicken and chips, until they arrived at the theatre in the heart of London.

He'd taken her to see her favourite musical, *Cats*, and she had been overwhelmed with the whole experience. She'd seen it when she was younger on a trip with the school, but she had always wanted to see it again someday. Today was the day she'd waited for, and he'd made this happen. Seated in a VIP booth, with the best view of the performance and more champagne on arrival too, it was a night they would never forget.

"Now I understand the dress and shoes. This is amazing, darling. Oh, my word, you've done all this for me?"

"For you, Jane, nothing is too much." He pulled out the red-cushioned velvet chair for her to take her seat, handed her a glass of fizz, and leaned down to kiss her as the lights dimmed and the musical experience began. She felt like the most special woman in the whole theatre that night.

It had been just the perfect birthday surprise, Sarah had babysat the twins. Jane's mum had also popped round for a bit to help Sarah out, but it hadn't been the end of the evening as Karl had arranged a night in one of the top hotels in London in a penthouse suite overlooking the city. Only the best for his wife, he'd thought when he had booked it all.

"What about the twins?" she whispered to him as he passed her some small gold binoculars from the shelf in front of them.

"Sarah and your mum have it all in hand. I've left them the full instruction book, and they have our numbers, but they won't need them. They are experts at this babysitting lark now," he'd joked reassuringly. "Just enjoy your night."

It was one of the best nights Jane had ever spent with him. One she knew she would treasure forever, and remembering it tonight made her smile as she lay looking up at the ceiling in the spare room.

With these thoughts running through her mind, she made a mental note of excuses, reasons, and predicaments to get out of telling him the truth about where she was disappearing to each time.

It was time to step it up. He couldn't find out. If he was to know, she would be the one telling him; but maybe not just yet. She still didn't feel ready for it but when would the time be right, when would she be ready to tell him the heartbreaking truth that she was so carefully trying to hide from him? She was only trying to protect him after all, but, if she wasn't more on top of things, more focused on the matter in hand, it could be out of her control at any moment. And even sooner than she hoped.

Chapter Seventeen

It was the anniversary of the day that Jane and Karl had met all those years ago at college and today he had planned to have the day off, so that he could surprise Jane at work with some flowers, personally this time. For the past few years, he had sent them to her office, by using the local florist in town. But this year, he wanted to do things a little differently, a heart-warming and romantic thought that was about to backfire in the most dramatic way for both of them and much sooner than she'd hoped.

"Have a nice day, darling. I'll see you about six after work," he lied to Jane as she kissed him goodbye at the door of the house that morning.

"Okay, honey, don't work too hard," she joked and watched him drive off up the road, wondering what she could get up to today. A visit to see James was on the cards, but she wanted to freshen up and have a shower first after spending half an hour clearing the breakfast plates and dishes. She also thought it might be a good idea to start trying out some headscarves that she had bought online as her hair was getting thinner each day now, and she wanted it to look more of a fashion accessory than the true fact of losing her hair and looking terrible.

Sitting in front of her mirror, she decided she would have to have an hour with Sarah for her to help with this. Not one for liking any type of headwear, including hats of any kind, this was proving to be more difficult than she had imagined. They just made her look ill, and she didn't like it at all, so she continued to get ready to go out for her chemo session at eleven, chucking the scarves into the back of the bottom drawer of her dresser, hoping maybe Sarah could help another day while everyone else was out the house.

Karl had gone straight to Jane's office on his lunch break where he had found none of his wife's belongings and someone else sitting at her desk. Walking in with a massive bunch of flowers to a complete stranger had been awkward for both of them, and he wasn't impressed with his findings, as well as being rather embarrassed. "I'm sorry, I thought this was Jane Walden's office. Did she move to a new one?" His wide smile turned to confusion as he lowered the flowers from in front of his face and his big smile disappeared.

"Oh. Sorry, no. I'm fairly new, but I moved in here when the previous lady here left the company a few months back," the strawberry blonde lady answered innocently, looking shocked at this man walking into her office flourishing an amazing bouquet.

Karl, silenced by the words 'when the previous lady here left' hung the flowers down by his side as her words hit him like the sharp punch of a fist in the stomach. He felt winded and completely taken aback. What did she mean, 'left a few months back?' Jane had been going to work every day for the past few months, or so he thought. If not, where had she been going? Where was she each day? What was going on? He was totally bewildered and needed answers. Turning back into the corridor and hastily making his way to Carol's office, his mind raced.

"Carol, can I have a word please?" he blurted as he entered the room in haste.

She was on a phone call as he barged into the room and reached her desk. "Sorry, I'll have to call you back," she said putting down the phone immediately.

"What's going on, Carol? There's someone in Jane's office who says she left a few months back. What does she mean she left?"

In shock, and not knowing where to go or what to say next, Carol replied, "Karl, you should speak to Jane. It's really not for me to discuss."

"What do you mean discuss? What's there to talk about? She's either left or that woman in my wife's office is lying to me, what is it, Carol?" He was fuming now.

"Just talk to Jane, please," she pleaded, holding her hands out to him.

"I will. Don't you worry!" He went to leave but paused and turned to face her again. "Just tell me this, does Jane still work here or not?"

Carol was heartbroken. She hadn't expected him to

turn up again so soon, and this was the worst thing that could have happened. "Look, why don't we get a coffee? Get you calmed down a bit. I'll call Jane, and…"

"I don't want bloody coffee. I want to know where my wife is and why she's not in her office!" His voice was shaky, full of confusion and anger. "So, does she still work here or not?"

Not knowing what else to do and certain that he wasn't going to let it go, she just shook her head. He looked at her in disbelief and stormed out, chucking the flowers in the reception bin as he left. He glanced towards the staff photo area and noticed that Jane's picture had been removed too. He rushed to his car, slamming the door with force, his heart pumping hard against his chest, his face sticky with sweat from the panic.

The drive home was vague, and he felt sick at the thought of what had been going on. He had looked stupid in front of all those people he'd seen so many times before when he had visited and wanted to know the truth. Why had she not been at her office? And why had she left months back and not told him? None of it made sense, but the more he thought about things, the worse the conclusions he began to come to. Was she having an affair? Where was she going each day, and if she wasn't working, where was the money coming from each month?

While this was all happening, Jane had been in the clinic having another draining chemo session, unaware of the events now unfolding for her husband and, of course, poor Carol. As soon as she finished, she quickly stopped by the cemetery and visited James as planned, still none the wiser.

Her phone had died so she didn't get the warning from Carol about the unexpected visit and what had just happened. For some reason, she didn't even have the charger with her today so, not thinking, resigned herself to charge it up when she got home.

"I'm tired this week, really bloody tired, and I'm sure my hair is getting thinner. What do you think?" She turned her head to look away from James and flicked her hair.

"It's fine, Jane. You still look gorgeous. Have you thought about a bandana or headscarf thing? You would rock one of those."

"Mmm, yes. I have a few to try out, but I'm not sure they suit me, to be honest. I tried a few headscarves this morning, but I don't have the knack with them yet. You will tell me when I need to cover the bald patches, won't you, James?"

"Of course." He smiled reassuringly.

"Look, I've got to go a bit earlier today. It's a bit of a special day for Karl and me. It's the anniversary of the day we met all those many years ago. The kids are going on sleepovers so we can have the whole evening together. I think I'll convince him to order food in so we can chill out a bit. I've not got the energy to go out tonight."

"Sounds just perfect, and congratulations to you both. You get off then. I'll see you tomorrow sometime. Maybe around three if you can make it then?" he said, and off into the shed he went, waving.

She was really looking forward to spending some quality time alone with Karl in the house by themselves. Although the children were no problem and did spend most of their time in their rooms, it was still nice to be alone now and again.

Food choices were on her mind. She'd suggest Indian as it was his favourite takeaway and she picked up a bottle of sparkling cava on her way back to the house. Sod it, she thought, a small glass can't hurt. It was their favourite type of sparkling wine too.

On the way home, she had visited a little underwear boutique to get something special to put on as a surprise for him after their meal. A little black and red number to add a bit of passion maybe. If she had the energy that was. Sarah had also sourced some great cover-up makeup to hide the bruises, and it was working a treat. He hadn't noticed, and she could barely see them herself now. Everything was ready in her head, and she couldn't wait to see him.

Their special night was going to be just perfect, or so she thought.

Jane noticed that Karl's car was in the driveway as she returned home. "It's nice that we both got the afternoon off," she said as she met him in the hallway excited for their special evening.

"Yeah, great," he answered abruptly, walking into the lounge.

"I thought we could order in some food tonight, how about an Indian, your favourite? Maybe have a cuddle on the sofa and watch a movie. There's something new on Netflix apparently, a romantic comedy, what do you think?" she said plugging her phone in to charge finally.

"Not that hungry," he sharply replied, shrugging his shoulders as he sat down on the sofa putting his feet up onto the coffee table.

"Oh. Okay? Maybe order later then, a glass of fizz first? I got our favourite cava too."

"Maybe." He didn't even look up at her as he switched on the TV with the remote control.

"I have a little something for you later too." She moved closer to him with a cheeky look in her eye but got no response. "Karl, is everything okay?"

"How was work this week?" he asked her, getting up and leaning on the wall.

"Erm, okay, I guess. Nothing special happened." She turned to face him.

"No visits from anyone then?" His voice was stern.

Before she had the chance to answer, he spoke a little louder and demanded, "Where were you today, Jane?" He pushed the lounge door shut and switched the TV off again, throwing the control onto the sofa beside her.

"I told you. I went into town after work to get some bits for tonight. I have a little surprise in store." She winked back at him, hoping to lift the murky atmosphere and change his mood. Something wasn't quite right.

"After work, yeah, from your office?" he asked, not even reacting to the surprise element of the conversation.

"Yes, after work from the office. Karl, what's this all about? What's going on? Why are you so angry?" Jane was concerned and worried he knew something.

"So, what time exactly did you leave work today?" he emphasised the word work and made quote marks with his fingers.

"Normal time. Christ, what's with all the questions?"

"You can't give me an exact time then? No? Not even a rough idea of when you left your office today?"

"Erm, about two-ish, I think. Maybe three o'clock. I had to pop and see a client quickly, why?"

"A client? Interesting. Well, do you want to know what I've been up to today?" Before she could reply, he continued, "I thought it would be nice to buy you a massive bunch of your favourite flowers and surprise you. I turn up at your office with them, yet it seems your office *isn't* there. Well, excuse me, no. The office was there, but you in the office? Erm, no!" He glared at her, now even more angry and continued, "There was someone else in your office, not you, and none of your stuff was there either. Even your staff photo had gone from reception. Why's that then? Mmmm, let's see…" Her heart sank as she realised what was going on. "Seems you haven't worked there for a couple of months now, so, again, I'll ask you, where were you today? Because you certainly weren't at work and haven't been there for weeks it turns out!" His voice deepened to an even angrier tone and she knew she had been caught. She'd completely forgotten about the office and the fact that he could turn up there. Even though he'd done it so many times before, her mind had been too busy lately to consider he might go there for this anniversary. How stupid she felt to have let this happen. The one thing she didn't want to happen now had, and she didn't know how to get around it.

Her heart ached as she realised what she had done, or more, what she hadn't done by not covering her tracks. Even after the recent visit that Carol had texted her about, she hadn't learned a valuable lesson. But still, she didn't have the heart to tell him the truth straight away so more lying now ensued to try and mend this mess and win him back, but would it work this time? She felt doubtful but it was worth a try, wasn't it?

"Look, okay… I didn't want to tell you, but… I left a while back to look for something else, to have a little change and break from it, I wasn't enjoying it anymore."

"So, you thought it would be better to just pretend to go to work each day? How long were you planning on lying to me with your new venture?"

"Well, sort of, yes, I had the money. A good pay-out which paid for our holiday…" she stopped as she realised what she had said.

"Pay-out? So, what about the lottery win?" he questioned, eyebrows frowning angrily.

There was an awful silence for what seemed like minutes as she gathered some story quickly in her head.

"It wasn't the lottery, Karl. I took redundancy and made up the lottery story, so I didn't have to tell you I was being let go at work."

He sniggered angrily. "I don't believe you, Jane… I want the truth, and I want it now! There is so much that doesn't add up lately. Private phone calls, texts in the night, and who is 'P'?" he asked, referring to the Post-it note he had seen in the bedroom a few nights back with an initial and a number on it. It was Paula's number from the clinic, but she couldn't bring herself to tell him that either. The situation was getting worse by the second and she was frantic with worry.

"It's just someone I met in the coffee shop who had a job going," she lied, and he knew it.

"Do you think I'm stupid? A phone number with a kiss on it and 'anytime' written below?" His voice grew louder, and she could feel herself shaking inside. "If you haven't been going to work, where have you been going each day then? All dressed up smart?"

She didn't know what to say, knowing that she needed to lie more, but the words wouldn't come out. "I er…" Her mind wasn't working quick enough today because of pure panic. She didn't want him to be in this situation of suspecting her, but she still couldn't bring herself to say what she really needed to.

Before she could say anything more or make something else up, he interrupted her with an irate but sad look on his face. "I don't believe this… after all these years, Jane. After all we've been through… just tell me. Are you seeing someone else? Who is it? Some toy boy from work? Is it that post guy? Just tell me the bloody truth, will you? Come on, I can take it. Who is he, Jane?"

"WHAT?" she cried. "No!" She should've known that question was coming. Why else would someone lie to their husband in this way? Most people lie because they are having an affair. She wasn't and this was churning her up inside. She'd never seen him react this way. He was angry but, at the same time, heartbroken, and she could see that. What the hell was she to do? Was it time she told the truth? What would he say?

As her mind wandered, her phone turned on and messages began coming through, but she could only glance over at it hearing it pinging.

"Is that him? Sending you more secret messages? Who is he, Jane?" He moved closer to her with rage in his eyes like she'd never seen before and didn't want to see again.

"Karl, you've got this all wrong. You really have. It's nothing like that…" She felt a little scared, not that he'd ever hurt her, but by the fact that she'd now hurt him so badly. His reaction was frightening and so upsetting for her. She'd never seen him like this. It was horrible.

"Have I got it wrong? Have I really? Then you tell me why you have lied to me all this time? Who keeps ringing you and texting you?" He grabbed her phone ripping it out from the charger, swiping furiously trying to get it to start up, he was too messed up to concentrate on what he was doing so threw it down and turned back to her. "And where are all these 'appointments' and 'clients' you have to go to? You have no job, so what appointments are they exactly? No more lies, Jane. Do you know how stupid I felt today turning up at your office with a massive bunch of flowers for my wife to find out that you don't even work there anymore? Carol looking at me like a complete idiot. Who is he, Jane? WHO IS HE, tell me, NOW!" he screamed in her now, very flushed and anxious face.

"It's no one!" she yelled back. "There's no one else. Look, I'm sorry, Karl… I just didn't want to tell you that I'd taken redundancy. I was embarrassed, so I just thought it would be easier for you to think I was still working until I found something else, then I was going to tell you."

He sat back down and slumped into the lounge chair, "Oh Jesus, come on then. What's the story? Let's have it now then. The whole sob story." He looked at her angrily. He was so hurt, and she knew she couldn't do this to him anymore. He thought she was having an affair, and he couldn't be more wrong. If only it had been as simple as that. It was time to set the record straight. It had gone too far now to continue with these horrid lies.

"Karl… please, just listen to me. There's no one else. I promise, honestly. No one, and I'm sorry I lied about the money, but I had to. I didn't know what else to do."

"Jane, for God's sake. After all these years together, I never thought we would end up like this. Lies after lies. No more. Just tell me the bloody truth!"

"Okay!" she screamed back suddenly, knowing she couldn't take this crazy situation any longer. She took a deep breath. The time was now. She had to tell him why she had lied, lies that had gone too far and hurt him so badly. Lies that had made him think this of her.

"I… took redundancy so that we could afford a decent holiday to Florida with the kids, and I carried on with the lie that I still had a job because I didn't want you worrying about money. You saw how much I got, and it should last until…" she paused, realising the moment had come.

"What… until what exactly, Jane? You run away with your toy boy? Or is he a sugar daddy?" His sarcasm hit her hard, and she couldn't stand it anymore.

"Oh, for Christ's sake, Karl, okay… you want the complete truth? Well, that's not it—"

"What, Jane?" he interrupted, "What can you hit me with now? More lies? Go on, shock me."

She took another deep breath as he glared at her. "I'm

ill Karl. Okay? I'm not well…" She began to shake with tension and anxiety. The adrenaline rushed through her body making her tremble, and she didn't like this feeling one little bit.

"Really? This whole situation isn't well!" He stood up to walk out the door.

Suddenly, the moment had arrived, the moment she had dreaded would come and she couldn't bear to lie to him any longer so shouted at him, "Bloody hell, I'm dying Karl, I'm bloody dying!"

She was looking straight at him with huge tears filling her eyes as he turned around to face her. After a short pause, he looked at her blankly. She lowered her voice a little. "I have cancer, and it's not going away, Karl." Tears flowed from her eyes down her flushed cheeks. "Instead of going to work every day, I've been going to chemotherapy, doctors, hospital appointments, visiting hospices, and shit like that. Happy you know the truth now?" Her chest was heaving, her voice raspy. "That's what I've been up to while you've been suspecting me of having an affair. Really. An affair. Does our marriage mean nothing? I thought we were stronger than that, seriously. How could you think that of me?" Her lips quivered. "I wish it was an affair instead of this bloody thing killing me." She lowered her voice and sat back down, exhausted. "So that's the truth. Okay, Karl. That's it. Now you know the whole truth about why I'm not working there anymore."

A silence of what seemed an hour ensued, although it was only minutes. Karl looked stunned by these words and stared at his beloved wife, who now looked pale and was shaking. He couldn't come to grips with what he had heard. Why would she have lied like this? He didn't understand her need for protecting her family. He just didn't get it and, for the moment, remained angry. "So, all this lottery nonsense was a lie?" he asked as she glanced up at him hoping to resolve things. "Why did you have to make that up? We could've helped you. We could've got you more help, more advice, more treatment. How long has this been going on?"

Jane tried to be brave, but tears kept escaping and streaming down her cheeks. She wiped them away over and over again. "I had to. I wanted us to enjoy the short time I have left by going away on our dream holiday with you all. You loved it, Karl, and I love you and the kids too much to have put you through it all. I was even having chemo out there while you and the kids went out. It has not been easy. I'm sorry, Karl. I just thought—"

Karl interrupted her. "No, Jane," he cried, "you didn't think. That's the problem here, you lied. To me, your husband, your kids. I thought we were worth more than that, and for something as important as this, what the hell were you actually thinking Jane…? I just don't, I can't deal with this, I need to get out of here!" With that, he stormed out, slamming the front door behind him, making a picture frame fall to the floor with the force.

"Karl!" she called after him but knew he wasn't going to stop and stay with her right now. She knew deep down that he just needed to go and calm down. Take in what she had told him and digest it. She felt overwhelmed with sadness and hated herself so much for keeping it from this wonderful man. What had she done and what would happen to their lives now? What a mess.

Chapter Eighteen

Jane listened to the screech of the car tyres as he sped away. She ran to the front window and just saw him turning out of the road. She hung her head, breathing heavily and then fell to the floor on her knees. Her head in her hands, she wept, wondering if things would ever be the same from now on. The remaining time she had left; how would he be able to love her after all the lies she'd been spinning for all these months? Would he forgive her? She hated herself right now for letting this happen.

Sobbing and looking up at the photographs in the beautiful ornate frames on the mantelpiece, Jane stood up carefully and went over to them. Her husband, her children, Mum and Pops, her best friend. She paused. Her best friend. That's who she needed right now. Sarah would know what to do; she always did.

"Sarah…" she gasped and went to the kitchen, grabbing her handbag. It fell to the floor, and the contents fell across the black matt floor tiles, making a loud ringing as coins hit them. Everything seemed to be against her right now, but she then remembered that her phone was being charged in the lounge. She went back into the room and fetched it from the floor where Karl had thrown it back down. Hurrying back to the kitchen, it slipped from her trembling hands and hit the floor. It had cracked the screen, but she didn't care. At the time, it didn't even register that it had got damaged. She just needed to get it turned back on and hit the speed dial and get Sarah there, and fast.

"I need you to explain it to him. He doesn't understand. He's so angry. I've messed up so badly, Sarah. Why didn't I just come clean? I… I can't do this… I just… oh God…" she spluttered out her words, weeping down the phone hysterically. "I can't do this anymore."

"Honey… calm down… I'm coming 'round now. Stay where you are. You're at home, right?" Sarah tried to console her best friend and calm her down a little, but it wasn't working this time. There had been so many times over the years that she had needed Jane, and she had been there in a flash; now her best friend needed her more than ever, and she would not fail her.

Around ten minutes later, Jane heard keys unlocking the front door, and she looked up from her arms where she had been resting her head on the table trying to comprehend what was happening and what mess she was now in.

Was it Karl? Had he come back and calmed down, ready to talk? Not yet. It was Sarah. She had given her best friend a set of keys some weeks ago after she had told her the truth about her illness, just in case she needed them, and this was definitely one of those times.

"Where are you, Jane?" Sarah called down the hallway, chucking the keys on the sideboard.

Jane ran out of the kitchen, bumping into the doorway on her way and knocking herself sideways. It hurt, but she needed to hug her best friend so didn't even care that she'd done it.

Wrapping their arms around each other, Sarah comforted her. "It's okay, it's okay. Come on. Let's sort this all out." Rubbing Jane gently on her back, she led her back into the kitchen and sat her down as Jane proceeded to tell her the conversation.

"So, you don't know where he's gone?" asked Sarah as she began to make strong black coffee for them both.

"No, he just stormed off in the car." Jane started picking up the contents of her bag that had fallen earlier. "He was so angry, Sarah. I've never seen him like that before. What have I done?" She slammed a notebook hard onto the floor in anger.

"Right, listen." Sarah reached down to hold Jane's head up. "He just needs to calm down and register what's going on. I'm sure he'll be back soon. He loves you more than anything in the world. He won't stay angry for long. I'll wait here until he comes back. What time are the kids due in from school?" she helped Jane up from the floor.

"Oh no, I forgot they were coming home to get their sleepover stuff after school. Probably about six-ish?" She glanced at her watch. "Maybe I could get Mum to collect them, take them back to hers for dinner. I'll call her." Jane did not want the kids to come back and see her in this state.

It was only a couple of hours before they finished school and their clubs.

"Jane, give it here. Let me call her. She will know you're upset by your voice. I'll tell her we are stuck in traffic in town shopping or something along those lines. Then, I'll go take their stuff to your mum's. Give me the phone." Sarah took hold of the phone and went into the hallway to make the call.

Jane listened to Sarah explaining some lie to her mum and began gnawing at her nails. She hadn't done that for years and had been trying hard to grow them back since they were now basically non-existent. Her life had changed by a massive scale today, and she was beside herself with worry and stress.

"Right, that's all sorted. Your mum will collect them from their school clubs, and I've texted them both to let them know to wait for her at the gates. I will drop their bags off to Janice before they go to their friends. Now, let's sort your face out… when he does come back, he does not want to see splodged mascara hitting him in the face."

Sarah always had a way of making Jane smile whatever the situation, and this was one of them. She knew she must've looked awful but hadn't even thought about it and didn't really care too much. She knew Sarah was right, and she needed to look better than this crumbled mess right now, for all their sakes.

They had seen each other in all sorts of states through their many years of friendship. When you have been best friends with someone since primary school, you go through a lot; good times, bad times, stupid times, messy times, all sorts, and that's when you find out who your true friends really are.

They calmly made their way upstairs, and Jane sat down in the bedroom at her dressing table, which had a large oval-shaped mirror on with all her makeup, perfume, and bits and bobs on it. This was one of Jane's favourite pieces in the house. She and Karl had seen it at a vintage furniture sale in a nearby town, and she'd fallen in love with it. It had needed a bit of sprucing up, but she didn't mind. She loved making good on old things and had spent weeks sanding it all down, priming it, glossing it white and changing the drawer knobs to some new-style fake glass ones that sparkled when the sun came through the window and hit them. The chair seat had then been covered in a vintage style material of cream and faded red roses to match her bed covers and curtains.

It was truly stunning, and over the years, Jane would often find Cassie sitting there pretending to do her makeup and doing her hair as she loved it too. Jane had always kept a lookout for another one to create for her but had not yet found one suitable. Maybe it was too late now though. Even Karl admitted when it was finished that she had transformed it, and he'd never been into refurbishing furniture. He'd always prefer to buy new as he just didn't have the time for it and wasn't a lover of DIY.

"Jane, your arm?" Sarah noticed a large red and raised mark, which must've been where she'd hit the doorway as she'd run out to meet Sarah. "Is it sore?"

Jane glanced down at the mark. "A bit, yes. I didn't even realise I'd hit it so hard, to be honest. It will bruise up nicely tomorrow I guess." There was a bruise already forming, the blood had rushed to the surface and it looked so tender.

"What are you like?" Sarah playfully swiped Jane on her chin. She didn't use to bruise that quickly, if at all, but this must be down to the chemo and everything else that she was going through right now. Time to get the cover-up makeup out again.

Sarah began brushing Jane's hair.

Glancing at her phone, Jane asked, "Do you think it may be worth ringing him or texting him?"

"Erm… maybe… or, as I said, I think he might need to just calm down first. Get used to the news in his head." Her voice graduated into a quieter tone at the end of the sentence, and a silent pause followed.

Jane looked up at Sarah's worried face in the reflection of the mirror. "What's wrong? Sarah, what is it?"

There were no words that could be said. She lifted the brush to show Jane. A big clump of hair had come out on the brush, and this was the first time Sarah had seen it happen. Knowing that one day it would, didn't make it any easier right now.

Jane had noticed it start happening a few weeks back, but it was nothing major. She had tried to ignore it by fixing it into a ponytail loosely so as not to need to brush it just in case. She stood up and held her friend's hands. "It's okay. It's been happening for weeks, and it's only going to get worse. My eyebrows are even beginning to go now too. Hey, maybe we should go wig shopping?" There was that cheeky smile again, although not as big as it usually was, and she spoke with a shaky voice trying not to break down yet again.

A lonely tear slowly trickled down Sarah's cheek. Her best friend was trying to be so strong. She didn't want to lose her, it seemed so unfair that this beautiful woman should have to go through this. And she'd kept it from so many people so far. Why her? At such a young age with two gorgeous children, who she should be seeing grow up, get married, have their own children and make Jane a nanna. She would have made an awesome grandparent, just as amazing as she was a mother.

The silence was broken by the sound of the front door opening. "Karl," Jane gasped as she looked at Sarah and crept to the bedroom door opening it slightly.

Everything seemed to move in slow motion and super quietly, but it was him. She could smell his aftershave drifting upstairs. He was back, and she wanted to see him, to explain, to embrace him, to kiss him, to say sorry. Would he let her? Had she ruined it all? Was this the end of them? Her mind was in bits.

"Do you want me to wait up here?" asked Sarah as she put her arms around Jane's tiny waist from behind.

"No, it's fine. I'll call you later. Thanks."

"Well, I'll wait till I know you're both okay and then take the kids stuff to your mum's. Just call me if you need me alright?"

They gave each other a reassuring smile, and Jane opened the door and slowly descended the staircase, running her hand along the smooth white bannister and staring at the figure in the doorway.

The sun shone through the stained-glass door and

created a dark silhouette of her gorgeous husband. She had decided to change into one of her favourite summer dresses, the one which she had worn when they had been to the zoo last summer.

Sarah had put Jane's hair in a loose and low ponytail, to hide the slightly balding patch from the loss of hair earlier, and sorted her makeup. Although still with reddened eyes from all the crying, she did look a little better.

As she reached the last step, Karl slowly approached her. He had obviously been crying too; his eyes were red and bloodshot. He looked slightly dishevelled, but she thought nothing less of him. She loved him so much. He was her dream man, her soulmate, and crying was not something he had ever hidden from her. It didn't happen often and, understandably, now was one of those times where it didn't matter either.

There were no words said in that deathly quiet moment. He just slowly placed his hands on her flushed, warm cheeks, pulled her gently toward him, and kissed her forehead for a few seconds, holding back more tears as he swallowed hard. They sat at the dining table opposite each other, holding hands, and Jane began to tell him the whole truth and everything she had been going through. There was no way she was going to hide it anymore. She couldn't do this to him. Seeing him that badly affected by it all was just too much for either of them to take, and the lies had to stop from now on.

Karl was struggling so much though. He was losing his best friend, his soulmate, the only person he had ever truly loved. He would've done anything to stop this for her, but he knew from what she was saying that there was nothing left he could do apart from being the best husband that would give her the most amazing last days, weeks, whatever the timescale was. He had to step up and be the man she'd always known he would be. He was determined he wouldn't let her down.

"I just wanted to protect you from the stress and worry of the illness. It's bad enough for one of us to know and go through it. Maybe now it seems wrong, but I need you to understand. I just didn't know what to do. I wanted our time together to be great without worrying about me dying or having to come to the treatments every week."

"I do understand, darling. Well, sort of. I just feel as though I should've been told. I could've been with you for every moment of this shit ordeal." He sounded slightly angry again, but he wasn't angry at her, he was angry at the cancer. Angry at the whole situation and what she had been through already, and all alone. This disease was taking one of the most precious things from his life, and their children would now be losing their mother, sooner than any child should lose a parent. There was nothing he could do. Not now. Not ever. He had to admit defeat to this awful illness but, at the same time, be strong for her and help her beat it for as long as possible. He felt hopeless but full of courage for her and how she was dealing with it.

The night hadn't gone to plan at all, but they spent the evening embracing and chatting into the early hours, trying to come to terms with the events of the day. They even cracked open the bottle of cava that Jane had brought home, but the lingerie remained in the box for the time being. Passion wasn't on the menu that night.

The following afternoon, the doorbell chimed. It was Jane's mother, back with the children.

"I can't face them all just now. Can you get it?" Karl asked as he went upstairs after having a very strong coffee together.

"Sure." She nodded and waited for him to shut the bathroom door before opening the front door to her twins and mum, Janice.

Jane had been able to keep strong so far and now had to maintain this façade for her mother and the kids.

"Hey, you two," She hugged them a little tighter than usual. "How did the sleepovers go?"

"It was great, we had spaghetti Bolognese and strawberries and ice cream for pudding," said Cassie, smiling up at her mum. "Thanks for picking us up, Grandma."

"Yeah. Thanks, Grandma," said Robbie, head down into his phone watching some video.

"That's okay, you two. See you soon, my darlings. They're always so good for their grandma, you know, and so polite. I heard them thanking their friends' parents when I picked them both up. So lovely to hear such good manners, isn't it, dear? You've done well with my wee grandchildren, Jane."

Both of them went up to their rooms, dropping their blazers and bags by the coat hooks. They hardly ever hung them up or took them upstairs with them straight away. Jane found it amusing that they both did the same. She had always thought it must be a twin thing.

"Thanks, Mum. Hope they were okay for you?" Jane gave her mum a kiss on the cheek.

"They've been angels as usual." Her mum loved having her grandchildren around and even enjoyed just picking them up from places. Whatever she could do to spend time with them, she didn't mind.

She was retired now but still enjoyed a busy life at art clubs and social dance classes. Since Pops had passed away, she had promised to keep active and enjoy life – which she was doing – and the grandchildren helped with that enjoyment of life a little bit more. She had made a promise to her husband before he died that she wouldn't be a lonely old girl on her own and ensure that she would make new friends, which she had. There was no new love on the horizon for her, but she had so many good friends to spend time with at the moment, it wasn't needed.

They'd always been out and about together until near the end when his cancer had taken hold. He had only found out two months before that it was terminal as he didn't much like going to the doctors and didn't get anything checked regularly. He had just thought it was his age but had kept upbeat about it even after the diagnosis and still went dancing twice a week with his wife and their friends. They both loved it so much, and it was hard for her to return to the club without him. But she'd made the promise and stuck to it, meeting lots of new people and enjoying it again too.

Janice lived about ten minutes away in a small bungalow that she had bought. She had found it too difficult to live in the house they'd shared as a couple for so many years. Too many memories around. Plus, the new bungalow was nearer to Jane and the children, so it was easier to pop over for dinner or just to see them for the afternoon.

"Did you get anything nice when you were out shopping with Sarah?" she asked.

"Shopping?" Jane said with a puzzled tone. "Oh, shopping, yes… to be honest, it was more like window shopping for Christmas ideas." She remembered that Sarah had told the lie to her mum the previous day about shopping in town and quickly came up with an answer.

"Christmas, crikey, you're planning ahead. That makes a change for you, dear," she chuckled. "Anyway, sorry, darling, but I really must dash. We have our new book club starting tonight, and I said I'd pop along with Rita, you know, from next door? Here are a few letters that the children gave me after school yesterday. You know they'd lose them if I hadn't taken them." She giggled as she handed over the letters. "You sure you're okay, Jane? You look a bit peaky this afternoon?"

"Yes, Mum. Honestly, I'm fine. Just a bit tired, it's been a hectic few days at work and that."

They hugged again, and Jane embraced her slightly longer. Every moment seemed precious now, and a hug meant even more. Just to watch her mother walking away was something she now treasured and enjoyed doing.

Karl emerged from the bathroom and looked over the banister as Jane glanced up toward him. He'd tidied his hair and given his face a wash, also applying a little more aftershave for Jane's benefit.

"You okay?" Jane asked as she met him at the top of the

stairs.

"I don't know. I guess so. Are the kids okay?" he said as he touched her hand resting on the top bannister.

"Yeah. They had a lovely time as usual, and Mum loved spending time with them again, she's an absolute diamond with them."

It was Saturday night, so the family decided to stay in and watch a film together. Karl went to the corner shop to get some chocolate, popcorn, and sweet snacks for the kids, and they settled in the lounge for the evening.

For the next few hours, everything seemed normal. Laughing, joking, and enjoying the film together like nothing was wrong. Like no one knew any different. No cancer and no sadness or bad thoughts. Just time well spent with three of the most special people in Jane's life. She wished the evening could last forever or be frozen in time and wondered how many more evenings they would get like this in the coming months. She knew it would be less than she'd like.

"Goodnight, Cassie, love you. Goodnight, Robbie, love you," Jane whispered into each of their rooms as she did every night.

"Night, love you," they both answered.

Karl popped his head into his and Jane's bedroom, where she was removing her makeup at her dressing table.

"I'll be back in a minute, babe." Karl liked to tuck the kids in, even at their age. He had done this every night since the day they were born. A kiss on the head and saying goodnight to his precious son and daughter.

Robbie preferred a fist punch rather than a kiss these

days. He was becoming a young man now, and Karl respected the more grown-up approach to the bedtime routine. He'd soon be too old to be tucked in, but the fist bump wouldn't age.

Jane and Karl got into bed not long after as it had been an exhausting and emotionally charged twenty-four hours. Slipping on one of her favourite pale pink, silk negligees that Karl had got her on their last wedding anniversary, Jane climbed into her side of the bed, gently pulling the sheets over her. As usual, Karl only had some black boxer shorts on. She had never minded the fact that he didn't wear much to bed as she liked to admire his toned torso and she rested her head on his chest.

"I need to get you a new one of those," he said as he ran his hand down her side, feeling the silk on his fingers as she lay next to him.

"No, you don't. This is my favourite and always will be. It has lots of memories." Jane giggled cheekily, which made Karl smile at her and he almost blushed a little.

They lay together for a few moments, then Jane pulled herself up from his chest, stroked his face, and whispered lovingly, "Make love to me, Karl." she kissed him gently on the lips as he looked back at her with a concerned look.

"I'm fine," she reassured him, "honestly."

With their bodies entwined and lost in that moment, it was tender and beautiful. Another moment she wished she could freeze, realising that they may not get many more romantic times like this. Making love to him was the best thing for both of them that night, and it felt extra special, full of emotion and most of all, love and gentleness.

Karl lay on his side while watching her sleeping peacefully, thinking she looked as beautiful as ever. If anything, he thought, more beautiful tonight for some reason. Deep down, he knew that he would not be able to see her lying next to him for much longer. He didn't want to take his eyes off her; why sleep when he could look at his gorgeous and brave wife? He carefully moved a strand of hair that had fallen onto her cheek and began thinking of the times they had gone through together. Their first meeting at the fancy dress party, the fairy-tale wedding in the castle grounds, the amazing honeymoon in Vegas. Then the miscarriage that had devastated them, then the utter joy of getting pregnant again a few months later with the exciting reveal of finding out at the second ultrasound scan that announced it was twins, the huge tummy when she was pregnant, the birth of the twins, the new house, the Florida holiday they had just had together… the thoughts went on. What an incredible journey it had been so far, and how cruel to not be able to enjoy twenty, thirty, forty more years together building even more amazing memories together.

He noticed the patch of hair that was missing as she moved slightly to get comfortable. He frowned as he wished he had not been so caught up with work stuff and had taken more notice of her over the past weeks. He felt confused, angry, sad but so in awe of this woman beside him. He smiled at her and whispered, "I love you so much Mrs Walden," then lay down slowly and gently so as not to wake her until the early hours when he too fell asleep.

Chapter Nineteen

"Hey there, you," Sarah called as she crossed the busy road, tottering along in her brand-new red heels on the rough cobbled path toward Jane.

"Hi, babe." They hugged and kissed each other on the cheek.

They had agreed to meet at the train station that morning to discuss a surprise shopping trip Jane had arranged for them.

"So where are we off to, Jane?" Sarah asked as they paid for their tickets and made their way over to the station platform.

"London, baby," laughed Jane, mimicking Austin Powers' funny moves from the film.

"You loon, stop that." They giggled. "Okay, so what are we getting? New shoes, makeup, Christmas bits, or some sexy lingerie?" Sarah mooched about the platform trying to do some sort of sexy move and made Jane laugh out loud.

"No, blimey, no time for all that sort of nonsense… well I may look at getting a new bra… no, something we've never had to shop for before. I need to get a wig."

"Oh, that's a bit disappointing… why? Just go with the bald look. You'll still be stunning," she joked back, holding her hair flat to her head.

"Thank you, darling, but no, I don't think so, I'm losing more of my hair each day, and these head scarves are just not cutting it for me. The kids think I'm having some sort of mid-life crisis, I'm sure."

"Bless them. They're such little cuties. Okay, well I can help with all this wig malarkey. My friend Danny does a drag act in London, he calls himself, Dani Doolligan." She shrugged her shoulders and continued, "Anyway, he's always getting different sorts of wigs for his act. Let me text him and find out if he knows some good places to go. I went to one shop with him last Christmas for a fancy dress do, and it had some really classy stuff."

"I don't want a bright pink bouffant wig, Sarah," Jane said as they boarded the train, taking their seats.

"Don't be silly; they do other styles… normal styles, sexy ones even." She wiggled her hips in a sexy move again.

Jane rolled her eyes at her friend with affection as she watched her swiftly tapping away on her phone and didn't even seem to be looking as she typed. Cassie must've learned this skill from Sarah, she thought.

The train wasn't too busy. They had chosen to go out of peak time to avoid any pushing and rushing about, so there were plenty of seats. They sat opposite each other with a small table between them, discussing wig colours and styles as Sarah Googled loads of images to show her.

"Karl did mention to me about maybe getting a redhead one," Jane said, raising her eyebrows and winking at Sarah.

"Mmm, I bet he'd love that. Does he have a thing for redheads then? How about going for a short style? It'll be much easier to maintain, quicker and easier to put on too I'd imagine?" Sarah suggested, showing her a short brunette bob style.

"Do you think it would be too different for me though? Not sure Cassie would like it. She's funny about my hair, and she loves it long."

"Maybe. Look, the best thing is for us to meet up with Danny and go to a few places, try some on, and see what you think. I'm sure you'll find something, Jane. And, as I said before, you'll still be stunning whatever style you go for. It's that gorgeous smile you have right there. You don't need hair," Sarah leant forward and gently grabbed Jane's cheeks playfully squeezing them.

"Oh, stop it, silly," Jane laughed as the train headed into Liverpool Street.

About half an hour later, they met with Danny, who took them to his local barbershop that had a wig store out the back. Soon Jane began trying all kinds of styles on before deciding on a particular one which suited her perfectly.

"Babe, it looks amazing. No one would know that was a wig. I might get one myself," Sarah exclaimed looking at the selection and opting to try a blonde, curly wig on.

They stared into the mirror as Sarah helped her to

slightly adjust it. They had been left to their own devices by Danny, who knew the shop owner very well and had asked for some privacy for them.

"I think I'll get this one. I really like it, and it doesn't look too different from my own hair, does it?" Jane smiled in relief. "Just adds a bit of thickness to it, so hopefully people won't notice that it's not my real hair."

"Yes, I agree. It looks brilliant. I'll go pay."

"Sarah, no. Here. Take my card." Jane rummaged quickly to find her purse, but Sarah had already gone out of the room.

Again, Jane looked in the mirror and touched her new hair, tousling it to the front and down the sides. Although there was relief there, she also felt a little sad. A single tear escaped, but this time she let it fall, sighing to herself and thinking how crazy her life had suddenly become and how much it had changed in just a few short months. In a few months, it would be Christmas so at least she could look half decent with the help of this new accessory.

Danny and Sarah reappeared, laughing away at some crazy bright yellow wig that she'd tried on. "Hey, Janey. How about this one for me?" A large afro in yellow with a red bow in it left them all in a heap of laughter.

"Thanks for today, Sarah. It's been a much better experience with you helping." Jane touched her friend's hand from across the table. They'd stopped in the nearby Nando's for a bite to eat before the train left for home.

"Sweetie, it was my absolute pleasure and, honestly, you looked gorgeous. The kids won't know the difference. Do you know what? Danny got it on his tab too. He really is a lovely bloke, he just needs to snag himself a decent husband now. He's been too busy building up his career at the minute, but he liked you and agreed that you looked stunning, hair or no hair. He also said if you need any more or any help with it, just give him a bell. I'll text you his mobile number, so you have it."

"Oh, bless him. How lovely. You should've told me, I could have thanked him properly for all his help."

"He's cool. He didn't want to embarrass you or put you on the spot. I've got a few tickets to his next show just before Christmas, so maybe you can chat to him then? Anyway, eat up. Our train leaves in an hour, and I want to pop into that little boutique over the road before we go. I know how slow you eat." Smiling at each other again, they tucked in.

~

"Wow, you look stunning. You have to get that one for sure," Jane remarked as Sarah appeared from the changing room in a strapless, blue, tight-fitting dress.

"I'm not sure about it. It's a bit…" she glanced up and down at herself in the mirror, tilting her head from side to side pondering the choice.

"A bit what? Sexy? Yes, it is. Very sexy. So get it. You may need it when I tell you what I have in store for you this week."

"Oh? Sounds ominous." Sarah slipped back into the changing room. "Tell me more," she called, popping her head over the door.

"Well, I've met this guy, and I think you two would be perfect together, we just need to arrange a meeting. He's very handsome and definitely your type. He's been through a lot and needs someone like you in his life, to get some fun in his life."

"Well, don't hold back, will you. Come on then. Let's get this dress, get on the train, and you can tell me more about the apparent mystery man of my dreams."

As they boarded the train with coffees from the station kiosk, they chatted all the way home about James and what had happened in his life so far.

"Do you really think I'm brave enough to take that shit on?" asked Sarah looking a little bewildered.

"Sarah, you're the most beautiful person I know. You'd be a fantastic match, and I want to know you're with someone totally awesome before I leave you. He's the one, he's lovely, and would be so good for you. I'm sure of it. How about it?" Jane eagerly awaited her reply.

Looking back into her excited friend's eyes, she agreed, "Alright, sort out a meeting then. I'm only doing it for you though and won't promise anything will come of it. You know how I like to be Miss Independent. I can't have anyone's toothbrush in the house without freaking out."

"YES!" Jane shrieked. She couldn't wait to tell James and went earlier than usual to meet with him the next day to give him the exciting news.

She hadn't managed to see him for a few days what with all that had been happening and had missed him and their chats and laughter. "Look what I got yesterday." Jane began rummaging through her bag, as she placed it on the bench, chuckling to herself.

"What the hell is that?" James cried as she showed him a bag of what looked like a ton of hair.

"It's my new, improved hair," she laughed, jiggling it under his nose in jest. "Do you like it?"

James laughed. "Very nice… are you going to have a fake name too? Will I have to call you madam or lady W?" he joked.

"Ha ha… no, it's just a wig for now. I'm going to need one soon, so I thought I'd better get one ready. It matches my hair well, don't you think? It'll just give my hair a bit of thickness as it's gotten so thin lately."

"Good idea. I'll look forward to seeing you in it. I'm sure it looks better on than stuffed in a bag." He'd brought new flowers today for his mum's grave and he began arranging them. "How's the chemo going? Do you have any sessions today?"

"Oh, it's okay. You know what it's like. Sit there bored, trying to concentrate on anything else but the needle pumping drugs into your arm. That book was great, but I finished it a few days back. I have a few days off then back on Tuesday. Hey, maybe you should come along, keep me company?" Jane realised right as she said it that it could be too difficult for him to be in that environment. It might bring back painful memories of his mother. "Sorry, that's a stupid thing to ask. Forget I said that" she corrected herself as she apologised.

"It's okay, Jane. Honestly. We didn't have much time for chemo. She didn't like it after the first few batches and then refused to go back; it just made her feel too ill for the short time she had left so she decided against it."

"Bless her. Sorry. Let's change the subject. Unless you want to talk about it?" Jane had always seemed to talk about herself and what she was going through. Maybe she should listen more to him and help him through it.

"No, it's cool, I'd rather talk about you." He smiled up at her from where he was kneeling on the ground, his floral display looking amazing yet again. She'd never known a man who could arrange flowers so well.

"You're so good at that." She nudged his arm as he sat down next to her.

"Mum used to love her flowers. She grew so many different types in the garden at home, so she always had a fresh bunch in the house. I'd watch her arranging them and I guess it just rubbed off on me."

"I need to get some fresh ones for Pops. Mum's not been this week. She's been so busy helping me out with the children and her clubs and that, so I said I'd get them for her this week."

"I have a few spare blooms here. I'll sort it out for you." he rearranged his bouquet and took a small bunch over to Pops' grave for her. How could she have been so lucky to have met someone so caring who was hurting at the same time too? You never get over a loved one dying, but he seemed to be coping so well with it, better than she was anyway. She hoped this would be Karl when the time came. That he would cope with losing her the way James was coping with losing his mother from the same horrid bloody illness.

"Did you visit any hospices with your mum?"

"No, she didn't want to be in one; she wanted to die at home. Because it all happened so quickly, she didn't seem to want the fuss and, to be honest, she was a lot happier knowing she was in her own bed when it happened. We sat with her till the end. It was peaceful for her, and she sort of looked happy as she went. She had asked us to print loads of photos and stick them on the ceiling so she could look at them and see everyone *on her way out*. They were her words, not mine."

This was the most he'd spoken about his mum dying, and she could see it hurt. He was strong and held it together, but it was lovely just to sit and listen to him talking for a change.

"That's a lovely idea, although we are visiting a hospice in a few days. I'm worried about the kids seeing me decline and how it will affect them. I know how quickly it can happen, as do you."

"Jane, from what you've told me about your kids, they are strong and love you very much. They may react completely differently when the time comes, and I'm sure your upbringing has made them who they are. They will want to be with you as much as possible. Hospices do amazing work, and I did think of working in one after Mum went. But I couldn't face the same sad situations day in, day out, you know? Maybe in a few years' time, I might change my mind and do something good for them like they do for so many people these days."

She watched him tidying and sweeping the area where they met each time as he spoke, thinking to herself how he always looked so together and organised. Then her thoughts turned to the children and how much they'd grown up in the last few months. Becoming teenagers had been tough. She was sure there would be much more teenage stress to come. How would Karl be, coping on his own dealing with all that? Boyfriends, girlfriends, driving lessons, clubbing, weddings, their babies one day? Would she be here to see any of that? Probably not.

He stood up and then sat next to her on the bench looking intently at her lap. "What are you writing there anyway?"

Jane had brought a special notepad with her today along with some coloured envelopes. "I'm writing letters to everyone for when, well, you know when I'm gone. A sort of goodbye to them all really, just so they know how much I loved them each individually."

"Wow, what a lovely thing to do, Jane, that really is and I'm sure they will appreciate it when the time comes, not that it's any time soon though, hey?" He nudged her shoulder with his.

"Hopefully not, but I just wanted to make sure I got everything down while I can. Tell them how they all meant the world to me, you know, that sort of gushy stuff." She smiled back at him with tears welling up in her eyes yet again. "I guess I had better get going actually, it's getting late." She stood up before she cracked again. Tears were escaping so easily and seemed to be all the time recently. It seemed she was helpless when their strength erupted whenever reality popped into her head about the future, or lack of it. "I'll pop by after lunch tomorrow. I'm meeting with Karl in the morning at the solicitors to make sure my will is all in order before… not a great morning, but I guess it needs to be done sooner rather than later. He found out the other day, that's why I've not been here for a few days or so, I had to tell him the whole truth, literally everything. He thought I'd been having an affair and it felt awful. He was so upset, James. I've never seen him so hurt and it was all my fault, I should have just been honest with him from the start of this bloody thing, but I couldn't."

"I'm sure he knows you had your reasons. You're a really solid couple from the stories you've told me. I'm sure it will all be okay. I'll see you tomorrow anyway. I'll be here from about half twelve. Oh, and would you like any flowers picked up?"

"No, I'll get some tomorrow as you shared today. See you then." She blew a kiss from her hand as she made her way to the car park. She had driven there today as she had felt too tired to walk after her London visit the day before.

The radio came on playing the *Friends'* theme tune, which seemed incredibly appropriate. James was her new friend this year and he was always being there for her. She sang along for the short drive home, feeling happy for once until she realised, that she had completely forgotten to ask James about setting up a meeting with Sarah. "Damn it!" she shouted, hitting the steering wheel in frustration. It was a job to complete when she saw him next. She couldn't forget. Her matchmaking skills wouldn't fail this time. She now had two best friends and she wanted them together, this was her mission.

Chapter Twenty

As they got into the car to head towards the solicitors that morning, Jane decided to ask Karl about visiting the hospice that Paula had talked about on a recent appointment at the clinic.

"They have suggested that I visit one of the local hospices to look at what it's like and what goes on. You know, for when the time comes. Do you want to come along? It's fine if you don't; Sarah can come if you'd prefer not to."

Looking slightly taken aback, he replied, "Erm. No, it's cool. I'm more than happy to come. When is it?"

"This afternoon actually. It's fine if it's too short notice with work and that. Honestly, Sarah has already said she's on standby in case you can't come."

"No, that's fine, I'll let work know. Adam said if I need any time at all to just let him know."

"Have you told him then?" she asked.

"Yes, darling. I had to talk to someone about it, and he's a mate too at the end of the day. He's been amazing. His sister had cervical cancer when she was just twenty-three, so he understands what we're going through, babe, and won't dock my pay either. He said, whatever time we need for any appointments and such, we can have."

"Oh, bless him. That's so lovely of him. How is she, his sister?"

He paused and shook his head. They looked at one another with sadness in their eyes and reached for each other's hands, sitting in thoughtful silence for the rest of the journey.

Jane glanced out of the window, leaning on her other hand, feeling awful that this damn disease could take someone so young with their whole lives ahead of them. At least she had had a little time to get married, have children and explore a bit of the world, unlike Adam's sister. How unfair.

~

"Well, that's all sorted then," Jane sighed as they left the solicitor's office.

"It's for the best, babe. I just needed to make sure you were happy with everything."

"Just wish I had more special things to give the kids. A few bits of jewellery and a wad of money each seems like nothing, does it?"

"Darling, I'll make sure they never go without, and they'll have plenty of people around them to help."

"Are you going to replace me then? Find yourself a younger model?" Jane jokingly replied.

"Jane. Don't say that." Karl looked at her seriously, frowning hard with sadness in his eyes.

"Oh, look, I'm sorry," she said as she saw his expression change. "I didn't mean anything by it. It's just… well, they won't have a mother unless you do find someone else. Which you will, but then, they might forget me, Karl. They might love their new mum more than they loved me, especially if she does a better job than me. And she'll probably last longer than I have." Jane almost fell onto the nearby bench in a state as the future thoughts of her beloved family being without her, carrying on without her, became all too real in that moment.

Karl knelt in front of her with his hands softly cupping her pale cheeks. "They will never forget this beautiful face, this gorgeous woman who brought them into the world and loved them unconditionally. Sweetheart, you will always be their mum, and no one will take your place, not ever, especially in my heart." He kissed her salty tears away and they spent a few moments sitting together on the bench in an embrace that neither wanted to end. Just the two of them it seemed, watching the world go by.

"Karl…" she snivelled.

"Yes, darling?"

"Don't be alone forever."

No words could be uttered at that moment. They both knew what the future held, and Jane knew that she couldn't expect him to be without someone in his life when she was gone. The children needed a mother figure in their lives for those times when a woman was needed, especially for her baby girl. She knew Sarah would always be there if no one else was, but deep down, she didn't want him to be alone for the rest of his life, like her mum was without Pops.

Karl touched her hand. "Come on, let's go and see this hospice place then get you home. You need to rest after today. It's been full-on for a few days now."

They got up and made their way to the car which was parked in a nearby multi-storey in town. Jane waited on the ground floor level while Karl went to fetch it, saving her energy and giving her time to clear her head.

She couldn't believe how she'd just lost it for a moment and the things that she'd said. Like he needed the extra stress. She decided that she must try and keep it together more and stop all this unnecessary nonsense and worry. For all of them.

~

As they drove into the hospice car park, Jane just sat there, she didn't want to take her seatbelt off. She looked straight ahead at the building, watching patients outside in the gardens, their loved ones sitting close by them. It looked peaceful and tranquil but also sad, a bit like a weepy movie scene if she was honest. Most of them looked so fragile and pale, covered with a blanket to keep them warm even though the sun was on them. She remembered how cold Pops used to get, even when they were all feeling hot.

These people knew they were nearing the end of their lives, and it was hard to see it in the flesh, happening right in front of her eyes now. She'd never seen a place like it before. After all, why would she? Pops never went to one.

Karl looked at her and could see she wasn't too happy, so he placed his hand on hers and gently squeezed it in reassurance. "You don't have to come here. I can care for you at home, no matter what, for however long you need me to. It's not a problem, darling."

"It's too much to ask of you and the kids. We watched my dad go through it all, and it wasn't nice for any of us to see him like that. It's hard work with the medication and washing me would be humiliating. You and the kids shouldn't have to go through that."

"I don't care. We made vows, till death do us part, in sickness and in health. Whatever you want, I'm here for you. We can have a look around but remember, I can have as much time as needed to be there for you. The kids are stronger than you think too. You underestimate them sometimes. They may be just teenagers, but they're a lot like you. I really think that they will want to be with you when they know what's going on." The words coming out of his mouth were heart-breaking but honest and supportive, and he'd accepted that she wasn't getting over this. He wanted to care for her, and he would, no matter what, but she didn't feel right about the children, especially, seeing her for her last weeks as she remembered seeing her dad pass away gradually.

~

The staff in the hospice were lovely, caring, and helpful, full of advice and knowledge as Jane asked what seemed like a hundred or more questions.

"We have a playroom, which is split into age groups. We know that teenagers don't want to play with LEGO and building bricks, so we set up this area for the older ones with a few consoles and games, etc," The nurse was showing them around the kids' areas when Karl touched Jane's arm gently.

"I'm just going to get a bit of air, sweetheart," he said, kissing her on the cheek. It had become a bit too much for him, and she could see it in his eyes. She followed the nurse, glancing back to see Karl going outside into the garden and shutting the door behind him.

Standing alone, taking a deep breath and gathering his composure, he heard a voice from behind him, "You okay there, mate?"

Karl turned to see another man about the same age standing behind him, leaning on the wall with a newspaper.

"Yeah, on a visit here with my wife and it just got a bit much for me for a moment. There's some great work going on in there, and the staff are lovely too."

"Yes, they are amazing people. My sister is in now," the guy replied.

"My wife is trying to decide what to do when, you know, when it's time. She doesn't want us to cope with it all near the end."

"Sorry to hear that. It's a tough time, but she would be in good hands here. Honestly. My mum, wife, and now my sister have been in here, and they've all had the dignity and peace they deserved. It's easier on the families too."

"Jesus, mate, I'm so sorry." Karl turned to face him. "How have you coped all those times?"

"You just do, mate. It's a right pain in the arse this cancer shit, but it's a relentless bugger, so you just have to stay strong for them and help them cope as best you can."

"I guess so. It's just been such a shock. She didn't tell me at first, and our kids don't know yet. We're both dreading that day when they have to be told. She's not even told her mother either."

"Women are stronger than we know. They want to manage alone, but ultimately, you have to be there for them every step of the way, no matter what they want or need. And the kids, I don't know them, obviously, but they will cope too. There's something about kids that makes them super resilient to things like this. Look, here's my info," he passed over his business card, "if you need a chat anytime, we can go for a beer or something. I didn't have many guys to chat to, so I know how hard it can be as a bloke. The offer is there if you want, and no worries if not. I understand you don't know me."

"That's good of you. Thanks, erm…" he glanced down at the name on the card, "Dave. I'm Karl, and that would be great. Look, I better get back in there, see how she's doing. I'm supposed to be the strong one after all. Take care, mate. I'll be in touch, thanks."

"No worries at all." They shook hands, and Karl knew he would take him up on his offer. It would be good to speak to someone who already had the experience of going through it and was going through it now yet again.

"Hey, sweetie, sorry about that." Jane looked tired and tearful. Karl put his arm around her waist. "You okay?"

"Yes, but I think I'm ready to go home now."

They thanked the nurse who had shown them around and made their way back out to the car park.

Karl noticed Dave getting into his car and put his thumb up to him.

"Who's that?" Jane asked, noticing the gesture between the men.

"I met him outside earlier. His name is Dave. He suggested meeting up for a chat and a beer. He's been through it three times here, and he gave me his number."

"Oh, that's nice of him." Jane laid her head on the car headrest and began dozing off. The busy day had taken it out of her more than she thought.

The drive home was quiet and thoughtful for Karl too. He kept looking over at his wife sleeping, thinking about how life would be without her there in that seat. He couldn't imagine it. He didn't really want to think too much about it, but he knew that the day would come soon. He'd already seen a decline in how she was since she told him the awful news that day.

They arrived home and made their way into the lounge. "Do you want a coffee, Jane?" he asked as she curled up slowly on the sofa.

"Just some water, please. I feel a headache coming on, and it's time for some more tablets, isn't it?" she replied.

"I'll sort it. Do you want anything to eat?" He pulled a blanket off the back of the sofa to put over her legs while passing her the tablet bottle from his jacket pocket.

"Maybe a bit of toast for now, if that's okay? Thanks, honey. I'm pretty whacked."

"Sure, no problem. I won't be long. Do you need any more pillows or cushions? Are you warm enough? Do you want the TV on? Another blanket? Magazine?"

"Karl... I'm fine," she snapped back and then, realising her shortness, smiled at him, knowing that he was just trying to cover all aspects of caring for her. It was sweet and he knew she wasn't cross.

A text message sound came through on her phone; it was from Sarah.

'*Hey gorgeous, how was the visit?*' it said.

'*It was lovely, but I'm not sure Karl liked it,*' she swiftly texted back.

'*He just wants the best for you, I'm sure.*'

'*I know, but it may be too hard for him near the end. I don't want him to have to deal with me.*'

'*I'm here too, and I'll move in if necessary.*'

'*That's not a bad idea. There's the spare room, LOL.*'

'*I'll be over later anyway. Got a client now.*'

'*Okay, lovely. See you around dinner time?*'

'*Oooh, yeah, food. LOL. Love u Xxxx.*'

'*Bye, babe, love u too. xxx.*'

When Karl returned with her toast a few minutes later, she'd already fallen asleep, phone in hand. He walked out to the garden, munching on the toast and put his hand in his pocket, pulling out the card from Dave at the hospice and decided to give him a quick text.

'*Hi, Dave, it's Karl. We met at the hospice earlier today. Would you be up for a beer and a chat tonight?*'

A few minutes later, he got a reply text back.

'*Sure thing. The Red Lion on Queens Street? Do you know it?*'

'*Yes, only about ten minutes from me, that's great. About 5pm okay for you?*' he typed back.

'*Fine, see you then. I'll get the beers in, Stella alright for you?*'

'*Perfect, cheers.*' Karl felt relieved in some way that he would have someone to talk to about everything. He'd been finding it difficult to cope but hadn't wanted to ask Jane too much in case it upset her. He placed his phone in his back pocket and kicked a ball around the garden for a bit to take his mind off things. Before long, an hour had passed, and Jane still slept peacefully while he began to think about what to have for dinner. As he reached the freezer, he heard the front door opening, it was Sarah.

"How is she doing today?" she asked as Karl made her a coffee.

"She's okay, a bit of a wobble after the solicitor's this morning, but I think she's okay now. She's been sleeping for a few hours. The solicitor's, then the visit to the hospice, took it out of her a bit. I asked her mum to have the kids until dinner so she could rest up."

"Oh, bless her. What do you mean a wobble? Not falling over?"

"No, no. Just… well she just lost it, you know, emotionally. She can explain later. Look, do you mind sitting with her? I'm going to meet a guy for a beer. We met at the hospice, and he's offered a bit of male support if I need it. I thought it would do me good to chat to another guy about it all, you know from a male perspective?"

"Sure, I'll sort the dinner out if you like. What time are the kids back?"

"Should be around half an hour or so. There's loads of options in the freezer, we stocked up yesterday, so just do something that can be shoved in the oven. Chicken pie and chips, I think there are some baked beans in the cupboard, the kids prefer them over peas and that. I'll have mine when I get back."

"Okay, Karl, no problem at all, have fun." She gave him a reassuring touch to his shoulder, and he left after kissing Jane gently on the cheek.

Ten minutes later, Jane began to stir. "Hey, sleepyhead, how's my gorgeous girl?" Sarah perched on the coffee table in front of the sofa.

"Oh, hello." Jane stretched her arms out above her head and yawned. "How long was I out for?"

"A few hours apparently. Dinner's in the oven, and the kids are due back in about five minutes."

"What? Oh, okay. Where's Karl?" Jane sat herself up and looked at the clock on the mantelpiece as Sarah got back up and went to the kitchen.

"He's popped out to see a guy he met earlier today at the hospice," shouted Sarah from the kitchen as she started taking the dinner from the oven just as the doorbell rang. "That'll be the little sweetpeas. I'll get it." Sarah ran to the door, giving the kids a massive hug and kissing Jane's mum on the cheek. "Come on into the kitchen, dinner is ready, I'm just serving up. Janice, are you staying for some? There's plenty of pie. Karl bought a large family one, would feed around ten of us I think," she chuckled.

The kids loved having Sarah around so much. They dropped all their school stuff and went straight to the table where Jane had now moved herself to.

"Hey, guys, how was school? Hi, Mum. You okay?" Jane asked all at once.

"No, I've had a bite to eat earlier. Thank you, Sarah, dear, and yes, my darling, I'm fine," replied Janice looking on. "I'll just have a cup of tea if that's okay? I can do it while you sort the dinner out."

The next hour or so was spent chatting and catching up with the kids, her mum, and Sarah. She really enjoyed it too, it had been a while since they'd all sat down together.

"So, do you have any homework tonight, kids?"

They both looked agonisingly at their mum and replied, "Yes," in unison and left to go upstairs, almost hanging their heads at the thought of more schoolwork.

The ladies laughed at their lack of enthusiasm and the woes of being a teenager with mounds of schoolwork ahead of them each night.

"How are you, Jane, dear? You look exhausted," Janice asked as they sat at the table drinking another round of tea and coffee.

"I'm okay, Mum. Just been a bit busy lately with one thing and another, you know how it can suddenly catch up with you."

Janice got up and closed the kitchen door. "Jane, dear, I'm your mother. I know there's something else going on here. Are you pregnant again? Ooh, do you have something exciting to tell me?" She smiled widely in anticipation of some baby news.

"Oh, Mum. No, sorry, no, I'm definitely not pregnant, it's too late for all that again. Look, I'm fine, aren't I, Sarah?" Jane glanced over to Sarah for some reassurance.

"Yeah, she's just been doing too much at work, plus, I've been running her to London, taking her Christmas shopping, and—"

Before Sarah could finish, Janice interrupted. "Girls, girls, please, I'm a grown woman, and I know when something is being hidden from me. Especially you two scallywags. Remember, I've known you both as teenagers and something's not adding up just recently, my dears, so, come on, what's going on?"

Sarah and Jane looked at each other as if to ask for help, but nothing happened. They both knew that Janice wouldn't give up asking questions and she was right; she had always known when something wasn't adding up with the two of them. Her sixth sense would always prevail.

"I think it's time, honey. You have to tell her the news," said Sarah, looking at her best friend and knowing that this mother meant business. Deep down in her heart, Sarah knew Janice deserved to know more than anyone, but Jane shook her head gently back at Sarah as if to say no, she didn't want to have to tell her.

"Tell me what news?" Janice asked, sitting down again.

"Look, it's nothing, Mum. Just work has been making me very tired lately."

"Jane, don't. For goodness sake, she's your mother. Just tell her. She needs to know, she'll understand more than any of us," Sarah demanded.

A short, empty silence followed as Jane thought for a moment and realised Sarah was right. It was time. She didn't want to, but this was it. Another heart-breaking conversation was to be had, telling her wonderful mum the awful truth that she had been hiding.

"Jane, dear, you're worrying me now, what on earth is going on?" she exclaimed, wide eyed.

Jane sat close to her mother and cupped hold of her hands. "Mum, it's not good news…"

The next few hours were tough for everyone. Tears streamed, but even more love and support existed now for Jane in the form of her loving parent. She'd known deep down from the start that all her family would always be there. She just didn't want them to hurt like was doing for longer than they needed. And the thought of speaking the actual 'dying' words to them was something she'd dreaded.

"We will get you through this, my dear. Just like we did with Pops." Janice held Jane's hand, and Sarah's hand was in the other. Sarah had always felt like a second daughter to her, and this was a time to pull together more than ever. "I knew something was up weeks ago, my dear. I noticed you had lost weight, your hair looks thinner, and you always seem so tired. I didn't like to pry as I know how you are about your figure. I just hoped you were going to say something along the lines of, hey, Mum, we're pregnant or something like that. You should've told me. You really should have, especially after your father."

She sounded hurt, which made Jane feel even more terrible about keeping it from her all this time.

"I'm sorry, Mum, I really am. I've just been trying to protect everyone from hurting for so long. Only Karl and Sarah know, oh and Carol from work, but I'm not ready to tell the kids the truth yet. Not by a long shot."

Janice looked intently at her daughter. "Well, you may need to think that through. They've asked a few times if you were poorly. I've just said you've been tired because of work, never imagining it to be this, and you've not even been going to work."

"Oh, Mum, I can't tell you how sorry I am. I hope you

understand. I guess I'll have to tell the kids sooner than I wanted to if they are asking questions." This was the worst feeling for Jane. Telling the children was the thing she had dreaded the most and she didn't want it to happen at all but knew it had to be done, especially if they'd been asking about her being poorly. The same situation might occur as with Karl where they'd come to other conclusions or find out another way, and she really didn't want that to happen. It had been awful when Karl had found out the way he did so she decided that it would have to be soon.

Karl returned home just before ten o'clock and crept slowly into bed trying not to wake anyone up. He'd only had a few beers; it had been more talking than drinking for a change. He'd wanted to have a clear head so he could learn to deal with this situation just a little bit more for all their sakes.

"You okay, darling?" whispered Jane, stirring from sleep as she felt his body draw close to hers, inhaling the wonderful smell of his aftershave.

"Yes. Sorry," he whispered back, "I didn't mean to wake you. I met that guy, Dave from the hospice. He's such a great bloke, and we're going to meet up next week if you're okay with that. He's certainly been through the mill with his family…" He stopped as he noticed that she had fallen back to sleep, so he lay on his back, wondering if he was going to cope as well as Dave was when the inevitable came. It wasn't a case of if he would though, he had to, for the sake of the children. They would need him when the time came and he wouldn't let them down. Nor would he let Jane down.

Chapter Twenty-One

"How are you doing, lovely lady?" The gentle and now familiar voice came from behind the bench, tapping her shoulder gently.

She turned to see James holding a big bunch of yellow flowers. "For you, madam." His smile and humour never failed to make her feel better.

"James. They're stunning, thank you. You really shouldn't have though."

"Leave them with your Pops then. He'll appreciate them," he joked as he glanced down. "Wouldn't you, Pops?"

"Silly," Jane said as she jokingly swiped his arm. "But, yes, you are right, he would love these. You know that's his favourite colour."

"No problem, I'll get them arranged for him while you fill me in on your news. I'm guessing you've got lots to tell me as usual, hey?"

"Thanks, well, yes I've got something to ask you actually, that I completely forgot about the other day, stupidly." Shaking her head, she continued, "there's someone I want you to meet. A lady. My best, and very single friend Sarah." She winked at him as he glanced up at her. "I've told her all about you and how lovely you are too, but I must warn you, she's a bit of a minx, well actually, she's a lot of a minx," she chuckled as he came and sat on their bench next to her.

"Sounds intriguing. I get the feeling you want to tell me more about this minx of a lady?"

She did have much more to say about her beautiful best friend, so she carried on telling him all about Sarah and how wonderful she was. How she'd already imagined them being together, and the fact that seeing her best friend happy with someone before she left this world would be amazing. James was just right for her, unattached, no children, and a bit of a free spirit like she was. They would get on like a house on fire, and Jane was determined to make this happen as soon as possible for them both. She felt a wave of excitement running through her body as she detailed every aspect of Sarah's life to him and how great they would be for each other.

"She sounds lovely…" he said but then paused, standing up putting his hands into his pockets.

"Is that it? 'She sounds lovely?'" Jane replied curiously.

"Listen… I don't know if I'm ready to start all that business yet. Dating, courting, whatever you call it now. I'm quite happy on my own, honestly."

"Of course you are ready. It's been two years, James. You deserve to be happy, and I'd…" she stopped for a moment of reflection, "I want to know that you have someone lovely in your life before… well, you know… before I can't see you or Sarah with anyone…"

"Look, please don't worry about me. You are all that matters to me at the minute. Now, shall we sort these flowers out? Pops is waiting, and you know he doesn't like to wait."

Jane was bemused by his words, but she didn't want to push it. His weird reaction seemed strange but the last thing she wanted to do was upset him or make him angry. He was about the only person she hadn't upset lately so she decided to leave it for now and began helping to decorate Pops' grave with the flowers. They looked amazing, and, yet again, James knew how to place them just right, and she enjoyed watching him.

Each visit, she was getting weaker and found it harder every time to kneel down, so he'd taken over that job. He had already moved the bench closer so now she could still help by passing the blooms to him.

"Anyway… listen, Mrs W, we do need to have a bit of a chat," he said, sitting back down next to her.

"Oh…do we? About Sarah?" She glanced hopefully at his now more serious face.

"Ha ha, no. Look, there's going to come a point when you don't need to see me, when you can't get here anymore, physically. Karl knows about the cancer now, and you should be with him and your gorgeous twins. Spending your time with them, not me." He paused to look at her surprised expression. "I can see it's getting harder for you to come here, and I don't want to cause you any more pain or stress than you need right now. I know how tough it gets near the end."

"What are you talking about? I don't understand, what's happened to make you say this?" She looked intently at him, frowning. "Have you spoken to someone? Have I done something wrong? And who says I'm near the end? Do you know something I don't? Is it the business with Sarah because I'm sorry if it was—"

"No, no," he interrupted. "Look, I just feel as though it's time to say goodbye to us and our meetings. Time for you to be with your family. I don't mean anything bad by it; I just feel it's the right time now that I leave you to it, to be with the ones you love."

Jane's eyes began to glisten over. "But… I need you. I like seeing you, meeting you. You've been the only one I can be with, tell everything to and not worry that I'm hurting you or causing you to be upset, or is that it? Have I upset you?" She was fraught with sadness and emotion, thinking about not seeing him was devastating and she felt overwhelmed by what he was saying to her.

"No, you haven't done anything or said anything either, of course, you haven't. I know it's been great, I've loved our chats, but… one day, you'll understand that sometimes you have to let go and—"

Jane interrupted him sternly, replying, "No, I will not say goodbye before I need to. It's not happening!" She slowly got off the bench and turned back round to face him, pleading, "James, please. Don't do this to me. Don't leave me. You can come to the house. Come and meet Karl, he'll understand. Have some dinner, and you can look at all my silly wigs and headscarves; meet the twins and Mum…" Her expression changed from confusion to anxiety. She couldn't lose him. Not now, not when she was still able to see him and get to the cemetery.

He looked down at the ground. "I can't do that, Jane. I just can't do that. It's time for me to go. I'm not going to come here anymore. I've spent too long in this place and need to crack on with other stuff, get on with my life and let you live the rest of yours."

"No!" she cried, "I don't want you out of my life. It's not far from here. Come on. Let me introduce you to the kids, Karl, my mum and especially Sarah. She's so up for meeting you, please? Take my phone number, I don't know why we haven't swapped numbers yet, what's yours and I can text you my address?" She frantically rummaged to find her phone in her bag, but he grabbed hold of her arm firmly to stop her searching.

"I'm sorry, Jane. It's not possible for me to do that at the moment. Please just understand and trust me, this is the right thing for us both right now."

She gave a heavy sigh as if to give in. His eyes looked serious and although she'd only known him a matter of months, she did trust him and respected his wishes. He didn't have to keep coming here and wasting his time talking the day away with her, taking in all her woes and tears but he had, and he had been amazing at it but she wasn't going to give up on the matchmaking she so wanted for him and her friend. "Okay, fine. Just one more meeting, to meet Sarah, and I'll leave you be. You should be together, and it would make me so happy to see two of my best friends happy before I pop my clogs. Please, James, for me? Just one last time?" she pleaded with him.

He took a deep breath and looked at her desperate and very tearful face. She winked at him cheekily as he nodded, and smiled secretly hoping he would change his mind over the next few days.

It was time to get home, so Jane reached for her walking stick. She had to use this now for even the smallest amount of walking. "This bloody thing," she said, wobbling. "See you tomorrow afternoon then?" She blew a kiss to him and made her way out of the cemetery towards home. He stood there watching her as she turned and waved. All the while, she was imagining how lovely it would be to see him and Sarah together.

Sarah was in the kitchen when she arrived, trying to decide on dinner with the kids. "Hey, lovely, where have you been?" she asked, hugging her and helping her sit on the kitchen barstool. Jane had left her stick in the hall cupboard, she didn't like the kids seeing it.

"Just visiting Pops again."

"Aww. You sure you need to do that so often, Jane? Let me know next time, and I'll take you. It's quite a walk there, isn't it?"

"It's fine. The walk does me good, but I do have something to talk to you about."

"Oh? What's that then?"

"Later…" Jane nodded towards the children. "How are my babies then?" They had both come and sat on either side of her. She loved having them close by, and they loved being there.

"When can you get rid of that thing?" asked Robbie, pointing to the headscarf.

"Hopefully soon, darling. Sorry if it makes Mum look funny. I'm just having issues with my hair right now, and I don't want to look like a bald old lady for you, do I?" She wished she had remembered to put her thickening wig on instead. They seemed to be noticing and before long, they'd ask about the stick if she wasn't careful.

"A friend's mum wears one but it's because she's not very well, Noah said she's got no hair and that she's going to die... you're not dying are you, Mum?"

Jane's eyes seemed to explode at the question now looming over her and Sarah froze on the spot after dropping the cutlery she had just got out of the drawer.

"No, Robbie, darling, of course not, it's just a fashion thing to cover my bird's nest hairstyle," Jane replied trying to reassure him.

He just nodded back and began showing her the science homework he had been doing before she arrived. Even though she didn't understand it, she still enjoyed hearing him talk about it and trying to explain things to her and was glad of the distraction. She glanced over to Sarah who just winced a smile.

"Cass, are you ready?" bellowed Karl as he ran down the stairs and into the kitchen. "Oh... hi, honey. I didn't know you were back. You okay?" He kissed Jane on the cheek and put his arm around her shoulders.

"Sorry. Yeah, I'm good, just a bit tired."

"Would you rather me drop her and come back? I can run you a nice bubble bath?"

"No, I'm good. It's dance tonight, isn't it?"

"Yes, but it's only an hour, so it's not too long. Come on, Cassie, we don't want to be late again this week. Mate, do you want to kick a ball about while she's dancing?" he ruffled Robbie's hair as he grabbed his hoody.

"Yeah, okay," Robbie replied, jumping down to go and fetch his football from the garden.

"See you later then, you lot," Jane called to them as they made their way to the front door. "Have fun."

"Do you want me to run you a bath instead, Jane?" asked Sarah as she began cutting the potatoes into wedges for dinner.

"That would be great actually, Sarah. Thanks. I'm so tired right now. It's been such a busy day."

"Maybe you need a lay down first. Come on, let's get you upstairs for a rest." She turned on the oven and then helped Jane up the stairs and into the bedroom. "There you go. Does that feel better?" Sarah plumped her pillows for her.

"Mmm, my bed always feels better," Jane replied as they snuggled down together.

"Now what was it you wanted to talk about?"

"Oh, yes. I've told James all about you, and he is up for a meeting as soon as you can. I get the feeling that he doesn't want to visit the cemetery anymore, so I need you to meet with him sooner rather than later."

"Seriously? He still wants to meet me after the stories you've told him about me?" she joked.

"Yes, he does." Jane looked at her sideways. "Can you make it tomorrow? He's up for it in the afternoon?"

"I have to go on a training day tomorrow, and the next day. Maybe the weekend would be better."

"Are you delaying this?" Jane asked smirking.

"No, honestly. I have to do a two-day course for work. There's me and three other beauticians who want to come and work for me. I wasn't going to go in case you needed me, but I've checked with Karl, and he's going to be around so thought it would be cool for me to go."

"Oh, don't be silly. But that's nice of you to check. I'll ask him tomorrow about the weekend then. Yes?"

"Okay. Now, you get some rest, and I'll let you know when dinner is ready, and then we can do your bath, I bought you some new relaxing bubbles to try." She pulled one of the soft blankets over her friend and went back downstairs.

Jane lay there thinking about how her two friends would look together, how amazing would it be to finally see Sarah with someone who could make her extremely happy. How great for this man, whom she'd met that day and had become another close friend in such weird circumstances, to be together with her best friend. Her mind wandered again as she slowly drifted off to sleep.

"Hey, sweetie, do you want anything to eat yet?" Karl was back with the kids, gently whispering as he knelt beside Jane's side of the bed.

She hadn't realised she'd been asleep for so long. It was dark outside now, and the kids had on their pyjamas, ready for bed. "Blimey, I must've been more tired than I thought.

Erm… yes. Just a little, please. I'm not that hungry, I'm thirsty more than anything." She sat up, reaching for the glass of water by her bedside, "Is Sarah still here?"

"No, she left about an hour ago when we got back. She said she had to pack her work stuff up for the course."

"Oh, right, yeah. She's going away for a few days training for her work."

"Do you want me to bring your dinner up here? Save you going downstairs?"

"Yes, please, darling. Can you send the kids in to say goodnight too before they go to bed?"

"Sure." He got up, kissed her on the top of her head and left the room, calling to the children, who were brushing their teeth on the way.

Cassie was first to pop in and say goodnight, shortly followed by Robbie who gave her a fist bump.

After she had finished most of her dinner, Karl joined her on the bed. "You have an appointment next week, don't you?" He was looking at his phone calendar.

"Yes, Monday. More of the same, I guess."

"I'd like to come with you if that's okay?"

"Sure. It's a bit boring there though. You'll just be sitting there doing nothing."

"I've booked the day off anyway, so I may as well be bored with you. Dave, you know from the hospice that day, said it helped him understand the whole process a bit more, so I said I'd try it with you." He smiled at her and held her hand, twiddling her wedding ring, which was getting very loose on her now fragile, thin finger.

"Robbie asked me if I was dying."

"What! Where did that come from?" Karl asked shocked and raising his eyebrows.

"Apparently, his friend's mum wears headscarves, and the friend has told Robbie it's because she's going to die; it was awful. I didn't know what to say but ended up lying, saying of course not."

"It's okay." Karl could see she was getting tearful. "He'll understand when the time comes and I can explain everything to him, don't worry, darling."

They talked for a while longer until Jane fell asleep again. The tiredness was getting worse each week, and she knew the time would come when she would have to tell more people, the children, friends but it was all coming sooner than she had anticipated.

Chapter Twenty-Two

After seeing James, the following day, he had reluctantly agreed to meet Sarah at the weekend and Jane felt such relief knowing she could see him one more time.

Saturday came, and she was so excited as Sarah drove up the driveway that afternoon, that she got to the front door before her, even with her silly walking stick. "What took you so long? Where have you been?" she asked impatiently.

"Sorry, next-door's dog escaped, so I had to help her get it back in. Bloody thing. Why do people have pets? I don't know. Anyway, come on then. Let's do this meeting." She took Jane's arm and helped her get into the car. "Where are we going for it anyway?"

"To the cemetery," answered Jane innocently.

"What! Are you having a laugh, seriously, are you joking me?" Sarah stopped and looked at her in amazement.

"No, why would it be a joke? That's where I met him in the first place, and it's nice and peaceful."

"A cemetery for a first meeting? Is he an undertaker or something? He's not one of those gravediggers, is he?" she sniggered.

"Don't be silly. Come on. Let's go. You'll see soon enough, and you'll love him. I just know you will." Jane smiled at her and nodded, directing the way forward with her hands.

They parked the car and began slowly walking to Jane's usual meeting spot by Pops' grave.

"Honestly, Jane, is this such a good idea? It's creeping me out a bit," Sarah said as they sat down on the bench.

"Yes. It's a great idea. He'll be here soon. Don't worry, it's not creepy, it's serene and lovely. I've spent hours here being able to think clearly while chatting to him. You look great by the way. Is that a new outfit you've got especially for today?"

"Well, I got it while we were away training. Although if I'd known we were coming here, I'd have worn something else. I feel rather overdressed for this place. You could've told me beforehand where we were going." Sarah was wearing black jeans, a smart grey blouse with a feather design, and she'd finished the look off with some strappy heels.

They sat and waited for an hour. "I don't understand," said Jane as she glanced at her watch again and looked around. "He said four o'clock. I'm sure he did."

"Maybe he's got held up somewhere or chickened out. Don't you have his number?"

Jane thought for a moment. She didn't. She hadn't even thought about swapping numbers in all the weeks and months they had been meeting there apart from when he'd said about not seeing her anymore and then he'd stopped her in her tracks. "Let's just give him another half hour," Jane replied anxiously. But nothing. He didn't show up.

"You okay, Jane?" asked Sarah as they drove home in awkward silence.

"Yes. I'm fine."

"You sure, darling? Maybe something just came up, and he couldn't get there?"

"Maybe." Jane couldn't stop wondering what had happened. Where was he? Why hadn't he turned up like he had promised he would? Had he been too nervous? Had something happened? Why hadn't she gotten his phone number before and why did he stop her that day? This wasn't making any sense and she felt angry and embarrassed. "I'm sorry to have wasted your time." She turned to look at Sarah as they approached the driveway of the house.

"Don't worry, sweetie. I'm sure there's a good reason, and there's always another day." She reached for Jane's hand and gently squeezed it. She always knew the right things to say. "I'm still up for it. You've intrigued me even more with this mystery guy. And if it makes you happy…"

Still puzzled and fraught with emotion, Jane decided she wanted to go back to see if she'd got the timings wrong, she had to work this out. "I'm going back again, Sarah. Can you take me back, please?"

"Jane, you need to rest. This is silly. Come on. Go

tomorrow. I'm sure he'll be there then, and I'll come with you again. It's no problem."

"No. I need to know what's happened. Please, Sarah, can we go back? Maybe I got the time wrong? You know what my mind's been like lately. I'll walk there if you don't want to take me in the car."

Sarah sighed but could see that her friend needed this closure. "Okay, but just for half an hour. Karl will kill me if I don't make you rest, you're looking worn out."

"Yes, half an hour, I promise, and then I'll rest."

They drove back again in silence. Sarah kept looking over at her friend, who looked upset and worried, but more than that, she looked disappointed. She hoped, more for Jane, that he would be there this time.

As they walked up the pathway towards the bench, Jane stumbled. She had forgotten to take her walking stick out of the car and was finding it difficult to walk today as if the emotional few hours had taken away some of her already dwindling strength.

"Sit here, Jane. I'll go back and get your stick." Sarah sat her down on a nearby bench while she made her way back to the car.

Jane was frustrated. "Damn it," she muttered under her breath, angry at the cancer for taking hold of her, making her so weak and fragile. As she looked over towards another bench just across from her, she noticed a man sitting and facing a gravestone near James' mother's grave. She used the last of her energy and managed to get up to walk over to him. Was it James sitting at a different bench for some reason? She glanced around at his face, and the man looked up at her in surprise.

"Sorry. I thought you were someone else," she said, standing back up straight. He looked familiar, but she didn't know why, and his eyes looked sad and tearful. He was a slighter, older man with a hat on and a smart, grey, pinstripe suit. "Are you okay?" she asked politely.

For a moment, it was like déjà vu. All those months ago, when James had done the same to her when she had found out the news and arrived at her father's grave upset, asking if she was okay. Now it was her turn to see if someone else was alright.

"Yes, I've just come to wish my brother a happy birthday," he sighed. "He would've been forty today," the man replied, looking back at the gravestone.

"Oh, I'm sorry." Jane sat beside him on the bench, looking at his face. Did she know him from somewhere? Why did he seem so familiar? Who was this man?

"We lost him a few years back now. He, er, took his own life, the fool."

"Oh my God. That's awful…" Jane gasped.

"It's okay. These things happen, but you just don't expect to bury your younger brother, do you?"

"No, not at all. I'm sorry for disturbing you." Jane began to get up carefully holding onto the bench.

"Please, it's fine, stay." He touched her hand. "My little brother loved to talk, couldn't shut him up sometimes. He's probably trying to get a word in edgewise now, aren't you, James?" he joked, glancing up towards the sky.

His words vibrated through her skin like a tornado sweeping up the air, as he mentioned the name James. He continued speaking, but she couldn't hear him properly. His voice was muffled to her as confusion set in. Was she hearing him right? Did he just say James? she thought. Was it just pure coincidence? She turned her head to listen more to this man sitting beside her.

"I carry this about for some reason, a picture of him. He was quite a looker. He got the looks, I got the brains," he chuckled while holding a photo in his hands and passed it over to Jane. It had been in his wallet, so was a little creased but obviously a lasting memory of this special person who had been in his life.

As she took hold of the photo, her blood ran cold, her whole world stood still for a second, and everything began moving in slow motion. The photo was of the man she now sat next to and another, younger version, standing together arm in arm. The younger guy was James. It was actually him in the picture. What was going on? She was totally confused, so she just continued to listen while looking closer at the photo, blinking hard.

The man went on. "His wife left him a few years before and went off, to be with another woman. We were all so shocked and it devastated him. Turned out she was pregnant too, only a few months into the pregnancy, but he was so looking forward to becoming a dad and settling down finally. He would have made an awesome daddy. Unfortunately, she made up a story that she had lost the baby, but she hadn't. She went to live in France with her new woman and then wouldn't let him see the baby. He found it so hard and just couldn't get over it. We tried everything to help him cope. Then one day, I went to check on him and found him in his garage…" He stopped and shook his head, clearly fighting back tears. "A sight I will never get out of my head. It is something that no one should ever have to see in their life. I tried so hard to bring him back, but it was just too late. He knew what he was doing that day, bloody idiot."

Jane was in total shock. The man was opening up to her about his brother, but James had been there with her for weeks, months now, talking to her, telling her his stories about his wife, the other woman, his mum, his family and everything apart from the baby, maybe he'd not come to terms with it at all? It just didn't make any sense, and she didn't know what to say to this man. She just continued to look at him in silence as she listened and glanced down at the photo every few minutes, trying to come to terms with the situation and attempting to work out in her head what it all meant.

Sarah had made her way back from the car. "Jane? Is everything alright? Here's your stick, sorry I took so long, had a phone call from the salon…"

"Oh, thanks. This is… sorry I didn't get your name?"

"Tom Cooper. Hi." He stood up and took Sarah's hand, gently kissing it like a true gentleman.

"Sarah…" she replied, blushing a little as she felt his soft lips touch her hand.

"And you are?" he looked at Jane, who was still sitting in shock. She was oblivious to the flirting that was happening right above her head.

"Jane… sorry… I was miles away." She couldn't explain her confusion as she didn't understand it herself.

"Well, ladies, it's been a pleasure meeting you both." He tilted his hat. "But I really must go now. I hope I haven't upset your day going on with my sob story."

"No, of course not, I'm sorry for your loss." Jane shook her head and tried her best to smile up at him.

He walked off, leaving Jane speechless and motionless, still holding the picture tightly in her hands. Had he forgotten it on purpose? She glanced down at it again, looking into the eyes of this man she had been chatting to and meeting with for so long. "Oh, Sarah, his photo…" she cried.

"Here, I'll take it to him." Sarah took the photo and quickly ran ahead to find Tom, who was just getting into his car. "Tom, you forgot your picture." She smiled sweetly at him.

"Wow, I'm such a dumbass sometimes, thank you." He took the picture and placed it back into his wallet and smiled back at Sarah nervously as she turned to get back to Jane who was still sat silently, trying to comprehend what had just happened. She looked ahead at the gravestone and read it out loud: James Michael Cooper. It was James' headstone. He'd died four years ago.

A heavy tear fell down her cheek as she began to realise what had been happening. Had he been an angel sent to her to keep her strong? The more she thought about it, the more things fell into place as she remembered certain aspects of their chats and meetings. He always wore the same outfit, his hair never changed, and he was always there, whatever the time, and that moment when she had said about swapping phone numbers and addresses. She had never even seen him with a phone! How could she have missed that one? Why hadn't they left the cemetery anytime? How did he know that she would be there? Why had this happened? Suddenly, the neck scarf that he always wore became clearer to her. To hide the marks on his neck from his untimely suicide. Jane was blown away with grief and just sat silently, staring at his name until Sarah returned, slightly out of breath from running. "You okay, sweetie?" she asked.

"Yes. I think so. Take me home now, please," Jane replied sharply.

"I take it that wasn't who we were supposed to meet?"

"No, it wasn't. Sorry. Best just forget that idea."

Just as they got to the cemetery gate, Jane glanced back one last time. Goodbye, James, she thought. And right there, she knew that would be the last time. James had known that his brother was coming, and that's why he had to go. His time for Jane was over, and there'd be no more. She knew the truth now and weirdly, she felt some closure for them both.

As painful as it was, she felt grateful to have had those moments with him; even if they were just between the two of them, and no one else knew. Even if they didn't really happen, or did they? She would never know, but he had helped her at the exact right time. He'd been there for her, and although he had not been Sarah's new man as she had wanted and ultimately planned, she felt privileged to have been there with him no matter what, in no matter what form. But she knew she would miss those times too and felt tremendous sadness. Also, how the hell would she explain who James was to Sarah now and would she think she had lost her mind?

Chapter Twenty-Three

The next few days were so hard. Jane had to get her head around what had happened at the cemetery that day with meeting Tom and failing at matchmaking for Sarah. She was trying her best to comprehend what she'd been told and what she had seen. She couldn't explain it to anyone but Sarah, and she was amazing about it too, as per usual.

"I feel so stupid, Sarah… do you think he was some sort of angel or a ghost?"

"Maybe Pops sent him to keep you strong? I don't know really." Sarah looked concerned at her bewildered and very sad-faced friend.

"Please don't tell Karl. He'll think I've finally lost the plot or something," Jane pleaded with her.

"I won't tell anyone, I promise."

Jane kept thinking back about the last conversation she'd had with James. About how he had said that he couldn't come to the house. It all started to make more sense. But she was heartbroken. Partly because of the whole situation, and also because she felt so silly and couldn't work out why he had been sent to her.

"You would've been so great together, Sarah. If only, if only he…"

"Jane… sweetheart… it's over now. He said his goodbyes when you think about it. What he said to you before, that was his way of telling you he had to go. He knew it was time for him to move on, maybe he was needed for someone else, to help them through something?"

"Yes, maybe you're right, but I miss him. How can I miss something or someone that wasn't even really there? I mean, he wasn't even alive for God's sake."

Sarah didn't have any words to help with this. She couldn't understand it either really but didn't want to admit that to Jane or make her feel any worse. Was it the medication that she was on that had made her imagine James; but then how could she have known all the information that Tom, his brother, had gone on to tell her afterwards that day in the cemetery? Unexplainable things had occurred, and neither of them really understood it but, James had been sent for some reason and maybe one day they'd find out why but for now, Jane had the fondest memories of him, and their time and she was happy with that forever.

~

"How are you feeling in general, Jane?" Paula had come to the house to visit as it was getting harder to go to the clinic for Jane apart from the odd chemo sessions; which she was trying to have much less of. She didn't think they were helping much anymore and had started feeling as though it was wasted time away from her family.

"I'm doing okay," she replied.

"Have you spoken to your mother yet?" Paula knew that Jane had been dreading telling Janice especially.

"Yes, she was upset, obviously, but was great about it actually, she understood why I hadn't told her straight away and between us all, we've decided it may be time to tell the children. I can't hide this pain anymore, and they're getting suspicious with all the headscarves I keep trying to wear. I don't want them to find out when it's too late, you know, and I can't speak to them properly?"

"Do you need any help with talking to them? I can be with you if you like, just there as support?"

"Paula, that's so kind of you, but I think Sarah will be here with Karl. My mum will also be on hand just in case."

"Well, if you or they need anything, any information, advice, anything, just call us, okay? That's what we are trained for and we're here for you whenever you need us, please don't forget that, you have all my contact numbers don't you?"

"Yes, I do… and thank you so much, you've all been wonderful throughout this horrid journey I've been on." She smiled.

"We have the booking-in visit at the hospice next Wednesday. Would you still like to meet us there?"

"Oh yes, Sarah is picking me up and bringing me along, and Karl is meeting us there after he's finished work."

They had decided to go for another visit and book a provisional bedroom for when Jane was ready to go in.

They all felt it wouldn't be long now.

Just as Paula left in her car, Sarah arrived with the children. Jane left the front door open as she watched them all get out and hurriedly walk towards the door. It wasn't the end of school time, so what were they doing home so early? Robbie walked straight past her, not even looking up at her; something wasn't right.

"Robbie!" shouted Sarah as Cassie followed close behind. "Robbie!" she yelled louder, but he didn't stop or acknowledge her call.

"What's happened, Sarah?" asked Jane in a panicked voice, watching the commotion.

Before Sarah could answer, Cassie approached the doorstep and looking up at her mum tearfully, asked abruptly, "Mum… are you dying?"

Jane's eyes widened with shock. "What?"

"Cassie, I told you to wait." Sarah looked crossly at her, ushering her inside.

"Sarah. What's going on?" Jane was confused.

Cassie ran upstairs, stamping her feet hard and loud on each step and then slamming her bedroom door with as much force as she could muster.

Sarah stepped in and shut the door behind Jane and sighed. "Some pesky kids have said something at school about your headscarves and the stick. You know what kids are like. They just blurt things out without thinking, giving it, 'has your mum got cancer or something' and 'why does she wear those silly scarves and have a walking stick?'. This is why I don't have any children, Jane, really? They can be so cruel at times, can't they?" She shook her head in anger.

"Oh shit. What… what am I going to do, Sarah? This is not how it was supposed to be for them."

"I know it's not, I've rung Karl for you, and he's on his way home now. It's time, Jane. You are going to have to tell them the truth. *Today*! They deserve to know from you what's going on, otherwise, the other kids will just carry on taunting them about it all."

"But… they will be so upset, Sarah. What if they can't deal with it, what if… and when I lied to Robbie that day, he's not going to forgive me—"

Sarah grasped Jane's arm, interrupting her. "Sweetheart, these are your children we are talking about. You don't know how long you have now. Let them in. Let them be with you, they will be alright once they know."

Jane had known that this day would come, but now, because of the way school children act sometimes it had been forced upon her, and she was dreading it so much. She just hoped they would forgive her.

Within minutes, Karl arrived home frantic with worry and called down the hallway, "Jane, where are you? Sarah?"

Jane had gone and sat down in the lounge scared of what the next few hours would bring, thinking of how she was going to explain this awful situation to her beloved and precious twins. Sarah went up to see if the children were okay.

"In the lounge, Karl," answered Jane, calling back to him in a quiet and timid voice.

Out of breath, he appeared in the doorway. "Did Sarah bring the children home? Are they alright?"

"Yes, she's upstairs with them." Her voice was shaking with anxiety and her hands were trembling with pure panic. "It's time we told them, isn't it?"

He sat beside her and held her hands in his lap, trying to calm them both down. "I think it is. It's going to be better coming from you than from someone at school just teasing them about it."

Sarah appeared with the children, holding their hands, and they looked distressed. Cassie had been crying, and Robbie looked bereft, his Florida cap was down covering part of his face. She'd already hurt them by hiding this thing from them. It was time to step up and be the strong mum that they loved and tell the truth now, as much as she dreaded it.

The discussion was emotional, as it had been telling Sarah, Karl, and then her mother, but revealing the truth to them both had made her realise that her children were much stronger than she had thought. Just as James had said they would be. They had taken it better than she had ever imagined they would and seemed, all of a sudden, even more grown-up and more beautiful in this moment of pure anguish and pain. She hated seeing their sweet eyes full of tears and looking at her in disbelief.

"Can the doctors make you better, Mum?" asked Robbie, holding her hand while they sat on the sofa together with Cassie on the other side of her.

Jane looked up at Sarah and Karl and then back at her scared little boy. "I'm afraid they can't, darling. There's nothing else they can do to make it go away. I'm having regular treatment and taking some tablets to help, but it's not going to get better now. They are just helping to give me a little more time with you guys." Her strength was shining through today; she knew she had to be strong in front of them. They needed her to be that courageous mother she had always been for them and she was determined to be brave and answer honestly any questions that they may have.

"So, it's like Noah's mum?" he asked looking up at her with tears in his eyes.

"I'm afraid so, yes."

Cassie hadn't said much, she just sat in silence and listened to all the details and information that her mum and dad were explaining. "Cass, do you understand what's happening to Mum, darling?" Sarah sat beside her and put her arm around her shuddering shoulders.

She just nodded slowly, then quietly asked in her sweet little voice, looking at her dad, "Can I go upstairs now?" Karl looked at Jane, and she nodded back at him in agreement.

"Yes, of course, darling. Just give us a shout or a text if you need anything. We will be straight up."

She walked to the door of the lounge, paused, spun around, and ran back to her mum, flinging her arms around her frail and still slightly shaking body.

Karl took a deep breath to avoid bursting into tears and looked up at the ceiling. It was so hard watching his beautiful children being so brave or at least trying their hardest to be. He could see everyone's hurt and pain today, and it was truly heart-breaking.

"I'll come with you, Cass." Robbie followed his sister

upstairs and Jane caught sight of him putting his arm around her as they reached the doorway.

"Wow," Sarah said, as Karl shut the lounge door. "You have the most amazing children, you guys."

"They are as strong as their mum. They've learned from the expert." Karl stroked Jane's cheek and smiled at her with tears in his eyes. "They will be okay, darling. I promise you. I won't let them down when…" He hung don his head to avoid her seeing even more tears brewing in his eyes.

She gently raised his head. "I know. You are an amazing father, Karl, and I know you'll do right by them, I know you both will."

This moment was tough for both of them like nothing before, and they knew what each other was saying without uttering the words. It was just so hard accepting the obvious. Time was against them now, more so than the past few weeks. Now everyone that mattered knew the situation, but it didn't make it any easier. It only seemed to bring everyone closer together as time went on.

~

By mid-November, Jane's health had deteriorated rapidly. She'd now lost all of her hair with just a few strands hanging on, and most of her eyebrows and eyelashes too. Her energy levels had dropped dramatically, and her weight had plummeted to just six stone. She no longer felt like herself and refused to look in the mirror anymore. She'd even asked Karl to remove her dressing table mirror, so she didn't have to look at herself when she woke up each day. She felt ugly and could see all her bones, and her gaunt face wasn't something she wanted to see on a daily basis. It wasn't even improved with a touch of makeup that she had asked Sarah to help her with one day. Well, she hadn't thought so anyway.

During the last few weeks, they had tried to spend as much quality time together as possible, visiting the parks and the zoo, but Jane had to be in a wheelchair.

She felt out of control and crippled by not being able to do things herself. She remembered how she had felt seeing Marie back in Florida looking so frail, how she'd thought at that moment that she would look like that; and now she did, what did people think? Her mind wandered aimlessly, fretting about everything and she couldn't help but worry.

Brad, in Miami, had phoned them with the news that Marie had passed away a few weeks back and it killed Jane even more inside knowing that her time would soon be coming.

The kids would sit and read various favourite books or magazines and discuss their school days at every opportunity, but she fell asleep so quickly each time, she never got to hear the full day's story or was able to think properly to help them with any homework.

Time was ticking by so fast and she felt completely helpless.

Chapter Twenty-Four

December crept up in what seemed like no time, and that meant Christmas would be upon them soon. Jane didn't want the family to have to deal with her illness when it was supposed to be a joyous and happy season and decided to book into the hospice, so they could get a little bit of respite before the festive period set in. She felt it was the best option at this time.

She mentioned it while Karl was running her bath that evening. "Karl, I think maybe I should book myself into the hospice?"

"Oh? I thought you were against the idea. You know we can look after you here." He turned the tap off and sat on the side of the bath looking at her perched in their special bathroom chair.

"Yes, I know I was, but it's just going to get harder for you and the kids each day now and you shouldn't have to deal with all this mess." She pointed to the pile of bandages

271

and medicines that now adorned the bathroom windowsill in place of the lovely candles and plants that used to sit there.

He went over to her and crouched down putting his hands onto her knees. "In sickness and in health, better or worse; remember?"

"I know you want to do this, Karl, but I really would like to go there and take some of the pressure off for you all. I'll ring them tomorrow and book in for next week. They had provisionally booked me in for around this time anyway."

Admiring the courage of his wife, he nodded, knowing that once she had set her mind on something that was it, so he would support her all he could at this crucial time in her life, however long she had.

The room was booked the next day and they all helped to get her moved in and comfortable with some pictures and ornaments from home. All the staff were friendly and made the children feel at ease. Karl, Sarah and Janice would take turns in sitting with Jane and sorting Cassie and Robbie out with whatever they needed.

Jane's room wasn't that big but why did she need a larger space, she thought; it's not like she could get up and move around. Sarah would entertain her with playing silly dance games or charades with the children and she tried hard to laugh but mostly only managed to grin at them and enjoy seeing them have fun.

Every day that passed, she felt more and more angry and frustrated and within a few weeks of being there, she started getting very agitated and upset and didn't want to see her last Christmas like this, she'd had enough of the stillness and quiet.

Although the hospice was peaceful, it was almost too quiet, for her especially. Jane didn't like it at all. She enjoyed hearing the buzz of her children, even when they were arguing or bickering, and she loved to hear the birds singing in her garden. Even hearing the droning sound of a lawnmower was better than this stillness every day.

The kids had brought in a small Christmas tree and decorated it in Jane's favourite colours, which she would admire all day. But did she want to look at that instead of the huge tree that they had always put up at home each year on the first of December? No, she didn't. She made the decision to speak to Karl alone that morning when he arrived.

"I want to go home, Karl. I don't want to be here anymore." She attempted to sit up suddenly but gasped in pain and scrunched her face up.

"Darling, this is the best place for you. I thought this is where you wanted to be?" He calmly and gently laid her back down. "Come on, lie down now, honey."

"No, it's not. I don't want to die here, Karl. Please... take me home. I want to be at home with you, I miss my house, my bed." Her eyes filled with tears, and her face was filled with agony.

"Sweetheart, please think about this. You have everything here, medication, help, and equipment that we don't have. There are certain things we can't do."

"Karl... all I want is you and my family in our home, not here. Don't let me die here. Take me home. No medication is going to help me now. I don't want to take anymore. I don't need it. I'm not having the chemo now. We know that's finished." She was in a frantic state. "I know you don't want to hear it, but I'm going to die soon, and I just want to be in my own bed, my own house, in our home. I want to see our Christmas tree one last time."   Tears were streaming down her pale, gaunt cheeks and Karl couldn't hold back his tears and anguish either. What should he do? His mind was racing, and he felt an urgent panic in the pit of his stomach. He knew deep down that the hospice might be able to keep her alive a bit longer, but his wife wasn't happy there now. He had to do something. He couldn't let her be so upset like this, he just couldn't.

"I'll be back in a minute," he said, and he left the room hurriedly, kissing her hand reassuringly and tucking it back under the blanket gently.

"Sarah, hi… I need you to come to the hospice right now." He'd phoned her from the courtyard outside.

"Oh God, she's not…?"

"No, no. It's not that. She wants to go home, and I need to get her there. She's really not happy staying here anymore. She wants to be at home with us in her own bed, Sarah. We need to do this for her."

"Karl, are you serious? Doesn't she need to be there?"

"Yes, she does, but she doesn't want to be, and I'm not going to force her to stay here, she's in a bit of a state right now. Can you grab a few things from home and bring them to me asap?"

"Sure, anything, what do you need? Just text me a list. I was just about to go to yours anyway with some new board games for the kids."

He typed away on his phone and sent her a list of things to bring, and she was there within half an hour.

Meanwhile, he checked back in on Jane and then went to go and find someone to talk to about her leaving, "Doctor Mitchell, could I have a word with you please?" he said to the doctor on duty, who was looking worried at his rushed manner.

"Yes, Mr Walden, is there a problem?"

"She wants to go home… and she wants to go now. Like as in, today."

"Okay, that's fine. We can gather some medication and equipment for you to take and send a nurse with you. Give me half an hour." As she turned to go back into her office, Karl grasped the doctor's arm.

"She doesn't want a nurse there. She just wants to go home and be with her family when… you know, when it happens. Please, understand… I have to do this for my wife right now. It's the only thing left I can do for her."

"Mr Walden, it's best for a nurse to be there, but I do understand how she feels. We have many patients who decide this near the end, but I do need to have a nurse nearby when the time comes, so please do call us when you think you need us there. We can have someone on call for as long as you need. Just let us know. I'll arrange the discharge papers for you to sign."

"I will. Thank you… and thank you for everything you've done for her so far, and for the children, they've really enjoyed their time here and made some new friends too which may help them in the long run." He held both of her hands and then returned to Jane's room where Sarah was helping her out of bed. "Here, let me do it." He went over to the bed and cupped Jane's face gently. "Let's get you home, see that bloody Christmas tree of yours," he said, smiling at her, sending as much love into her eyes as humanly possible during this tense moment.

She managed a small smile but said nothing as he picked her up in his arms. "Sarah, grab that big blanket please?" He indicated with his head to Jane's favourite new one that the kids and her mum had knitted for her a few weeks back at one of Janice's new craft groups.

Sarah placed it over Jane's frail body in his arms and kissed her head, tidying the headscarf and placing her furry slippers on her feet.

Jane laid her head on his shoulder as he carried her out of the room and down the corridor towards the entrance.

The doctor appeared with a wheelchair. "Do you need any help?" she asked, pointing to the chair.

"We're good, thank you," replied Karl as Jane held him just that little bit tighter as if to say she didn't want the chair and not to let go of her.

"I just need your signature," replied the doctor.

"Sarah, can you?" asked Karl turning to face her.

"Yep, sure." She signed the forms and then followed them out, thinking what a tragic, yet beautiful scene it was to witness. He looked like a hero trying to save his wife. He wasn't saving her from what was rapidly creeping up on them all, but he was doing his best and doing what Jane wanted, so in her eyes, he was her best friend's true hero.

The sun shone brightly outside, and Jane squinted at the

light, turning her face into Karl's chest a little bit more and closing her eyes tightly. Karl lifted the blanket to slightly cover her face as he noticed her struggling with the light.

"Nearly there, my darling." He laid her in the back seat of the car and straightened the blanket. "We're going home now. I'm taking you home." He closed the car door as quietly as he could and took a deep breath as Sarah glanced at him.

Reaching for his hand, she whispered, "You're doing the right thing, Karl. This is right for her, it's what she wants and what she needs. I'll go ahead of you and start getting things ready." She put the suitcase containing the few of Jane's things from her room into the boot of her car.

He smiled back at her and started for home, not uttering a word until they neared the cemetery.

"Karl," Jane whispered. "Please stop so I can see Pops for a few minutes."

He nodded in silence and parked the car near the entrance, helping her to sit up, so she could see out of the window.

As she looked towards her secret meeting place, there he was. James was standing there, looking straight at her with what seemed like a glow around him. They both smiled sweetly at each other, and with a slow blink of her eyes, he was gone. She was happy that he'd come to say a final goodbye. No one else knew or could see him apart from her, but it was magical, and she felt peace for him and indeed for herself. They had now said their final goodbyes.

She lay back down. "Okay, let's go home," she murmured sleepily.

Sarah had phoned Janice in advance, and she had gotten everything in the bedroom ready for her. She and the children were waiting anxiously at the doorway as they arrived, with Sarah in the kitchen making some fresh coffee.

Karl carried his wife straight upstairs, where the children joined them a few minutes later once she had settled in her bed.

As she lay down, she saw them walk towards her. She was exhausted but so happy to see them and relieved to be finally at home in her bed with the people that really mattered in her life. They'd even moved the Christmas tree into her bedroom in place of the dressing table and stool, so she could see it all day long for as much time as she had left.

That evening, she felt more at peace and relaxed than she had done in a long time. Karl had downloaded the musical, *Cats*, for them to watch together to remind her of the special evening they'd had at the theatre in London and she had managed to stay awake the whole way through. When it finished, she turned to Karl and whispered, "Talk to me, Karl. Tell me some of our stories," as he lay beside her admiring the full moon beaming through the open curtains.

"Stories… about us?" he replied softly.

She just nodded slowly.

"Okay. Oh, here's one. Do you remember that night we went to that posh do in the countryside? Some mansion in Hertfordshire? We made love in their wine cellar." Karl sniggered. "What were we thinking?"

Jane was struggling to smile back at him. She felt so weak tonight, a laugh wouldn't come out. It had been an emotional and tiring day.

"What about the journey home when you threw up all over my hired tuxedo? Telling the driver off for driving too fast." He laughed again. "You and country roads never really got on, did you?" He glanced down at Jane's face; her eyes were heavy, and she was blinking slowly. He continued, "Here's another one. Our wedding night, do you remember how we sat up most of the night opening the cards and gifts that we'd got from everyone? Can you believe how many we got, Jane, and the cash? People were so generous weren't they, sweetheart?" He beamed a big smile down to her face, but she had fallen asleep. She looked so still, so peaceful, and for a second, his heart missed a beat, thinking the worst. He concentrated hard and could see her chest moving up and down very slowly. Although her breathing was deep and had become slightly noisy, he had to check. "I love you so much, darling," he whispered, kissing her head gently as he got up and pulled the bed covers up to her neck.

He stood up and stared at her, thinking she was the most beautiful thing he had ever seen, even with little hair left, weight loss, head scarves, and the dreaded walking stick. She was still his beloved, gorgeous wife, and his heart was breaking into a million or more pieces right now. He couldn't begin to fathom how he would cope without the love of his life. How would he be able to support the kids? How would they cope without their mum? How would he be without his soulmate and best friend? These questions would have to wait for now. Questions didn't matter right at this moment. All that mattered was Jane and helping her live her last days in the comfort of her home with her family by her side as she wanted and needed it to be.

He sat in the armchair next to the bed. They'd brought the special one in from the bathroom, so people were more comfortable sitting beside her instead of on the bed. He had a newspaper to read, but he just wanted to watch her sleeping, watch her breathing peacefully. All the time she slept, she looked out of pain and at ease from all the stress and worry. When she was awake, her eyes sparkled as the Christmas fairy lights gleamed in the room at night.

They hadn't even thought about getting each other any presents this year, and Christmas was only a matter of days away now. They would all rather spend time with her than go out shopping, but Jane had suggested that they arrange a date in the new year when they could celebrate again knowing deep down, she wouldn't be there to enjoy that time. Her life was drawing to an end, but she still had some unfinished business to tend to and she needed someone to help with the task.

Chapter Twenty-Five

The following morning, Sarah came strolling into the bedroom with a vase full of flowers that Jane's former work colleagues had just arranged to be delivered to the house.

"Hey, gorgeous. Look at these beauties that arrived for you. Aren't they stunning? You're a lucky lady."

Jane smiled as she glanced toward the enormous bouquet of roses.

"Do you want them any nearer to the bed or shall I put them here?" Sarah asked, smelling them deeply as she placed them on the drawers.

Jane shook her head and gently reached out her hand to get Sarah to come nearer, whispering, "Read the card for me."

Sarah reached into the bouquet for the small pink envelope, opened it up and began to read, "*Sending all our love to you at Christmas and always, Carol & Co. PS turn over.*" Sarah turned the card over and continued, "*Perry had a little girl, and they have called her Courtney-Jane.* Aww. How lovely is that? Is that the postie guy you used to tell me about?"

A tear escaped from Jane's right eye as she nodded back slowly. How sweet Perry was, adding her name to his new baby's, and how lovely to hear the news before her big leaving day arrived. All of Jane's colleagues had been told the news a few weeks back and she'd had so many cards and flowers sent. Perry had been overwhelmed by the news and had sent her a long letter saying how much he missed seeing her in the office and how sorry he was.

"Sarah," she whispered as Sarah sat gently on the bed and leant forward towards Jane's face, "I love you."

"I love you too, honey," Sarah replied with sadness in her voice. "Move over bed-hogger," she joked, squishing herself onto the bed.

"It's nearly time." Jane's voice was so quiet, and she was finding it really hard to give strength or volume to her words.

"No, don't be silly. You're not going anywhere anytime soon," Sarah said in jest as she held back tears while stroking her best friend's frail hand. But she knew that Jane was probably right. She usually was. They had all noticed the rapid decline in her health over the past few days. The breathing had got deeper and noisier and Jane's energy was dwindling so quickly each day. The nurses had to take over Jane's personal hygiene as she had felt too embarrassed to have the family do it and Paula had been on hand to discuss the timescales with the adults.

Whispering again, Jane squeezed Sarah's hand with as much energy as she could muster up. "I need you to do something, Sarah, and you mustn't forget." She breathed hard. "It's really important you don't forget. Promise me?"

"Of course, anything. What is it?" Sarah looked down toward Jane's now very serious looking face.

"I've written letters for everyone. They are in the shed by Pops' grave. The key is under the gnome with the green hat on." She took another gasp of breath. "There's a gold tin with them all in, just under some books. The code for the box is nineteen eighty." Pausing to try and moisten her dry lips, she continued, "Only get them…" she paused again, "once I'm gone, you know… left the building." She tried to smile but only managed a very tiny grin and her eyes felt very heavy.

Sarah inhaled deeply to avoid crying, "Sure, no problem. I can do that for you." She was trying to be brave for Jane, but inside, she was crumbling faster as each hour went by, thinking of the moment that everyone was dreading and knowing it could be coming very soon.

Jane just smiled in her head, knowing that her best friend would do this important job for her when the time was right. "I'm cold, Sarah," she whispered as she closed her eyes and fell asleep, still holding her friend's hand.

Hanging her head, Sarah couldn't believe how strong this woman beside her was being right now, at this tragic time in her life. How was she really coping inside her head, such a beautiful person ripped apart at the seams.

"You alright?" Karl whispered as he quietly walked into the room and gently put his hand on her shoulder.

Wiping the tears away, Sarah sat up. "Yeah, just this bloody woman. She gets deep into my heart. It's so unfair,

Karl, so bloody unfair. I wish I could fix it," she answered.

"Yes, I know, me too, God how I wish I could fix it. She's truly amazing though. Through all these months, she's been stronger than all of us put together."

"She just said that she thinks it's not going to be long now, you know, the end. I can't believe it."

"You know Jane. She's always right." He gulped as a large lump appeared in his throat with another realisation of what was happening all too soon and the fact that she knew it better than all of them.

"She said she's cold too, maybe another blanket would be good. Where are the spares? I'll grab one for her."

"It's okay, there's a few in the wardrobe."

"Look, do you mind if I… I mean… I need a minute alone, Karl. I'll be back in a bit."

He stood there with tears in his eyes and sadness in his heart watching her leave the room distraught. They all knew the time was coming soon. It just didn't seem fair. Didn't even seem real, but it was, and it sucked, big time.

"Aunty Sarah, are you okay?" Cassie had noticed Sarah come down and go into the garden alone looking upset, so she left her phone in the kitchen and followed her.

"Oh, Cassie. Sorry, sweetie, I didn't know you were here, I thought you'd gone to Grandmas." She wiped her tears and blew her nose as she jumped, a little startled by Cassie's sudden appearance. She didn't want the kids seeing her upset; she was trying to be brave for them.

"No, Dad said we could stay off school today, spend a bit more time with Mum. We've just been in our rooms."

"Right, good idea. It's nice for us all to be together."

"What was Mum like when she was young?" Cassie passed her the box of tissues that she'd brought from inside.

"What was your mum like?" Sarah looked up at the bedroom window. "Wonderful, Cass, blooming wonderful. The bestest friend anyone could hope for."

"Do you have any fun stories you can tell me?"

"Blimey. Do I have stories, I can tell you hundreds about your mum and what she was like but, well, maybe not all of them until you're a little bit older and a bit wiser, hey? Come here, munchkin." She wrapped her arms around Cassie as they sat on the wooden swinging chair and began telling her a few funny stories of their childhood together, as teenagers, going on double dates, and then as they grew up, and the horrendous fashion disasters that they often had during their many years as friends.

Cassie loved hearing them and they shared some laughter together. "I wish I could find a best friend like that," she said swinging her legs.

"Aww, darling. I'll be your best friend until you find one if you want. Aunty Sarah can take you clubbing when you're old enough," she laughed, and it made Cassie giggle too.

Before they knew it, an hour had passed, and it had started to get dark. "We better go in, Cass, and get some dinner started for everyone. The boys will be getting hangry." They held each other's hands tightly and began walking towards the kitchen.

Suddenly Karl's voice shrieked through the house, "SARAH!" he cried.

A mad rush ensued as everyone ran upstairs to see why

285

he was shouting so loudly.

Time seemed to be moving in slow motion. Sarah swung the bedroom door open to see Karl cradling Jane in his arms, sobbing his heart out. He looked up at Sarah, as Janice and the twins now entered the room in a panicked silence together.

In his arms, Jane lay motionless and so pale, they knew from his face, that it was all over. She had gone.

He shook his head as tears streamed down his cheeks, rocking her frail body and stroking her head. "She's gone, she's gone," he wept.

Sarah stood with the children on each side of her, pulling them close, as floods of tears fell uncontrollably from each of them. Robbie stood motionless, unable to speak, and Cassie just sobbed silently.

Janice left the room and leaned against the landing wall, her hands covering her mouth in shock and utter grief. Her baby girl had died, and it felt rotten to the core. No one should see their child go before them. This wasn't how she had imagined her life would turn out. She wasn't supposed to outlive her daughter. Never should this happen, not ever.

About five minutes passed by and Karl gestured for the children to come over, once he had regained some composure himself. Bravely, he lay Jane's fragile body back onto the bed and turned to face his children. "Come and say goodbye to Mum." He paused to look at them, still standing motionless and blank faced. "It's okay. Mum's at peace now. No more pain for her," he told them, sniffing hard and wiping his face of the tears that refused to stop running down his cheeks.

It took Robbie a few minutes before he managed to join his sister and dad, leaving Sarah watching in heartbroken agony.

As they got onto the bed and lay beside their mum, Sarah turned and left the room to check on Janice, who was standing alone, contemplating and trying to deal with what had happened and what she had been witnessing in those dramatic few moments.

They hugged each other tightly. "Oh, Sarah, my baby girl," she sobbed, "my little butterfly has flown."

"I know, I know, let's go say goodbye to her, hey? We all need to pull together now," Sarah said as she wiped her tears away and led Janice to the bedroom once more.

Standing in the doorway, looking at this beautiful little family in so much pain, Sarah fought hard to try and hold back her emotions but failed miserably. It was too much for anyone to deal with, let alone this amazing family. There wasn't a sound to be heard, and it seemed like hours before anyone spoke or moved. There were just no words that could be uttered in these final moments of Jane's life. They all just needed peace and time to say goodbye and be together. Just one last time.

The next few days were filled with a range of low ebbs of sadness, highly emotional smiles, tears, laughter, and mixed feelings as they tried to come to terms with the loss that they felt so deeply; all the while discussing Jane and what an amazing person and beautiful character, she had been throughout the years.

Christmas came and went without the usual fun celebrations, but the family stuck together and exchanged the few gifts that Sarah and Jane had secretly bought on their various Christmas shopping trips together before she'd got too ill to go out, but it just wasn't the same without her there. The usual sparkle had gone this year.

Cassie and Robbie were brave and strong, just like their mum had taught them to be. Sarah and Janice both decided that they would stay at the house for a few days, helping Karl prepare for the funeral and supporting the children, who couldn't face going to school full time after the festive break. The school had offered amazing support for them, and the head of year had been great in keeping Karl up to date with how they were doing when they did go to school part time, to begin with. They'd also had a few of their friends invite them around to their houses, which helped to take their minds off things for an hour or so. It gave them some sort of normality, and this was the only way the adults knew how to help them cope with it.

Cassie had created a few paintings and made a paper flower bouquet to place on the coffin. She knew how much her mum enjoyed looking at her artwork and didn't want fresh flowers to just die and then be gone forever. She wanted her mum to have them with her for always.

A few days after the funeral, Sarah remembered the job she had been asked to do – to collect the special letters that Jane had written and hidden in the shed for them all.

Arriving at the cemetery that morning, she noticed someone familiar sitting on the bench nearby to Pops' gravestone. "Hi… Tom, isn't it?" She'd realised on approach that she recognised him from a few weeks back when they had gone to meet James for the blind date which ended up never happening.

"Hi, yes… erm… Sarah, right?" he replied nervously, hoping he hadn't got her name wrong.

"Yes, that's me, we met here a few weeks back with my friend, Jane."

"Yes, I remember. I er… was meaning to call you actually," he said, stumbling over his words awkwardly.

"Oh, really?" she responded in surprise.

"Yes, I got your number from the graphics on your car that day, being the only car in the place, but… well, I just haven't plucked up the courage to ring," he continued. "Silly really, at my age, feeling nervous about ringing a lady."

She blushed a little and chuckled. "Oh, okay. Did you want to book some beauty treatments? I've got some leaflets back in the car that I can sort out for you if you like. We have men's treatments available now," Sarah replied, assuming he'd seen her business number and details from the car and that was the reason for taking down her number.

"Erm, no, it wasn't for that actually. I think I'm beyond help in that department," he laughed back. "No, well, tell me if this is a bit too forward but, I just wondered if you might like to go for a coffee with me sometime? I wanted to ask you that day we met, you know when you came to the car with my photo, but I got the impression you were both a bit preoccupied with something else and didn't want to intrude or seem rude and annoying."

Sarah blushed even more, remembering that she had quite fancied him that day especially after he'd kissed her hand so romantically and when they chatted briefly in the car park after she'd run his photo to him, but she hadn't really wanted to act on it either. She was too concerned with looking after Jane, meeting James, and hadn't had a second after the events of that day. "Erm, yes, that would be lovely actually. Do you need my number again?" she chuckled as she replied.

"No, it's cool, I've saved it, just not had the courage to ring it as yet, as I said, but you've saved me from that embarrassment now," he laughed. "Are you on your own today?" he asked, looking over at her car, which was parked just outside the grounds, near to the entrance gates.

"Yes, I've just come to collect something for Jane. She erm, she passed away the week before Christmas." Sarah's head hung down slightly as she held back tears. It still hurt so much to utter those words to anyone and if she was honest, it still didn't feel real.

"Oh, I'm so sorry for your loss," he apologised. "She seemed like such a lovely person."

"Thanks. She was absolutely the loveliest person I ever knew. She was my best friend, the bestest friend ever. I can't believe she's not here anymore. It still doesn't seem real, you know?"

He reached forward and gently placed his hand onto hers. "It does get easier as time passes. Believe me, when James died, my heart felt completely crushed, and I never thought I would be able to cope without him. We were always so close. He was all the family that me and Dad had left. I just wish he'd have talked to me before…" He paused to take a breath and glanced over at her sad eyes. "Look, is there anything I can help you with, anything you need? I'm happy to just be your shoulder to cry on if that's what you need at the moment, but I'll understand if you'd rather tell me to bugger off." He smiled nervously at her hoping to not offend.

Smiling back, she said, "Look, let me grab this thing out of the shed, and maybe we could pop into that coffee shop over the road for a bit? A friendly chat over a drink would be great right now, to be honest."

"Sure. That would be awesome. Do you need any help with anything?"

"Well, she just said it's in the shed in a gold tin, under some books. The gnome in the green hat has the key apparently. That's all I know, but hopefully, I will be able to find it, shall we go and have a look?"

With Jane being the organised person she was, everything was in exactly the places she'd said. As soon as they got into the shed, Sarah could see the tin gleaming, under some of her workbooks, but she didn't want to open it just yet. She knew she had to at some point and had promised Jane she would deliver the letters to everyone, but right now, the collection of it would do and the opening could be done later in the day.

She clasped it close to her heart, then placed it into a shopping bag, carefully putting it into the car before they made their way to the coffee shop after locking the shed.

As Sarah stared thoughtfully out the window, wondering what the letters would say, she caught the reflection of Tom standing at the counter. How strange that he should be there today at the gravesite. It's like Jane had known and sent her there today. Maybe she'd finally managed to matchmake after all her other failed attempts over the years. She shouldn't assume it though. It was just a coincidence, after all.

Her thoughts were interrupted as Tom approached the table with a tray. "I hope you don't mind, but I got us a chocolate chip cookie to share. Is that wrong to assume ladies need chocolate at stressful times?"

Chuckling a little, she replied, "Not at all. It's actually the exact thing that me and Jane always get with coffee—" Realising her words were in the present tense instead of the past, she stopped for a moment. "Well, we did, you know, before…" She sighed and just shook her head. "Thank you, that's really sweet of you and weirdly strange at the same time."

Tom could see she had gotten flustered, so he quickly changed the subject. "So, what's in the box? Do you have any ideas?" he asked as he placed the coffee on the table and discarded the tray on a chair next to them.

"Jane said she'd written special letters to everyone for when the time came, and I've got to give them out to each person so that's my job for this weekend."

"Oh, I see. That's a really thoughtful thing for her to have done. I'm sure she knew you were the right person for the job." He broke the cookie in half and passed her share to her.

She smiled sweetly back at him, taking it. "I just don't know the appropriate time to pass them on. Knowing Jane and how good she was with words, they're not going to be an easy read. God, I miss her so much already. Her gorgeous little twins are in bits most of the time, and Karl, her husband, the poor man, I just wish I could make it easier for him. I really do. He's such a sweetheart and he's trying to be so brave for the children, and Jane's mum, well, she's crushed."

"It's probably Jane's way of saying goodbye to you all. I wish we'd had that opportunity, you know, to say goodbye. Although I wish James had asked for help but as they say, everything happens for a reason." He looked straight into her eyes as she chewed on her cookie. "As I said earlier, it will get easier, Sarah. Right now, it's fresh and raw, and everyone is hurting but I'm sure you'll do the right thing by Jane and get those letters delivered at the right time." He reached across and stroked her hand as she held her coffee. She felt sincere warmth from him and was even more attracted to this friendly stranger.

Sarah continued to see Tom during that weekend, and they began to fall for each other almost immediately, much to Sarah's surprise.

"I think Jane had something to do with our first meeting that day at the gravesides," Sarah commented as they sat beside each other on a bench in the park eating some chips, trying to keep warm from the chilly January weather.

"What do you mean, Sarah?" questioned Tom, turning and brushing her hair away from her face.

She paused for a moment as she remembered the day Jane had been so excited to get her to meet someone at the cemetery, that someone being James. It hadn't gone to plan at all, but maybe… just maybe… it was fate playing a hand in their lives, and as Tom had said at their first 'date' in the coffee shop, everything happens for a reason. That was why he was in her life right now. James' brother had come into the picture on that strangely, weird day, but now, she was so glad he had, and it felt perfect in every way that she'd never had imagined it could.

"Oh, don't worry. I just have a feeling she knew we'd meet somehow, someday." She leaned onto his shoulder and smiled to herself, thinking of her best friend and how happy she would be if she were here right now. Knowing that her crazy, best friend had finally found someone that she really cared for and she didn't even mind the thought of having his things in her house like she had been worried about before. All those years where Jane had tried to get her matched with someone, and it had happened like this. Her best friend was with her. She felt her near, and it began to fix her broken heart just a little more each day.

The day they were supposed to meet James, ended up being the moment Sarah had met Tom, and that was no accident. Jane had a part in this beautiful new relationship, she just knew it, so now she had to get herself together and deliver these important messages for her.

Chapter Twenty-Six

The following afternoon, Sarah went over to the Walden family home feeling a little bit stronger with the tin in her hands. The time had come for the letters to be distributed to Jane's very special people.

She opened the lid of the tin carefully to find five individual envelopes all in different colours, labelled with the names; Karl, Cassie, Robbie, Mum, and the last one, to Sarah you cheeky minx, which made her laugh quietly.

As she laid them all out carefully, one by one, on the dining table, Karl walked into the kitchen. "Hey, trouble, I didn't hear you come in. What are these?" he asked, noticing the envelopes. "Been doing some creative writing?"

"Hi. No, not me. These are from Jane. She asked me to collect them and give them out after, well, you know, after…" She handed the blue one to Karl, taking her own envelope and holding it close to her heart. "They are letters she wrote to everyone. I thought it best to get the funeral over before we had to read them."

"Letters, when did she do these?" he asked, looking at them a bit puzzled.

"I guess whenever she could get some time to herself and probably when she was at the cemetery. I know she found it a good place to reflect and concentrate, nice and peaceful, I suppose. She didn't really say, to be honest, just asked me to fetch them for her and give them out. She had spent a lot of time down there during the past few months, so it must have been then. I never saw her writing here."

"Right. Yes, she did tell me briefly about going there more often, but I didn't realise how much time it had been. When do you think we should do these?" he asked her, staring down and pointing at the envelopes with the children's names on.

"I think they should have theirs as soon as possible to be honest. It may help them cope a bit more. They've been so brave about it all, haven't they, and so strong, bless them. Cassie did tell me that her and Robbie had a bit of a heart to heart about it all, told me that they are still struggling a little bit, especially Rob, so, it may give them a tad more comfort, if you like, *hearing* from their mum in some sort of way, I don't know, I'm no expert when it comes to kids."

"Yeah, no, you're right. I'll go up and speak to them now, give them theirs. I think Cassie is working on a painting to put on Jane's grave when we visit at the weekend, it's keeping her mind occupied and you know how she loved painting for her mum."

"Do you want me to stick around? I can sit with them if

they need me to after they've had a read?"

"Erm… maybe, yeah. If you don't mind, that is?"

"Of course I don't mind. I'll put the kettle on and get something sorted for dinner too if you like?" She patted his arm as he left the room, clutching his letter to his chest and smelling it as he made his way upstairs. It smelled of Jane's perfume, the beautiful aroma of his beautiful wife, and his heart panged again with pain from not having that wonderful soul by his side anymore. How thoughtful had she been in doing this for them all. Even facing death, she was still thinking of everyone but herself and now they could read her last words in these personal notes, something he would treasure.

As Sarah turned to the sink to fill the kettle up with water, she noticed a photo on the windowsill of Jane with the kids on their holiday in Florida back in summer. She was smiling broadly. Her face was sparkling with joy, and all the time, she'd known what was happening, and the rest of the family hadn't had a clue. This wonderful woman had brought so much joy to all their lives, as much as they had to hers, and what an amazing holiday they'd all had together. She'd never forget the generosity of her ticket to join them; even though it was their last family holiday together, Jane had wanted her there. She'd known it would probably be their last time away together too.

The kettle began overflowing as Sarah was staring at the image and lost in her train of thought, recalling the amazing memories of the holiday and the fabulous time they had all spent together out there, even knowing what the two of them had at that time. "For goodness' sake, woman. See what you've made me do now, I'm a bloody mess without you here." She managed a slight chuckle as again, she stared into her best friend's eyes, whispering, "I miss you so much, honey, I really do."

~

Karl had reached the top of the stairs and looked towards his bedroom, glancing at the large empty bed. It looked so lonely and now, strangely small in there. How he wished she was still lying in it, looking at him as she used to in her stunning lingerie or even her silly fluffy pyjamas and funky slippers. Anything just to see her again. How would that bedroom, once full of happiness and passion and the touch of Jane's decor ever feel the same without her? He'd not been able to sleep a whole night since she had died. He kept having recurring dreams that she was suddenly back in the room, waking up in a sweat, then feeling the heartbroken shock of the realisation that she was gone and no longer in his life. The days had dragged on and he hadn't felt any better from that awful day when she had left for good, and he couldn't imagine it getting any better anytime soon.

Sighing, and closing his eyes for a moment to compose himself, he went to Robbie's door and knocked. "Hey, son. Is it okay to come in a minute and have a chat?"

He got a quiet but prompt reply of "Yeah," and pushed the door ajar, stepping inside. Robbie was playing a football game on his computer.

"Can you pause that a minute, mate? I've got something here for you. Mum has left you a letter."

Robbie paused his game and chucked the controller

onto the bed. He then reached to take the envelope and after a short pause, asked, "Dad, do you think Mum will always be with us, you know, in spirit? Not like a ghost or anything but just, with us?"

"Yes, I think so, son. You and Cass meant the world to her, and she loved you both more than anything. I'm sure she is watching over you right now and will continue to enjoy seeing you grow and become amazing adults," Karl tried to reassure him.

Robbie managed a tiny smile and Karl held out his fist for their father-son fist bump gesture, but Robbie leant forward and hugged him, not needing to say anything back.

"Do you want me to stay while you read it?" Karl asked him as they still embraced.

"Nah, I'm cool," he bravely answered glancing down at the green envelope and reading his name. "I'll finish my game first."

"Okay, mate. Just let me know if you need me, alright? I've got Cassie's letter to take into her and then I'll be downstairs with Sarah having a cuppa. She's cooking us some dinner." As Robbie sat back, Karl rubbed his son's head gently and left him to it, leaving the door slightly open. He looked back for a moment, thinking how brilliantly they were coping with all this heartache. He couldn't imagine being a child and losing his mum or dad at such a young age. His parents were still going strong in their late eighties and were living their dream, setting up home in Australia five years ago after finally retiring from their jobs as a chef and a teacher. Karl had been secretly planning to take Jane and the kids over to see them this year, but everything had changed so dramatically during the past few months, all plans were on hold. His parents had come over to England instead for Jane's funeral. He'd enjoyed spending the time with them and discussed about going over to Oz with the kids later that year, during the school summer holidays.

He made his way over to Cassie's room where she was busy creating. There were piles of paper and painting mess everywhere, but it didn't matter. She was doing what she loved. Being creative. Karl didn't care either, he loved to see her with her artwork, and these were extra special pieces today.

Noticing her father's appearance in the doorway, she asked, "Hey, Dad, do you think Mum would like this one or this one?" She showed him two paintings that she'd been working on all afternoon as she gestured him in.

"I think she'd love them both, sweetheart. They are beautiful. Well done. Mum loved all your paintings and drawings, didn't she?"

"Thanks. Yeah, maybe she can have them both." She started tidying up as she carefully placed the chosen art pieces on her bed on top of some old newspapers.

"Yeah, I think both of them is a great idea. Talking of Mum, she has left something for you. Do you want it now or shall I pin it up on your board while you finish up?"

Cassie glanced over to see the yellow envelope in his hands. "Erm, yes. Please put it on the board but use the special pins so it doesn't fall off. Some of the old ones are a bit rubbish and don't hold stuff up there properly, I need some new ones. Thanks, Dad," she replied, busily moving paintbrushes into a jar of water to soak and chucking some old paper into the bin under her desk.

As requested, he pinned the letter on her board with one of the glitter pins, admiring the range of crazy selfie photos of Cassie and her mum together in all sorts of poses and Snapchat disguises. He chuckled to himself as he left the room, thinking of all the times he had tried to jump in and photobomb their shots but was always getting told off for it by the girls. They'd loved taking photos together.

Jane had thought of everything she possibly could in the children's letters and had told them her memories of her pregnancy, their birth, first steps, first birthdays, holidays, and many more special moments that they'd all shared during her shortened life. She'd also recounted the amazing times in Florida that they'd enjoyed before everyone knew the truth and she had included a photo of each of them with her before she got so ill. During happier times, much healthier times.

As the strong children they were, they would take their time to read each of their letters over and over, crying, laughing and remembering with the help of their mum's written words.

Going back downstairs, Karl decided to go outside to read his letter on the garden bench on which they'd shared many a glass of wine over the years.

With a deep breath, he carefully opened the envelope and immediately the aroma of Jane's perfume flooded out once again from the pages. He lifted the papers to his nose to take it in just a bit more and closed his eyes, remembering how he used to watch her getting ready at her dressing table and puffing her atomizer of scent onto her neck and wrists.

He wished so much that he could see that image right now in their bedroom that now felt like a deserted, empty, and unloved room.

Opening his eyes, he glanced up at their bedroom window, then holding back the tears, he began to read his letter, slowly taking in every word.

'My darling Karl…' it began. *'I know that if you are reading this, I'm no longer with you, and this makes my heart bleed so hard. Well, as I'm now gone, I suppose it can't bleed anymore, but, oh, you know what I mean.'* He sniggered at her sense of humour. Even in this situation, she was still cracking jokes and making him smile. He continued reading. *"I cannot imagine life without you, but apparently, this is how it must be. I wanted to let you know that I'm so grateful for all the fun and crazy years we did have together and the absolute joy and happiness that you gave me during that time…"* He gasped a deep breath to stop the tears flowing again. This was not easy, but he continued reading and found at the end of the letter, that she had attached a copy of their wedding photo and one of her with the twins' moments after they'd been born with a Post-it note attached on which she'd written, *"Thank you for being an amazing husband and father, and especially, thank you for my two little babies, take care of them for me… x"*

Stapled to the letter was a voucher for his aftershave that she had promised herself she was going to stock up for him but hadn't managed to sort out in time. He chuckled to himself at her organisation even to the end and he wouldn't forget to get it next time he was in town.

Looking in awe at these beautiful people in the photos before him, he paused for a while to reflect on it all.

Sarah came into the garden and sat down beside him, handing him a mug of coffee. "Hey," she said gently, "you okay, mister?"

"Yeah, I'm fine, well I think so, sort of. It's just so hard to read these words but not be able to hear them out loud, you know, hear her voice again," he replied, taking hold of the mug. "She was such an amazing wife. I miss her so much already. I just don't know how I'll cope, Sarah, honestly, it's not getting any easier. She was my soulmate, my best friend, my everything, and it's just not the same without her here, seeing, hearing, touching her." He glanced down at the photo again, swallowing the hard lump in his throat that was making his voice crack. "She said she'd grow old with me."

Lovingly, Sarah replied, "I know it's hard, but your kids need you to be strong, Karl. They will help you through it, and I'll be here for you and them for as long as you'll have me around. I promise." She grasped his hand and squeezed it gently. They had such a good relationship, like brother and sister and he knew deep down that she would be there for him and especially for the children.

They sat together, swinging on the bench in silence, holding their letters and looking at the special photos that Jane had left for them both.

"Look at this crazy chick. It had to be that photo, didn't it? She really chose a good one for me to look back on." They laughed as they checked out Sarah's photo of the two of them at a hen party during their twenties, dressed as the superheroes, Catwoman and Wonder Woman. "I'm going to read the letter a bit later tonight though," she said as she put the photos back into the envelope carefully. "I'll get lunch sorted," she said and left him to finish his coffee.

The next morning, Janice came over with some homemade chocolate brownies for everyone and some muffins for the twins. When they had all finished indulging, and the kids had gone upstairs, Karl gave Janice the letter labelled Mum and explained where it had come from. She sat at the kitchen table looking at the gold envelope from her daughter and decided she wanted to go and be with Pops, so she could read it to him. Somehow it felt right to include him in this special moment.

"I think I should go and read this with Pops," she finally spoke standing up.

"Do you want a lift, Janice?" asked Sarah as she finished cleaning up the dishes. "It's on my way."

"That would be great. Thank you, my dear. Save my little old legs. I'll pop over tomorrow, Karl, I have some presents for the children from my book group. Bye for now, dear." She kissed him on the cheek before leaving.

The drive to the cemetery for Janice was a bit of a blur. She didn't recall much of the journey there as she'd spent most of the time staring down at the envelope, stroking the pen scribble of her name, Mum.

Once she had arrived, she felt more at ease. She was with her husband, and now her daughter's last words were in her hands to tell him all about.

"Hello, my darling," she said as she crouched down to rub Pops' headstone. "I have a little letter from our baby girl, so I thought I'd bring it along to read to you. Is she okay up there with you, my darling? Are you both okay?"

As she stared motionless for a few minutes, a tiny white butterfly landed on the top of the bench close to her fingers and displayed its' pretty wings, flapping them open and closed as if waving, then fluttered away silently into the trees above. Mesmerised, Janice watched it land once more on a branch and then it just vanished like something magical. It wasn't the season for butterflies, so how could it be there at all? The moment felt so special and Janice knew instantly, somehow, it was her daughter telling her that she was okay. She smiled up into the sky, and whispered, "Goodbye, my darling little butterfly, you take care of your Pops up there."

The atmosphere was intense but beautiful. All she could hear were the birds chirping and singing in the trees above, but everything else, including the heavy drone of constant traffic in the busy Cambridge streets outside, seemed to fall silent so she could savour this moment for a few minutes more.

Janice sat herself down on the bench, opened the envelope, and started reading, *'My dearest Mum…'* it began. *'I'm with Pops now as you probably already know, because you have this in your hands, but I am finally at peace. No more pain or horrible chemo and medication to contend with. I'm not hurting anymore, and hopefully, my hair has come back to its former glory. Never much liked the idea of being a baldy forever. Apparently, they say you return to your beautiful self after life has failed you, and you go on to other places, so here's hoping for a new head of hair especially.'* Janice chuckled at her daughter's humour as she noticed the smiley face that Jane had scribbled. *'Mum, I'm so sorry again that I didn't tell you about being poorly straight away. I never wanted to hurt you by lying and not telling the truth, but I'm sure you understand as you always did with everything I chose to do in life and I love you so much for that kindness and all the love you gave me over the years no matter what I got up to, especially those crazy times that me and Sarah put you through. Sorry about that., You really have been the best mother to me, the best any child could ask for and an even more amazing grandparent to our beautiful children. They absolutely adore you, as do I, as I did… well, you know…'* She stopped reading to gulp some air. It was too emotional, so she sat there for a short time to take it all in, to wipe her eyes clear of tears, and then continued reading to herself for the rest of it.

Her letter was five pages long, and she read it over and over. She could almost hear her daughter's voice become clearer, the more she read it, making her feel more at ease and at peace. She knew that Jane had put her whole heart into the letter, and she felt an amazing flurry of love for the closure it had brought to her at this moment in time. It was such a special and loving thing for her daughter to have done and must've been so hard knowing they would be her last words.

The final few words in the letter read, *'I love you for all eternity, Mum, from your little butterfly, Jane. XX.'*

Glancing to the sky once more, she took a huge breath of air as a tear trickled down her cheek, then looked towards Pops' gravestone. "Our daughter was truly amazing, wasn't she, my dear? She grew up to be so like you, brave until the very end. You were such a beautiful person, Jane, my little butterfly, now you must spread your wings and be at peace with your father. He'll take care of you now, my darling, until I can be with you both." She placed the envelope on the grave and used a heavy cobblestone on top of it to hold it in place. "I'm going to leave it with you tonight, my dear husband. Look after her up there, won't you? I love you both very much. I'll be back to see you both soon." She blew them both a final kiss.

Chapter Twenty-Seven

The following year, Jane's long-term dreams and wishes came true in more than one way for two of the most special people she'd had in her life.

"Tom, do you have a second?" asked Sarah as they strolled along the seaside promenade in Norfolk one weekend in May.

They'd decided to visit the place where she and Jane had stayed that hen weekend when the tragic news had been revealed. Sarah felt closer to her that day for some reason and had an overwhelming feeling of love come over her in that moment in the gleaming sunlight.

"Sure, honey, what's up?" Tom pointed to a nearby picnic bench and they sat opposite each other. "Is everything alright?" he asked, looking at her now thoughtful face.

"Yes, everything is fine, Tom. It's just that, well, you know what happened to Jane?" She glanced down at her hands as she reached out to touch his across the table and continued, "You see, Jane had always tried to match me up with someone, and I always messed it up or didn't take it seriously enough, but this time it's different. I feel like she had something to do with us getting together, like, she knew we would meet eventually. Somehow, she finally made it happen."

"You're not sick, are you, Sarah?" Concerned she was about to tell him something bad, he squeezed her hand.

"No, no. Sorry. I'm rambling on a bit, aren't I?" She paused and glanced back into his worried but loving green eyes. "It's just, well, she always wished for me to meet that special someone and settle down, and I never took her advice. I was never one for just being with one person, a free spirit most of my life, but…"

"But what? Are you breaking up with me?" Tom's face reminded her of other faces she had seen many times before at that pivotal moment of the 'it's not you, it's me' conversations that she'd had plenty of with other men throughout the years.

"No. God no. I just wanted to let you know that, for the first time in my life, I feel… well… I feel really secure with you, and if we hadn't met that day, you know, when Jane took me to the cemetery and you were there, we might never have met at all, and…" Sarah's words became flustered again, she was rambling on now, so he moved around to sit next to her and stroked her flushed cheek as if to say it was okay.

"Sarah, honey, it's fine. I know what you mean."

"I just get the feeling Jane knew. She must have. She

knew we had to meet because of…" She was about to say James, but swiftly realising she couldn't, she continued, "I want to make her proud and grant her one of her eternal wishes, Tom. But I'm going to need your help to do that."

"Whatever you want, gorgeous. I'm here for you. What do you need me to do?"

In a split second, everything became clear to Sarah. The visit to James that eventful day, the fact that Tom was there, that he'd left the photo behind, that she'd had to run after him to give it back; he'd taken her number from her car. Jane had made this relationship happen. She felt sure that she was now looking down on the two of them as the sun began gleaming through some puffy white clouds above, and the sky became suddenly brighter than usual. She gazed up, squinting at the luminous sun rays shining down on them, then turned back to face Tom with pure emotion and joy. "Marry me, Tom. Let's do it." She excitedly jumped up from her seat. "Let's do it for Jane."

He stood up swiftly, nearly tripping on the bench, held both her hands, and embraced her with a long, sumptuous and electrified kiss, like no other kiss they'd ever shared. Her heart was thumping like a drum through her chest, so hard, he could feel it on his.

She'd never felt like this in her life before and as he whispered softly into her ear, "Tell you what, you marry me," she peered up at the sky and winked, smiling with utter glee. Jane had finally got her wish for Sarah to find that special someone, to be happy and content and settle down at last. It was the most amazing moment she had ever experienced, and she felt sure it was all because of her one and only best friend in the whole world. There would never be another person like Jane Walden in her life and how she wished she could see her and Tom right now. She would have been so happy.

Tom lifted her up and swung her around as passers-by looked on wondering what they were doing. They didn't have a care in the world and embraced their special moment for the rest of the day.

~

After only eight months of planning, the wedding day arrived, and it was exactly how Jane had planned it when they were kids at primary school. Sarah had asked Karl to give her away – the plan had been for Jane to have that honour as Sarah didn't have any living parents for this job.

"Wow! Look at you. You look bloody gorgeous," Karl remarked when he saw Sarah arrive at the church. "Jane would've been so proud to see you marrying Tom. He's such a good bloke. She would have really got on well with him, wouldn't she?"

"Aww, thanks, darling, yes she would have loved him for sure," replied Sarah, slightly blushing while standing in front of him as she was admiring her fifties-style wedding dress and small bouquet of lilies in the mirror at the side of the entrance. It was a gorgeous February afternoon and the sun was shining for them. It didn't even feel cold which was strange for this time of year in England.

"Here, I wondered if you would like to wear this as your 'something borrowed' thing?" He reached into his suit jacket pocket, pulling out a small black velvet box and opened it to show her. "It was one of Jane's favourite pieces to wear to weddings and special occasions." He unhooked the bracelet from the box and handed it to her.

"Karl, that's stunning. Are you sure you're okay about me wearing it? I mean, it's Jane's."

"Definitely. I'm sure. She can sort of walk you down the aisle as she had always planned, well, with me." He looked into her eyes which were welling up with tears. "Yes, she did tell me the things you two had planned since childhood." He smiled back at her, fastening it onto her wrist, then held out his arm. "Now, come on. Let's get you hitched before you change your mind. Tom is waiting very patiently in there for his new wife."

They began the walk down the aisle towards an emotional Tom, with Cassie and Robbie, following as bridesmaid and page boy. Sarah couldn't help but beam a massive smile all the way, knowing that Jane was there in spirit for this perfect moment as she was always supposed to be. As she reached Tom, he kissed her cheek and she gushed, glancing down at the bracelet and smiling knowingly at it for a few seconds. Thank you, bestie, she thought and met Tom's eyes once again with utter heart-pounding joy and excitement for their big day.

~

"How was the honeymoon then?" asked Janice as they all sat around the dining table to celebrate the twins' fifteenth birthday that evening.

"Oh, Janice, it was so fabulous. It really was amazing, wasn't it, Tom, tell them about the heat."

"It was incredible, yes. Jamaica is somewhere you should try out," he replied, kissing Sarah's cheek. "Just fantastic. I've never been anywhere like it. And the heat. Phew. It was pretty intense at times."

"Can we go and try out the PS4 now, Dad?" asked Robbie as they finished their slices of birthday cake.

"Sure. Go on. Tom and I will be in soon to thrash you at that football game," he joked.

"Yeah, whatever," Robbie laughed back, playfully punching his dad in the arm.

As the children left the kitchen, Karl got a bottle of sparkling cava from the fridge. "Grab some wine glasses, Tom." He pointed to the glass cabinet. "Let's have a toast for Jane and for the twins' big day. This was one of her favourite bottles of fizz."

A short pause of silence and reflection followed with just the sound of bubbles fizzing in the glasses as they all stood up together in thought.

"To our babies' birthday, darling." Karl glanced up at the photo canvas on the wall of the four of them just after the twins had been born. It was a copy of one of the photos she had put into his special letter. He'd loved looking at it so much, he had decided to get it printed onto a canvas, so he had it to admire whenever he was in the kitchen. They all raised their glasses to it.

Sipping at the bubbly and smiling, each reminisced with their own memories of her. Everyone had such different recollections of this wonderful lady, but all were loving and fun times together.

Tom remembered the day he had met her briefly and had told her all about his brother, James, thinking that had been the most perfect day because that's where he'd met his now beautiful wife, thanks to Jane.

Sarah had way too many memories to get through but couldn't help but think of the night they'd spent in Norfolk after Jane was brave enough to finally reveal the truth but still had the strength to carry on with her many lies knowing how much it must've hurt her to do so.

Karl just looked in awe at his wife's face knowing he'd miss her eternally and would never love anyone quite the same as he'd loved her.

Janice remembered a night when Jane had discovered a hedgehog in the garden when she was around seven and kept trying to touch it, getting pricked in the process but continuing to carry on trying. This made her chuckle, breaking the silence, so she thought it would be a good time to make her announcement. "Well, while we have the bubbly out, my dears. I have a little bit of news to tell you all about too." She sat back down on the dining chair placing her glass triumphantly on the table.

They all turned to face her in expectation as she continued, "I've been seeing someone. A man no less, my dears." She paused to take in their shocked faces and laughed. "Jane always said Pops didn't want me to be alone forever. I never really took any notice, but you know, as usual, my little butterfly was right so, you'll all be glad to know that I'm not a lonely old spinster anymore. I think I might be in love again. After all these years."

Everyone looked in amazement and sat down quietly in unison. This was not something they had expected to come out of her mouth. Not ever. She had always been so adamant that she would never be with anyone else after

Pops. But, again, maybe Jane had something to do with this too, as if they'd all come to realise that she was right all along for all of them.

"Seriously, Janice? When did this happen?" asked Karl, still a little bemused by the announcement.

"She is definitely serious, mate," said Tom knowingly, "and I, for one, couldn't be happier for you both." He put his arms around Janice as he got up to grab another bottle of sparkly that he'd hidden, smiling knowingly.

Sarah and Karl looked at each other. "Are we missing something here?" Sarah shrugged her shoulders, looking puzzled.

"It's Henry, my dears, Tom's father." A massive smile appeared on Janice's face as she winked at Tom. "We met just a few months before the wedding and just sort of, what do you say these days, clicked, hit it off? We've been meeting every day since, and I even took him to one of my dance classes. He's a natural, you know, and my friends love him. We'll have to show you our new dance moves one evening." She chuckled, smooching a waltzing dance move in her chair.

"That's amazing news, Janice. How lovely. Jane would be so happy with this." Karl got up to give her a big cuddle. "She really would've been thrilled. I'm so happy for you, honestly, amazing." He grinned from ear to ear.

"Why, thank you, my dear. I was a little worried about telling you but, well, I sort of knew you'd all be happy for us. I'd like to think Jane is watching us all and loving what she sees, bless her little cotton socks."

They all raised their glasses once more knowing she was

absolutely right in every way. Jane would be watching them and loving it and it was exactly what she would've loved to have seen. She had, yet again, gotten a final wish come true for herself and for her dad.

"To Jane," they all cried and clinked their glasses together.

Chapter Twenty-Eight

So, that's the story of our amazing Mum, Jane Walden. Our beautiful, strong, and courageous mother who fought the awful disease right up to the very end as best she could.

My name is Cassie Walden, and I'm now twenty-three, attending Cambridge art school as a teacher while training to become a Macmillan nurse at our local hospice where Mum spent a few weeks when she was poorly. More importantly, I have regular mammograms to ensure that I keep a check on my breasts and that bloody awful C-word that took my mum doesn't have any chance of getting me.

Since Mum was diagnosed before she was forty years old, I can have regular three-year check-ups, and I'm obsessed with checking my breasts every week too, something that all women of any age should be taught to do. It's never too early to start thinking of it, something that I was made aware of because of my mum.

Being somebody who was hardly ever poorly, just the

odd cold during the wintertime mainly, Mum only found out that she had breast cancer because of her work planning an awareness event, too late in the day to do anything for her, unfortunately for her and us.

I have my own health insurance and I am now heavily involved in regular fundraising for breast cancer awareness especially, being so close to our hearts.

Dad: Well, my dad is my true hero in all this, and we'll never forget the relationship that they had together. What a magical time they must have had, even if it was cut too short. He'll always be my hero and someone Robbie aspired to be just like and has since become. He's not been able to get into another serious relationship as yet, but we do keep trying to set him up from time to time as Mum didn't want him to be alone for the rest of his life, and neither do we. I think he just can't bring himself to let go entirely from Mum, and that's sweet, but we will keep trying and helping him along the way to find a new lady to share the rest of his life with.

Robbie: My brilliant and sometimes annoying twin brother. He's doing okay and has just got engaged to a lovely girl, Lucy, who he met on his first day at college, just like Mum and Dad met all those years ago. She's lovely and we get on really well. It's like having a sister, as we spend time going out, swapping clothes, and shopping together. A bit like Mum and Sarah used to do. She's a wonderful person and has really helped Robbie cope with everything. He was still struggling quite badly with losing Mum, losing his way a little bit, so she came along at just the right time. They have already asked me to be a bridesmaid at the wedding, planned for next year, something Grandma is extremely excited about too and she's already been shopping for her hat and outfit.

Grandma: Her and Tom's dad, Henry, are still very much together. She has now moved in with him, and they go dancing every other week like she used to do with our grandpa, Pops. It's lovely to see her so happy too, and they are such a fun couple to have around. She has slowed down a little bit more but is still our wonderful and crazy grandma who we love dearly. Mum would've loved Henry, and Grandpa Pops would've approved. I visit them every Sunday for lunch with Dad, Robbie, Lucy, Sarah and Tom.

Sarah and Tom: Our wonderful 'aunt' Sarah is still crazy and fun-filled but now has someone special again to be crazy with in the form of Tom. We all love him. Robbie and I call him uncle. He and Dad go out every other weekend together for a pint down the local or a kick about of football with Robbie. They've got four dogs, in place of children I think, and they spoil them rotten. We are so happy for them.

Mum: What can I say? My mum was the best. She was also my friend. As a teenager losing her mother, I never thought I would be able to cope without her by my side, but I've learned from her that you have to be strong whatever life throws at you, and she was just that. Our super strong and beautiful mother fought as hard as she could against this damned horrible disease, but it beat her within six months of finding out. She didn't even get to see Christmas, which she absolutely loved. We have a special bauble with a photo of her in it which we place on her favourite

Christmas tree every year. The tree is looking a bit tired now after all these years, but she loved it, so it stays.

For months, she hid the illness and coped by herself to protect us as a family. Yes, she lied many times about the treatment, the working, the money, the headscarves and the walking stick that she thought we didn't know about, but she had her reasons, and we all understood why she did it in the end, even as young as we were at the time. Dad told us everything that she'd gone through to try and protect us and we completely understood her reasons.

She thought we didn't know until the day we came home with Sarah and sat down with her but me and Robbie had chatted about it many times before that day. We had researched on the internet, as you do, and had sort of come to the conclusion that she was very poorly, we just didn't want to ask her and cause her any upset. We also secretly hoped that what we had read, via Dr Google, wasn't going to be the truth or not as bad as actually losing her at the end of it.

If I have learned anything from my mum and this situation we went through, it's to be strong, to be resilient, and to love your family as much as you can every day of your life because you just never know what life is going to throw at you or indeed what someone may be going through in secret.

She had just six months after finding out, six months and that was it, all over. But she used those months to make plans, to write our special letters and try and make that remaining time with us full of great memories, with no more upset and tears than we needed to experience. She did good. We always chat about our last family holiday to Florida and how amazing it was even though we never knew the truth behind the reason for going at that time.

It's never something we want to live through again, but we will treasure those last months that we had with her forever. Although sad, they are still so precious to us.

My brother and I will always remember how hard she fought right till the end and how her lies were tough but understandable as a struggling mother, wife, daughter, and friend trying to protect her loved ones for as long as possible from the heart-breaking truth she faced alone for so long.

Yes, she told lies, but…

We call them, Mum's Reasonable Lies.

If you enjoyed this book, please take a few minutes
to post a review on Amazon as that will help
even more readers enjoy Reasonable Lies.

Simply go to Amazon, search for 'Reasonable Lies'
and click the number next to the review stars
to write your own customer review.

Thank you so much x

Acknowledgements

To my mum – your strength has been an inspiration.

To my three children and granddaughter – I love you with all my heart.

To my husband – who has supported me on this journey, with his guidance, love, and most of all patience.

To all those who kindly read one, two, three or even more drafts of this book – your feedback and comments have helped me so much in completing this book and achieving my dream of seeing it in print.

My family & Supporters – You know who you are.

A very special thank you to everyone

How It All Began

Traci, who writes under the name, T.A. Rosewood, wrote her first short story when she was just thirteen years old, which was called, *Looks Aren't Everything*.

For her GCSE English exam, Traci had to write a two-page story, but couldn't stop once she'd started writing, and was marked down for that English exam. Like the girl in her thirty-page story, *The Runaway*, Traci just can't help bending the rules.

In her twenties, Traci began writing and publishing poetry but had to stop writing as her family and children grew.

Almost two decades later, she was inspired to write again, when she met bestselling author Jojo Moyes at the open evening of Harts Books store in Saffron Walden, Essex.

Traci and her husband went along to show their support for the new bookshop in town and listened intently as local author, Jojo Moyes described how it felt when her bestselling book *Me Before You* was turned into a Hollywood film.

At that precise moment, Traci was inspired. She turned to her husband and said, "I'm going to start writing again."

That evening, she couldn't sleep for excitement and came up with a fictional storyline for *Reasonable Lies*, which would highlight a sensitive women's health issue.

Sadly, one month into writing her novel, Traci's mum, Pauline, was diagnosed with the same disease as the lead character in *Reasonable Lies*, which put an immediate stop to her writing, as it was just too painful to continue.

Thankfully, after two operations and eighteen months of treatment, her mum, having been given the all clear, then encouraged Traci to continue writing her book using her experience as research.

In October of 2019, Traci and her husband, Leonardo, attended a Harts Books 'Meet the Author' event, to hear Jojo Moyes talk about her latest book, *The Giver of Stars*.

During questions, Leonardo raised his hand to thank both Jojo Moyes and Harts Books, explaining how Traci was inspired to write her first novel at the previous visit.

JoJo was first to applaud, leading to a round of applause from the audience, which then kick-started lots of followers on social media, requests from local book clubs wanting to read Traci's book, and subsequently, lots of orders for *Reasonable Lies*.

Family, friends, local people, other authors, and the wide writing community and book reviewers, continue to be incredibly supportive of Traci's new venture.

Traci is a wife, mum and nanny living in North Essex.

I would love to hear from you,
so please tag me on
Instagram, Facebook or Twitter:
@TARosewood and use the hashtags
#tarosewood or #reasonablelies.

For more news, updates,
book signing events,
and competitions,
please visit my website:
www.tarosewood.com

Printed in Great Britain
by Amazon